# Lone
# Crow

## EA Porter

Cover model: Rick Mora

Cover Design: Olde Crow Publishing

I would like to thank two important people who made this cover possible:
The incredibly talented Rick Mora for his likeness,
and my PA, Christy Sassmen, for all she does to keep me on track.

*A woman's highest calling is to lead a man to his soul, so as to unite him with Source. A man's highest calling is to protect woman, so she is free to walk the earth unharmed.*

Cherokee Proverb

# Chapter One

Lone Crow had been riding lazily, enjoying the warm, spring morning and looking forward to visiting one of his favorite ponds when, just as his destination came into view, the serenity was interrupted by two wagons parked at the calm water's edge. He quickly considered turning back and traveling toward the river. The Warrior was not prepared to let a run-in with settlers ruin the beautiful day. As he turned his horse, his keen eye caught the sight of a woman bathing in the smooth, clear waters. He slid quietly from his pony's back and sent her away from the pond. The obedient horse walked to a close clearing with fresh, thick grass and stopped to nibble on the lush meadow, patiently waiting for its rider.

The Indian crouched down on the balls of his feet and thoughtfully considered the situation. The white woman was the picture of beauty with porcelain skin and long hair the color of fire. He watched as she plunged her head into the waist-deep water then came back up quickly, slinging her locks up and over her head.

Crouched and expertly hidden, Lone Crow moved effortlessly with the swaying of the wind through the tall grass.

The Warrior held a deep disdain for the white man. For the past ten years, he had done everything in his power to avoid all contact with the people. But something about the woman bathing in the water was different - familiar even.

Moving closer, he scanned the area. There were four others in the group, all resting lazily around a small fire while the woman enjoyed the cool water. All he could see of her was the long red hair that clung to the wet skin of her back.

Lone Crow knew watching at such a close distance was chancy. He knew he should return to his pony and continue his day without giving another thought to the fire-haired woman bathing in the pond. Still, he remained, watching, waiting, hoping she would turn and allow him to see her face.

He slid deeper into the landscape when he heard one of the men call out to the woman.

The name the man used surprised the Warrior. It was a name from his past, and he remembered it well. The knowledge made it even more challenging to return to his ride. A small part of him wanted to stay – stay and take the chance that he might be caught, just to hear the girl's name one more time. But he fought the desire and returned to his pony.

Hearing the name caused him to experience regret, and a plethora of other emotions he'd thought he'd locked away years earlier.

Faith.

It was a simple, short name, but it was jarring.

While Lone Crow and his pony moved further from the scene, he attempted to convince himself that many women shared the name. It was not an uncommon name for white women. However, the buried memories still scratched at his mind.

Instead of continuing his leisurely ride, he returned to his village and after seeing to his pony, walked toward the council house.

His village was not unlike others in the region. There were about thirty homes, all made from wood, clay, and different types of grasses. At the center was a dirt field used for games and gatherings surrounded by several benches for spectators. Numerous homes had small fires glowing near the entrance and several racks for tanning hides dotted the area. Young children chased each other gleefully while their mothers either worked on hides or tended crops. The camp remained in a constant state of activity until the dark took hold.

The night was Lone Crow's favorite time to be awake. Most others slept while he moved freely in the dark. He was an unusual man but it was not the Cherokee way to point out one's differences.

When he was escorted into the camp ten years earlier, the people took him in and helped him heal without questioning him or commenting on his strange ways. They had also shielded him when there were white men afoot, so he felt it was his duty to alert the Chief of the presence of white people so close to the village.

"Pathkiller," Lone Crow called as he stood beside the doorway.

While waiting to be invited inside, he found himself anxious to be alone and far away from the village.

"Lone Crow," the Chief acknowledged from inside the dwelling. "Come, sit, smoke with us."

The invitation was rare and Lone Crow did not want to appear to be ungrateful but he wanted to alert the Chief and then ride away for the next few days.

The Warrior walked in and bowed his head slightly in reverence to the older men who were gathered.

One of the men flanking the Chief scooted so that Lone Crow could sit.

Pathkiller nodded his head and motioned for the Warrior to make himself comfortable.

Lone Crow clenched his teeth and did as he was directed.

"What brings you here?" Pathkiller asked before lighting the pipe.

Lone Crow readied his response but was cut off by the Spiritual Leader, Bear Paw.

"Did you feel that we were talking about you?" he asked, leaning toward Lone Crow.

Lone Crow shook his head and again started to answer the Chief's question.

"I don't suppose it matters why you are here," the Chief continued, smoke emanating from his nose and mouth. "You are here and that saves me from sending someone to find you. You are not easy to locate when you are on your own."

Lone Crow had no idea what response was expected so he stayed silent and wished for the conversation to be over quickly.

"A few missionaries are coming into the village. We need you to stay close and interpret for us," the Chief explained, watching Lone Crow closely.

Lone Crow shook his head and began moving to a standing posture.

"Son," came a familiar voice from the darkness.

Lone Crow stayed on his feet but didn't move toward the exit.

"Sit down," the voice gently ordered.

Lone Crow did as he was told and squinted to look at his adopted father.

Between the darkness and the smoke, most of the men gathered were concealed until they leaned closer to the light of the fire.

As soon as Lone Crow's eyes were adjusted, he saw that his father's face was set. The man had made his decision and there would be no negotiation. But behind the stern look, Lone Crow could also see a sad understanding in the old man's eyes.

"I know this is asking a lot. But we cannot trust anyone else. The men and women of the group say they come in peace and want to teach us about the white man's God. We will listen because they say they also have goods to trade. We will continue to show them kindness as long as they have come in peace."

Lone Crow was not in favor of doing what his father wanted. But he knew he owed it to the man and to the village. They had done nothing but show him love and understanding since his arrival.

The older men had some idea of what had happened to him as a child. But he had never shared the whole of the story with anyone.

The scars he carried, both physical and mental, were his and his alone, to bear.

As he grew to adulthood, he learned the way of the warrior and was proficient in every task he attempted to learn. He fought with wild abandon and could disappear into the land easily. The people of his village called him brave but Lone Crow wasn't brave. He was burdened by the experiences he'd been forced to endure and didn't care if he lived or died.

The council had no idea how strongly Lone Crow felt because he'd never revealed his darkest secrets to anyone. The deep creases in his face told of hardships he'd endured – far more than most had experienced at such a young age. He was a man who was respected but never approached without invitation. Lone Crow wasn't rude or unkind; he just didn't enjoy company. The

Warrior was happiest when he was riding the land alone and enjoying the bounty she provided.

The men of the council were asking him to change his way of life and participate in an event that would collide with his character. And in doing so, they knew they were asking much from the Warrior. If the circumstances had been different, if there was killing to do, or raiding, he would be the first to volunteer. But they were asking him not only to stay in the camp, they were asking him to be in the prolonged company of white men. The whites were not ordinary trappers or traders either. The people for whom he was being asked to interpret were the same ilk of men who set the foundation for the person he became. It was a man proclaiming to be doing God's work. A man like the one which haunted his sleep and played the protagonist in his nightmares.

## Chapter Two

My life was not what I would consider a happy one.

I had endured much as a child and just when the opportunity to escape arose, my Aunt swooped in to save the day. At least, that was what she hoped others in town would think.

Her brand of parenting was much the same as my father's had been. As soon as I reached marriageable age, I was wed to the Godliest man Aunt Hazel could locate.

For the last seven years, I bore more bruises than I did babies. The only child I delivered alive, died in my arms only days later. For months I was inconsolable. The one silver lining of my loss was my husband stopped sharing his amorous desires with me. He still showed me attention by way of his fists, though.

Only while my husband was conducting church service was I allowed to visit with other people. In the beginning, I looked forward to the break from my husband and the chance to converse with anyone other than him. Once, I'd even honestly answered a woman when she asked what happened to my face. It was the last time I didn't attribute my bruises to my clumsiness. But over the previous six months, I hadn't even gone to the service. I stayed at home and, when everyone was in the church, I rode my horse and relaxed. The experience was more enjoyable than any church service I had ever attended.

Over the last year, my husband, Tobias Moore, had taken up with one of the women of the congregation. There was not one part of me that was jealous. I was grateful for his distraction but was still confused and angered by his kind treatment of the woman. She smiled when he neared and never, ever cowered. I was pleased she wasn't being hurt by my husband but still confused. I had never seen a mark on her. His behavior only served to make me hate him more and continue to question if there weren't some truth behind both my husband's and my late father's repeated insistence that my treatment was really my fault.

When he returned from his latest "prayer meeting" with Wilma, he was flush with excitement. That particular emotion usually didn't bode well for me so I was hesitant to inquire about the reason for his mood.

"Faith," he acknowledged my presence as he sat at the small dining room table, waiting for me to serve him dinner. "I have news. I have been selected to make the next trip into Indian territory. We are gonna go help those poor people see the light."

I had just turned when he informed me of his news and, try as I might, I couldn't stop the china plate full of food from falling to the floor when he'd finished the declaration.

Tobias' news caused all the memories of my childhood to come flooding back, recollections that I had done my best to keep locked away.

I was so stunned by the news that I was still standing with my mouth hanging open when Tobias grabbed me by the hair and forced me to the ground.

"What did you do that for?!" he raged as he pushed me further into the floor.

My eyes were watering but I was doing my best not to cry. "I'm … sorry," I mumbled, quickly regaining my senses and pulling away before he could slap me.

He huffed and ran his hand through his thick black hair. "Clean that up and get me another plate. I swear, I think you are mentally stunted, woman. No one else makes me as mad as you do," Tobias continued ranting as he retook his seat and placed the cloth napkin across his lap. "Get me some more first. Then clean your mess," he demanded.

I nodded and quickly did as he ordered.

His actions had buffered my ability to fixate on his news but that blessing did come at a cost. My head ached and I was feeling a little queasy.

"Now, as I was saying," Tobias continued as I resumed cleaning without looking up at him. "We are going to travel by wagon with another couple and another man. I think the change in scenery will be nice and I do believe I can make a difference to those poor people."

"You don't want me to accompany you, do you?" I asked after the mess was cleaned.

I hoped his answer was no. I didn't want to leave but found myself growing excited at the thought he would be gone.

My hopes were dashed when he smiled and reached for my waist to draw me close to his side.

"Your comin'," he assured me. "There are a couple of reasons why I need your pretty face. We will be traveling with three others. Of course, Wilma and her husband, Howard, are coming. They are both holy and full of Christ's word. With us will be a young man from another town who has been on a missionary trip before. You know how I feel about Wilma but no one else does so I need ya for that. I also think, if you don't make me discipline you, the Indians might find you something pretty to look at. The village is Cherokee and last I heard we were on friendly terms with the Chief so there will be little danger. Unless you choose not to behave. And I still believe you will see the light one day soon. I don't enjoy beating you. You just don't seem to learn."

While he was telling me what his plans were, I moved away and stood at the washbasin with my back to him.

I was sure he knew he was scratching at the scab that was my childhood and yet I still didn't have the courage to tell him to shut up. In my mind I was yelling at him but on the exterior, I was doing my best not to cry.

"You not hungry?" he asked, changing the subject.

I didn't turn around to face him but I did shake my head.

"Good. Fix me another plate," he demanded. "We are gonna leave in three days so I will be busy until then. I think the less I have to talk to you, the better your chances are," he added with humor in his voice.

I gritted my teeth and reached for the knife. It was becoming a ritual for me. The last time I'd had the weapon in my hand, I was almost strong enough to turn to him. Although I knew it was wrong, I had dreamt of his death many times. The simple truth was, I wanted him dead. But I knew if I killed him, the town's folk would surely hang me. I was miserable and had little hope of that fact ever changing but I still did not want to die.

"Well? Aren't you gonna say anything?" he asked as he grabbed my arm when I took his empty plate.

I grimaced and tried to pull away from him. I had no idea what he expected me to say and I was growing angry with him toying with me. There was not much I could do with my anger but it was present none the less.

"See, this right here," he began as he stood and knocked the chair back with his legs.

The noise made by the flimsy piece of furniture when it contacted the wooden floor made me jump.

Tobias clamped down harder on my arm and pulled me into his chest. "You make me do this, ya know."

I closed my eyes and bit the inside of my cheek in preparation for whatever was to come next.

I was shocked and relieved when he pushed me from him and kicked the chair before walking to the door.

"I am gonna stay as far from you as possible until we leave. All I got to say is you better behave on this trip. I don't know if others will understand the reason I have to constantly discipline you. Don't think I won't. I just don't want to look unchristian like in their eyes. Some don't cotton to the old ways as much as in the past. Your dad was a true believer and I learned much from him before he was murdered by that dirty little Indian boy," he continued his warnings and reasoning for beating me before leaving me in peace.

I leaned against the wooden counter and did everything in my power not to break down.

My mind was screaming questions no one could answer. Why? Why now? I had been able to force the recurring dream from continuing only the year earlier.

Was the trip a good way to finally kill me? Or was he planning to continue to torture me with my past? Or maybe barter me to the Natives?

Tobias knew everything about me when he asked my aunt for my hand in marriage. But as brutal as he had been over the years, he had not mentioned my past at all. He preferred physical pain to mental pain. And I wasn't sure I didn't as well.

Instead of cleaning the dishes, I sat in the middle of the room and took several deep breaths. As hard as I tried to stop the voice growing louder in my head, I couldn't. The flimsy grasp I had on the present was slipping and it quickly became impossible to stop my father's voice from growing stronger. My father's angry, labored voice slurring his words so badly I couldn't understand what he was saying.

It was not unusual for him to beat me when he'd been drinking but the look on his face the last time he came after me was different.

I was always terrified when I knew a beating was coming but the expression on his face forced my panic to a new level.

"No, Father. I did as you asked. The church is clean," I began rambling as I took small steps backward. "Moses is sleeping and I was just leaving."

"Ya cull thiiss clean?" he asked as he began picking up and throwing the bibles I had just placed neatly on the wooden pews.

I noticed some of the spines broke when they landed and knew he would blame their destruction on me.

"You and me are gonna play a game," he slurred as he began moving closer to me.

I continued to back up and prayed to God to intervene.

My father reached out and fell into me. There was nothing I could do to stop from falling when the weight of the man crashed into me.

My breath left me when we hit the floor but I managed to quickly squirm from underneath him and scoot away.

The fall had caused the back of my head to bleed but I didn't have time to worry about my injury. All I wanted to do was get away.

Even in a highly inebriated state, my father was quick. He grabbed me by my hair and threw me back down before I could make it to the door. I attempted to stand before he kicked me. His boot made contact with my stomach and I laid on the floor in a fetal position.

"Father Silas," I heard Moses' voice call.

My best friend, the only male who treated me with kindness, was standing with a gun in his hand. He was shaking but the weapon was aimed at my father.

Moses had bruises on his face and was bleeding from his lip. His expression was one I hadn't seen before. I was frightened for him, not my father.

My father turned and started walking toward Moses. "Boy, I will kill you for this," he warned.

Moses kept his aim true and ignored my father's words.

"Faith," he stated in a surprisingly calm manner.

I wiped my eyes and looked at him.

"We will never see each other again. But he will never hurt you again either," my only friend assured me before pulling the trigger.

My father didn't fall immediately but when he did, I was sure he was already dead.

I wasn't sad. I was afraid of what was going to happen to Moses.

"I have to leave now. I will never forget you," he spoke as he picked up a sack made from a sheet and threw it across his shoulder.

Moses was a year older than me but for a ten-year-old, he was handling what he had done with great calmness.

"Take me with you," I begged as I attempted to stand and run to him.

"I cannot. I am going home. My people are all dead but there are others. I need to find my way back to whom I was two years ago," he explained as he slid into the shadows.

The sounds of the townspeople approaching became clearer.

"What is going to happen to me?" I asked, allowing the tears to flow.

Moses abandoning me wasn't the first time I'd felt helpless but I'd never felt it quite so deeply.

"You live. Be happy," he answered before disappearing from my life forever.

Chapter Three

"The missionaries will be here tomorrow. Can we count on your help?" Pathkiller asked after a lengthy silence.

"He will do as he is asked," Lone Crow's adopted father assured.

"This must be Lone Crow's decision, Otter," the Chief argued gently.

"How long will you need me?" Lone Crow asked hesitantly before giving his father an apologetic look.

Pathkiller cleared his throat and looked to all those gathered before answering.

"They will stay until we ask them to leave. They are on a mission from their God. I understand that you do not enjoy using the white man's language but you are the only one of us who can. So, you are needed."

Lone Crow nodded his head and again rose to a standing posture. "I will be back with the sunrise. But I will seek solitude until then," he stated, walking from the enclosure.

As soon as the sun and wind hit his face, he felt better. When he was in the open, he was free.

Instead of going to his home, he found his pony and rode to his favorite spot.

The area was not easy to get to but it was the one place he felt he could allow the memories to play out without fear of being interrupted.

While he rode, he blocked the simmering memories by singing a song he'd learned from Faith. The Warrior was well aware it was a song about the white man's God but it was the only thing he allowed to stay with him since he'd escaped.

Once he had unburdened the horse of his packs, he lightly patted it on the rump. The pony was accustomed to Lone Crow's ways so he walked lazily toward a lush patch of grass and began eating.

Only after laying out his fur and lighting a small fire did the Warrior allow his mind to relax.

Lone Crow knew the next few hours were going to be punishing. But also knew if he didn't allow the memories to play out, he had no chance of helping his people.

Before he allowed his mind to be completely taken over with the recollections, he again questioned the possibility that the woman he had seen at the watering hole could be the girl he'd left in town all those years ago. As soon as he realized just how impossible that was, he laid down in the lush underbrush, crossed his hands behind his head, closed his eyes, and reluctantly entered into a past he'd sworn to forget.

***

Lone Crow was like many other young boys. He feared little and relished exploring the land. That particular day he had traveled to the river even after being warned against it.

While he was mindlessly playing in the water, he heard the sounds of gunfire and the screams of people. Frightened, he ran from the water and didn't stop until the smoke hanging in the air burnt his eyes.

His village had never been raided so the scene was challenging to understand. It was as if his mind would not allow him to grasp the devastation.

Instead of wailing and looking for his family, he picked up a bow and arrow quiver that was lying nearby and moved to the cover of one of the few homes not burning.

He knew little of warfare or hunting because he was still in the care of his mother and aunts. But he was sure he could kill.

Lone Crow's arms shook as he stood at the ready and tried to control his breathing.

The boy's focus was on what was happening in front of him. He was scared but still desperately trying to get a good shot at any of the numerous white men riding wildly through his town when he was grabbed from behind.

He kicked and yelled and fought but whoever had him did not let go until he was placed in the back of an open, wooden wagon.

After trying to run several times, he was tied and gagged.

For the next three days he was ungagged only when the soldiers offered him food.

He hadn't eaten any of it and calmly accepted that he would soon join his family in the Spirit World. He was young and had little hope of escape. He wasn't afraid of death as much as he feared what the men had in store for him. Apprehension and guilt consumed him and he remained rooted in his place in the wagon until the company of soldiers stopped in front of a bright white, ornate building at the center of the town.

He was weak from hunger but slowly made his way to the back of the wagon when he saw a man peering in at him curiously.

Lone Crow had no idea what the man was saying but he was sure he didn't want to go with him.

After being dragged from the wagon and beat until he was sure he was taking his last breath, he was placed in a small room beside the white building. It was tiny and more room was given to the chopped wood than to the boy.

The first night he was there, he allowed himself to cry. He even asked the Great Creator to end his suffering. Still, he woke the next morning. The pain he was enduring was something he hoped would end soon.

By midday, he found himself sweating and struggling to breathe. In his young mind, it was a good sign that he was dying. So he pulled his legs to his chest and waited for death.

When the door opened, a cold breeze blew in, his skin broke out in goosebumps, and a shiver consumed his body.

The man who had beat him and placed him in the small room was smiling and holding his hand out to Lone Crow.

He shook his head and tensed his muscles as he held his ground.

The man's smile disappeared and he grabbed Lone Crow's crossed arms before pulling him outside.

After being thrown to the ground, Lone Crow could feel the tissue and muscles being bruised and damaged by the man's boots mercilessly being thrust onto any exposed part of the boy's body.

He was quickly losing the ability to feel when he heard a girl's voice in the distance.

Again, he was unaware of what was being said but the girl's tone was one of begging.

The beating stopped and Lone Crow watched through swollen eyes as the man turned and used the back of his large hand to silence the small girl and knock her to the ground.

It was at that very moment he knew he had to live. If for no other reason than to keep his savior alive.

The beatings weren't an everyday occurrence but they happened often. And Lone Crow was usually the one who received the brunt of the man's anger.

Over the next few months, the man who proclaimed himself Lone Crow's liberator cut the young boy's long hair and burnt his native clothing. He was forced to wear the white man's clothes and learn the language. At first, Lone Crow fought but soon discovered the less he struggled, the easier his life was. The man's name, Father Silas, was the second word he learned to speak. The first was Faith.

Faith was shy, scared, lonely, and broken. Lone Crow thought of her as a wounded bird and always attempted to protect her.

She was a year younger than he but was smart and helped him learn to read and write. Most nights, after Father Silas fell into a drunken stupor, he and Faith took the opportunity to talk into the wee hours.

Faith taught him to speak English. And before Lone Crow accepted the tongue as his own, he taught Faith one Cherokee word. He taught her how to say bird: "tsisqua." The longer he was away from his people, the less he spoke of them. He learned much about the ways of the white people because he was forced to live as one. But Faith seemed to make everything a little easier, talking to her and listening as she read stories from the bible. It didn't matter what she was reading. Her voice was soft and full of caring and he knew he would never tire of hearing it.

At the time, Lone Crow was too young to understand that Faith would be the only woman he would ever love. But the older he grew, the more he realized just how true it was.

As the years passed, the beatings became more intense and frequent. The only time the two were spared from Father Silas' brand of discipline was on Sundays and that quickly became the time the two would sit and plan their future.

The night he took action was two years later. Lone Crow was in the middle of his twelfth year. If he were still among his people, he would be ready to accompany his father and uncles on his first raid. But Lone Crow was forced to work the small plot of land beside the church and was expected to complete any task that was labor-intensive. Because he was not an idle child, he grew in strength every day. And because he was always planning his escape, he began to pay more attention to things around him. Knowing patience was all he needed did not make his life any easier. Every night before going to sleep, he prayed to the Great Creator and asked for the discipline to continue to take the beatings without fighting back.

The night that Lone Crow was forced to alter his plan, Father Silas came back from the shed where he'd sat and drank in solitude.

"Moses, boy," Silas yelled between blows. "That is my daughter and I don't like the way you are looking at her. I have tried and tried to get the devil out of you but it seems there is no helping you people," he spat.

Lone Crow was balled up on the floor, doing his best to catch his breath.

He did have feelings for Faith. They had spoken of leaving together for at least a year. Helping her was the only reason he hadn't run before. But he was still too young to take her from the only way of life she knew. That plan would surely end in disaster. The boy didn't have the luxury of thinking through his next action. He had vowed to protect Faith and he knew where the Father was going when Silas ceased beating him and closed the door. What he had just endured was not a regular beating and Lone Crow wasn't sure Father Silas' attack on Faith wouldn't kill her.

After several attempts that ended up with him back on the ground, he was able to stand. Once he was steady on his feet, he located the closest weapon and stumbled his way toward the chapel.

Killing Father Silas had always been an inevitability. But Lone Crow had hoped he could postpone the act until it was safe for him to take Faith with him.

The barbarity of Father Silas' last attack had been the final straw. He knew he couldn't postpone his next action any longer. He wasn't sure he would reach Faith in time to stop her from being 'disciplined,' but he was going to make sure it was the last time she had to endure a beating at the hands of the man who called himself her father.

Pulling the trigger and sending the bullet into Silas was effortless. He hesitated only long enough to assure Faith she would be fine. Telling the girl, who had been his only sanity, that he couldn't take her with him, was immensely difficult.

Lone Crow was convinced the townsfolk were aware of the treatment he and Faith endured and hoped she would not be blamed in any way for her father's murder. He prayed she would be able to find the joy her life had been lacking.

Knowing he had to leave her didn't make the task any easier. But once he heard the sounds of people coming toward the church, he knew he had no other choice.

Only a few weeks earlier had he packed some supplies into a blanket. At that moment, he was glad he'd had the forethought to do so. He was weak, badly bruised, and still bleeding from his mouth so any extra comfort was a plus.

Lone Crow walked for the better part of three days before a Native hunting party found him sleeping in the thick roots of a tree.

A tall, painted man approached him cautiously and held out a piece of dried meat to Lone Crow.

"What happened to you?" he asked when Lone Crow took the offered meal quickly and began savoring the taste of it.

Lone Crow recalled the language but it still took a minute for the meaning of the words to sink in.

Instead of answering the man's inquiry, he shook his head and finished what he was so eagerly chewing on.

"Who cut your hair and beat you?" the man continued his gentle interrogation as he reached to hold Lone Crow's face in his hands.

Lone Crow cowered and pulled away.

A look of understanding crossed the man's face. "Do you have a home?" he asked, standing and backing away a step.

Lone Crow took a deep breath and looked up at the man. "No," he answered, searching his memory for the right word.

"You do now," the man decided, holding his hand out to aid Lone Crow in standing. "That is, if you want to come along."

"I do," Lone Crow replied, gritting his teeth as he took the man's outstretched hand.

"From this day forward, you are the adoptive son of Otter. When you are ready, you can tell me what happened to you."

That was ten years earlier and although the Warrior loved and respected his adopted father, he still hadn't shared any of his childhood with the man.

## Chapter Four

The days leading up to our departure were unusually quiet and uneventful.

I was still concerned as to the reason why Tobias wanted me to accompany him but knew there was nothing I could do to change his mind.

My husband had stopped returning home for meals two days before we left.

His absence was a godsend on the one hand. On the other, it allowed me too much time to think about my childhood. And as the flashes of scenes turned to full-blown memories, I realized Moses was the only person who had shown me any kindness. The understanding made me both angry and heartbroken. The more I thought about my life, the less I understood. Why had no other person seen me as important? The true, brutally-honest reality of my situation hit me hard.

In between tears and anger, I packed and readied everything while I waited for Tobias' return. While attempting to keep busy, I decided to escape from the traveling party as soon as the opportunity arose. I wasn't sure if my plan wasn't a direct reaction to my anger at the world but the reason really wasn't important. It was a need that grew with each breath, almost like a whisper in the back of my mind, a warning that I may never get another opportunity like the one I was being given again.

The way I saw it was, Tobias was not taking me for any other reason than to be a buffer to his ongoing relationship with Wilma. I was of the mind that Wilma's husband should know what was happening. The only thing that stopped me from sharing my knowledge with Howard was I was afraid Tobias might kill the man, or me, or both of us.

If we were away from the town and in a small group, I thought chances were better that the information would end up getting Tobias killed. And I was alright with that thought. But I knew it was not Christian to wish for the death of your husband. Still, after the life I had been given, it was difficult for me to believe I was important to God. I had been praying for his help as long as I could remember, begging him to allow me some peace. He never heard or answered my prayers. Or if he did hear them, he didn't see my pleas as important.

I never spoke my beliefs out loud but, when riding my horse on the Sunday mornings I wasn't forced to stand by Tobias' side, I felt a peacefulness that I didn't feel anywhere else.

While I fought with the emotions that accompanied the memories of my past, I didn't allow myself too much hope. My reality was most probably not going to be any different when we returned. That was, unless he really was planning on either killing me or leaving me. I was well aware the man could have killed me many times and hadn't. But things had changed. Tobias had found another woman. One who apparently didn't bring out the evil in him. Maybe the only reason he wanted me to go was to kill me. Between the memories, my plan to run, and all the unsavory reasons my husband wanted me to be by his side, my brain was entirely too busy to allow me to sleep the night before our departure.

I heard Tobias come into the house before dawn and listened as he hummed one of his favorite hymns and walked around the house.

Hearing him not stumble was a hopeful sign but I still worried he might have had too much to drink. So, I stayed silent and kept my eyes closed when he opened the bedroom door.

"Faith?" he asked in a calm, almost caring voice.

Over the years I had been able to train my body not to flinch when he spoke. He seemed to get enjoyment from my frightened reactions so I did my best to hide them. Even with the gentle tone he was employing, my muscles were tense and my eyes remained closed.

"You need to get up. We are meeting in the sanctuary for prayer before we leave," my husband continued speaking, sounding as if he were moving nearer to me with every word. "From now on, we will have to be close. Do not make me have to hurt you."

His calm tone was tinged with anger when I felt him sit on the bed beside me. I continued stubbornly feigning sleep until he moved to pull the hair from my face.

"I will behave," I promised when my eyes opened widely because of his touch.

He smiled sadly and stood before walking back to the doorway.

"Good. Now get dressed. Wilma has breakfast made and we need to pick up the last of the supplies before we head out. Hurry up."

I nodded and quickly rose from the bed.

Tobias stood in the open entryway and watched as I put my dress over my undergarments.

"You need to eat more," he informed me. "But those bruises are healing nicely," he continued as I went about my morning ritual. "The man coming with us, the one that is known to these people, his name is Adam. He is probably gonna want to talk to you since you haven't met yet. Remember to watch your tongue and do not talk too much," he warned as I waited for him to move from the doorway.

I wasn't slumber hazed because sleep had evaded me but he wasn't making much sense and I fought with the notion of asking him why he felt the need to warn me. We had been married for seven long years and I had only once made the mistake of being honest and open. I wondered why he felt the need to reinforce his belief. But I stayed silent, bowed my head, and waited for him to move.

"I'm gonna need to hear you say you understand me, Faith," Tobias growled as he angrily grabbed my arms, not giving thought to the bruises he was surely leaving.

While he shook me like a ragdoll, I relaxed into the motion. It was a trick I'd learned early. If I didn't fight the sway, it was not as jarring.

When he finally ceased jolting me, I nodded and looked up at him.

"I will do my best not to anger you during this trip, husband," I stated, hoping he didn't hear the anger in my voice when I spoke the word 'husband.'

He grumbled and moved from my path but stayed one step behind me until we were walking from the small house.

Once we were outside, I saw the wagons were lined up outside the church and several of the congregants were making their way inside the chapel.

I hadn't been in the company of Tobias' parishioners for months and was a bit apprehensive. My knee jerk reaction to all the company caused my step to slow.

"Oh no, Faith," Tobias whispered as he grabbed my hand in his. He squeezed so tightly, tears formed in my eyes.

At the same time he was reaching to turn me to face him, I heard someone clear their throat loudly.

Tobias quickly removed his hand from my arm before smiling and acknowledging the man.

"This must be your lovely wife, Faith," the stranger smiled warmly and held his hand out to me.

I had been around people who claimed to be Christians all my life. But the man standing in front of me reaching out was the calmest, warmest soul I'd ever encountered. Love and understanding radiated from him.

He was taller than me but not as tall as Tobias. Still, his presence was huge.

Tobias was tall and slender. His face was thin and his features were sharp. His hair was brown and his eyes were blue. He was a handsome man. At least, I was sure I once considered him attractive.

Adam, on the other hand, was what I could only describe as beautiful. He had long, curly, black hair, deep green eyes, and a short beard.

His smile was almost hypnotic and I felt as if I were moving in slow motion when I placed my hand in his.

"Adam," Tobias greeted, regaining his composure. "This is Faith," he stated as he grabbed me around the waist in a move that I was sure was unnecessary.

My hand lingered in Adam's and he kept the smile on his face as he searched my eyes.

"It is nice to meet you. I look forward to many talks along the trail," he said, looking from me to Tobias. "I believe the town has prepared a going away feast. Shall we?" he asked, gesturing for Tobias and me to take the lead.

I turned only because Tobias was still holding me.

"Do not be fooled by the man," my husband whispered. "And do not let your guard down around him."

I nodded and walked beside Tobias into the church.

The breakfast was painful to endure. No one sought me out to speak. Most women avoided eye contact with me entirely. When I did catch one of their glances, they looked sad and much like they felt sorry for me.

I quickly learned I did not care for their pity or their remoteness.

The longer we were there, the more I attempted to sneak out the door.

By the time I had moved close enough to the exit to make my escape, Adam was walking my way.

"Were you thinking about taking some air?" he asked.

"I ... I ... no. I was looking for my husband," I both stammered and lied.

"There you are," I heard Tobias voice. "Shall we gather the last of the supplies?" he asked, again placing his arm around me. "Adam, are you traveling with us or Howard and Wilma this time?"

"I do appreciate the offer. But we are going to get mighty tired of each other before we reach the village. I brought my horse. I will follow your lead," he informed Tobias before lifting his hat from his head, looking at me, and bowing slightly. "It has been a pleasure, Faith. I am sure we will find time to speak soon. Maybe around the fire tonight."

I felt Tobias' grip tightening and was doing my best not to allow Adam to see that my husband was causing me pain.

A strange look crossed his face but he quickly recovered and smiled at Tobias.

"Tobias, I do believe this trip will be lifechanging for you," Adam decreed before leaving us.

"What did he ask you?" Tobias asked, pulling me through the doorway, not stopping until he was practically dragging me to the waiting wagon.

"He asked if I was going for some fresh air," I answered, doing my best to stay on my feet.

"I know we need him but I don't like him," he informed me as he pushed me to the wooden seat and climbed up to sit beside me.

I failed to notice the people from the church had gathered around the two wagons and was deeply embarrassed when I did.

Tobias did seem slightly concerned with his lapse in behavior when we were in public. And I found I quite enjoyed his discomfort.

"Keep us in your prayers. We are doing the Lord's work," he said before nudging the animals forward.

I sat beside him, silently picking at the skin around my fingernails.

"Faith, you better cheer up," he warned when we made our last stop before leaving the town.

I nodded but didn't look up until he had left my side.

While waiting for Tobias to return, I took a deep breath and told myself that the trip would not end in my death and that I still had the beginnings of a plan. It wasn't as easy to convince myself of those things as it should have been.

Chapter Five

Lone Crow did not sleep. Instead, he decided to get a better look at the people who were causing his anxiety. Fear was one emotion he would have rather left dead. He had not shaken from fear since he'd escaped the white man's town.

Again, he allowed the memory of his fleeing to fill his mind. As soon as he felt he had run far enough, a sense of relief and calmness overtook him. He knew he was lost and also couldn't be sure he would be able to locate a friendly face before he died. But he was free. It was a feeling he'd forgotten and it brought him great joy. As he lay in the tree roots, dried blood on his face and muscles fatigued to exhaustion, he promised himself that he would never interact with the whites again.

And yet that was precisely what he was going to do because the man who allowed him to be free for the last ten years wanted him to.

Instead of fighting with his sleeplessness, he placed his packs on the pony and rode back toward the location he had last seen the wagons.

Lone Crow did not know how he would react when faced with a white man, let alone one who claimed he was doing God's work. So he thought watching them from afar might settle his nerves. If his initial reactions were fear and self-preservation, at least his family would not be present to witness it. If nothing else, he needed to be hard and guarded when he was forced to interact with the people.

The trip to the watering hole took less time than Lone Crow expected. As hard as he tried to calm his nerves, he remained atop his pony for the better part of an hour after reaching the destination.

· As soon as he was able to quell his fear and stress, he saw that the sun was just beginning its daily battle with the darkness. He knew he had taken too much time to adjust. The travelers would be waking soon and he was expected back at camp before they arrived. Fearing he still didn't have a good grip on his emotions, he slid from his ride's back and began sneaking closer.

Lone Crow knew someone was awake and from the sounds coming from near the water, it was not one but two people. A couple had separated themselves in the hopes of attaining privacy.

The thought of interrupting the two was fleeting.

Instead of finishing his task, he began backing toward his pony.

As he departed, he saw the two stand and begin to dress.

Neither saw him as they giggled and wiped the dirt from one another's clothing but he was able to get a good look at them.

The fear he had been feeling was short-lived but it was intense.

As soon as the fear was gone, he was washed in an understanding that had evaded him until then.

He was no longer a child and the people he was going to have to speak for were not as big as he remembered Father Silas to be. In fact, the man was shorter and looked as if he didn't work the land.

The woman was not the flame-haired one he'd seen earlier. She had blond hair and although he couldn't explain the disappointment that ran through him when he realized that, it did just the same.

While riding back to the camp, he began to feel stronger and more confident that he would be able to do as his elders asked. The trip may not have turned out like he wanted but it did, in fact, allow Lone Crow to understand he was not that helpless child any longer. He was a man and had no reason to fear the visitors. He was still free and was surrounded by people who cared for him.

By the time he reached the outskirts of his village, the Warrior felt he had the task well in hand.

"Lone Crow," Otter called.

Lone Crow patted his pony and left him to mingle with the other horses before looking toward his adopted father.

The look on Otter's face was a mixture of pride and apprehension. And Lone Crow knew there was no way to prevent his father from accompanying him to the council house.

"I am pleased to see you, my son," Otter greeted as he slipped his arm around Lone Crow's neck.

"I don't believe this will be a problem," Lone Crow informed Otter quickly, hoping he was correct in his thoughts.

"I know you are strong. I have watched you grow from a frightened, shy child into a warrior we are all thankful and proud to ride with. You may have kept what you've endured to yourself but, whatever it was, as horrific as I believe it was, you have grown and should not allow those shadows to dance in your mind. If I didn't believe doing this would help you put it all behind you once and for all, I would have never agreed to ask for your help."

Otter's declaration was the most the two had spoken in months and it felt good to hear the old man's thoughts.

"Father," he said, stopping and looking at the man. "You have been the best father I could have hoped for. Maybe when the missionaries are gone, I will tell you the whole story. And I thank you for understanding and letting me be who I am. Now, shall we get this over with?" Lone Crow asked, smiling, hopeful his optimistic attitude would hold.

"I will be beside you. Do not forget that," Otter said, hugging Lone Crow quickly before gesturing for his son to take the lead.

Lone Crow felt the slight hesitation in his step but ignored it and forged on.

Once they were inside the large building, Lone Crow moved to a corner and removed the beaded leather vest he wore. What should have been a simple task was anything but. Still, it was one he felt he was finally ready to perform.

Since he'd arrived in the village, the only people who had seen him without a covering were his parents. He knew he carried scars on his back from the beatings. Until the moment of clarity he'd experienced earlier, he would have never dreamt of allowing others to see them. But he felt strong and determined and the scars were his to carry.

"Are you sure?" Otter asked, touching his son on the shoulder as Lone Crow placed the vest on the ground.

"I am," Lone Crow answered, smiling at his father. "I survived the beatings and I have been ashamed for too long. The one thing I can promise you is that I will never be beaten again."

"That is good. Now let us see what Pathkiller has to say," Otter urged as he escorted Lone Crow to the circle of men gathered at the center of the building.

A large fire burned in the center of the circle and prayers were being offered up.

The two men sat and waited for the prayers to end.

"Since this is our first contact with God's people, I turn to you, Lone Crow," Pathkiller began speaking, looking at all those gathered, before landing his attention on the Warrior.

Lone Crow cleared his throat and waited for Pathkiller to finish the rest of the thought.

"We know you were treated badly by the man who took you. But you were with him for a time. Anything you can tell us about these people would be helpful."

Lone Crow found he was uncomfortable with all the things the Chief knew about his childhood trauma. He honestly thought most were unaware of anything that had transpired.

"What do you want to know?" he asked, after taking a deep breath.

"What do they really want?" Pathkiller questioned, sounding as if he were genuinely confused by the visit.

Lone Crow knew little of the white world outside of the church but was sure the white men did want something.

He had been forced to listen to the stories from the book they called the Bible. It was the only book he ever read but the reading and suggestions the text set forth where not how the people acted. The one thing he was sure of was the church did offer their way of life to anyone who would listen. Still he felt there was more to the visit than just hearing scriptures.

"I had limited interaction with most of them," Lone Crow began his answer after giving it some thought. "I do not believe they are all of the same breed as the man who took me. I have proof that some people are good and innocent and looking for a higher power to explain their lives. But I do not believe they all are," he continued before realizing he might be giving too much information in his reply. "I suggest we act as if we believe they are here to teach of the ways of their God, just as they said. And I will listen when they think I am not."

"Why would we need to know about their God?" A man asked as he leaned closer to the fire. "We have our own Creator."

Lone Crow did not have an answer to the man's question.

"Do you believe our Creator and theirs are not the same?" another voice piped in.

The questions were not easy to answer at the best of times. Lone Crow was not spiritual. He had prayed to every being he knew of and the beatings continued so he had quit attempting to communicate with any higher power.

"What are your thoughts," Pathkiller asked.

"They will want to read their verses and sing songs. At least that is what I expect. But I will be able to tell you more when I have met them. I still do not think mixing with them for long is a good idea." Lone Crow stated, finding himself falling back into nervousness.

If the people visiting felt the same as the people who had stolen him when he was a boy, he didn't trust them. Silas began changing Lone Crow the minute he took him in. The man changed his name, cut his hair, burnt his clothes, and some of the worst beatings Lone Crow endured were because he had fallen back into his mother tongue. Lone Crow accepted that all white men were not like Silas but he wasn't sure they didn't believe the same as him.

Why a race of people would intentionally go out of their way to change another was a query that he very much wanted an answer to. It wasn't the only inquiry the Warrior had but those questions were too deep and better saved for another time.

Otter nudged his son with his knee and pulled him from his thoughts.

"Well?" he heard Pathkiller ask.

Since he hadn't heard the last question, he looked to his father for help.

"He asked why you think the length of their stay is important," Otter informed his son in a whisper as he leaned closer to Lone Crow's ear.

"I believe the less we interact with them, the better. But my experience was my own. You will make your own decision once you have spoken with them."

Pathkiller looked confused but didn't continue his interrogation.

The sounds of whoops from the warriors alerted those gathered that the missionary party had entered the outskirts of the village.

Lone Crow fought the desire to run but quickly calmed himself again.

"Do you want me to go with you when you meet them?" he asked, only because he knew that was what was expected.

As angry as it made him, he felt his strength waning.

Otter patted his son on the leg in a comforting gesture.

"Yes," Pathkiller decided as he stood and waited for Lone Crow to rise. "We will return and smoke the pipe."

The dust the wagons kicked up made it difficult to see the people but Lone Crow could make out the flame-haired woman.

"Why did they bring women?" Pathkiller asked, clearly perplexed by the fact.

"I do not know. Maybe they think we will be swayed by their beauty," Lone Crow offered, wondering where that attitude had come from.

"Huh. Our women are beautiful. So comely that they are often the object of trapper's and trader's affection," Pathkiller stated, sounding both confused and a little angry. "We will leave them with the women while we talk," the Chief decided as the dust settled.

Lone Crow stopped in his tracks and fought for breath.

The flame-haired woman *was* his Faith. He would know her anywhere. She was just as beautiful as she had been when they last saw one another.

Pathkiller stopped two steps ahead and glanced back at Lone Crow, looking expectantly at the Warrior.

Lone Crow was not about to enlighten the man to his discovery.

"I am ready," Lone Crow lied, as he walked to Pathkiller's side.

Lone Crow steeled himself for the meeting the best he could.

His heart was racing and his palms were sweating. His body hadn't reacted that way since he left her so many years earlier.

While they walked closer, the man sitting beside Faith jumped from the wagon seat and began to walk toward them.

A smile was plastered on his face and he was quickly followed by another man.

Lone Crow wasn't concerned with either of the men. He wanted to make eye contact with Faith. In fact, he was determined to make it happen.

Right before the leading man held his hand out to the Warrior, Faith's eyes focused on Lone Crow.

Fear and excitement crossed her face but no recognition.

Lone Crow was both extremely disappointed and concerned that the woman might not be who he was sure she was.

"My name is Tobias Moore and this is Adam. I believe you may have met him before," the man introduced and greeted the two.

Lone Crow understood every word that the man spoke but was still too shocked to speak, let alone inform the strange white man that he had not seen the one called Adam before.

Pathkiller nudged the Warrior.

"This is the Chief, Pathkiller, and I am called Lone Crow," the Warrior spoke, still paying more attention to the lost looking woman than the men standing in front of him.

## Chapter Six

The trip was not as bad as I expected but it wasn't conducive to me dropping my tensed state either.

Tobias appeared to be biting his tongue and was absolutely attempting to look good in Adam's eyes. But his calmness lasted only until we retired for the night.

He hadn't laid a hand on me other than grabbing my arm to show me just how strongly he felt about whatever was bothering him that night. But he had continued to hone his new form of torture. The change from physical to mental abuse was seamless but I still preferred being hit to reliving my childhood.

By the third day it was abundantly clear that Tobias was growing unsettled. I knew the man well enough to understand if he didn't get an opportunity to visit with Wilma soon, he would turn his unrequited amorousness to me. And I wasn't sure if he forced me, I wouldn't scream. So as we rode in silence, I prayed for an answer to my latest obstacle. My track record with having prayers answered was nonexistent but that never stopped me from trying.

For the last few hours, the only thing that left Tobias' mouth were grumbles and his left leg went from calm to bouncing. Both were signs that he was experiencing great difficulty keeping his temper in check.

I won't lie. His discomfort was something I savored, to a point. So, I remained silent and enjoyed the beauty the land provided.

Every day we traveled further from the towns and outposts, the scenery grew more breathtaking. And instead of planning my escape or worrying that I might never return from the trip, I focused on the wonders of my surroundings.

Trees grew into one another, resulting in beautiful, mangled works of art. It was the first time I had seen nature that wasn't altered by man and was surprised to learn that grass frequently grew as tall as the wagon. Flowers dotted the landscape and the air smelled sweet. It was a nice relief from the odor which greeted you each morning back home. Our town was established only ten years earlier and yet it still reeked of dirt and animal droppings. There were days when the wind blew in our favor and the smell wasn't overpowering but those days were few and far between.

I had never traveled more than a few hours from town, and even then, the land had been cleared to make room for new homes and buildings. There were a few trees and plots of grass but nature had been curbed to allow the people to live in 'comfort.'

Because the beauty was so breathtaking and seemingly endless, I didn't miss talking. And due to the happiness nature was providing me, I hoped the memory would stay with me long after we returned to civilization.

But as calm as I was feeling, I knew I needed to try to speak to Tobias. His unhappiness was still simmering but the man had a limit and I knew it well. And yet, it still took another hour before I turned my attention to him.

After rehearsing the question over and over in my mind, and changing the phrasing several times, I opened my mouth and broke the proverbial ice.

"I am sure I can keep Howard and Adam busy if you want to try to speak to Wilma alone," I offered, wincing once my statement was spoken.

Tobias tightened his jaw and slowly turned to me. "I don't need you feeling sorry for me."

I didn't. In fact, I couldn't see a circumstance ever arising where I would feel sorry for the man. But he did sound on edge and my top priority was to keep our contact to a minimum. Even if Tobias and Wilma were breaking one of the commandments, I was sure their behavior would not reflect poorly on me.

"I was just offering you a way of relief," I spoke in a whisper before biting my fingernail and turning away from the man.

"Why?" he asked, sounding more interested in my answer than he had at any other time in our life together.

The question caught me off guard and it took a moment for me to answer.

"Why do you want to help me?" he repeated in a furious tone.

I bit my bottom lip and slowly turned to look at him.

Tobias' expression was one I'd seen often and it was usually followed up by a right hook or stiff kick.

"I will not offer help again," I assured him, keeping any anger from my voice.

A deep grumbled began at the base of Tobias' gut and slowly grew in intensity as it rose to his throat.

While he was embracing his anger, I was faced with a choice. I could sit there and allow him to hit me, or I could jump from the wagon and take my chances.

I chose to jump. It wasn't much of a jump, really. I moved quickly and tried to actually step from the ride.

Before I could release my grip, I felt myself being gently grabbed by my waist before being placed on Adam's horse.

"Are you alright?" he asked, concern thick in his voice.

"She is fine," Tobias answered, slowing the wagon to a stop. "She was just saying she needed to have a moment alone and was waiting for me to stop."

"Oh, I see," Adam replied, clearly not believing the story my husband was offering.

I stayed quiet until the two were finished speaking.

"Thank you for your help, but I believe I can manage from here," I explained in the most even tone I could manage.

"Tobias, why don't you follow the others. I will accompany Faith back to you when she has seen to herself," Adam offered.

His suggestion was just that. A mere recommendation and yet, there was a commanding undertone.

Tobias huffed quietly at the man's offer. "She is my woman and how would it look if you walked off with her?" he asked quickly.

Adam appeared both insulted and slightly puzzled by Tobias' question.

"Tobias?" he asked as he slid from his horse before offering me his hand. "I thought we were among friends. A Christian would never touch another man's wife. I was merely attempting to be helpful. If that is how you truly feel, I would suggest you pray on it. Now, I will return your lovely wife in a short time."

I could see Tobias fuming inside but he managed to smile a tight grin and nod his head in agreement before giving me a familiar warning look.

"You are the only one of us who knows where we are. Are we getting close?" Tobias asked, still not spurring the animals to move.

My husband was clearly concerned about leaving me alone but not for the reasons Adam assumed.

"I can return to the wagon and wait if it won't be long before we arrive," I offered, feeling as if there was no way I was going to come out of my new predicament without at least a few bruises.

Tobias visibly relaxed when he leaned toward me and offered his hand.

"I am sure your husband does not want to put you in any kind of discomfort," Adam stated as he gently pushed my outstretched hand to my side before looking up at Tobias and smiling one of the most genuine grins I had ever seen. "I will have her back before you miss her." Adam continued, as he walked to the horses pulling the wagon and slapped one of them gently on the rump.

They began moving before Tobias was able to digest what had happened.

"Now," Adam said as he turned his attention to me. "Let's see about finding you some privacy."

When he reached for me, I recoiled. I hadn't meant to do it but my body was always in a defensive mode.

Adam shook his head and forced a sad smile to cross his face. "Has he always beat you?" he asked easily.

No one except Moses had ever asked me such a blunt question and I was taken aback by the man's forthrightness.

I had always maintained that people knew how I was being treated but, for one reason or another, decided to ignore it.

Even if I wanted to, I couldn't change the response I gave him. It was hardwired into me.

"He doesn't beat me. He is on edge but he would never beat me. I am his wife," I explained as I walked further from the man in search of a thick clump of grass.

I hadn't needed to relieve myself but knew if I didn't pretend, it would only cause me more trouble.

"Faith," he continued speaking to me after turning his back. "You do not need to lie to me. I have seen men like Tobias before. They profess to be Christian but do not understand the meaning of the word. I want you to appreciate that I am on your side."

"Faith!" I heard Tobias' voice growing louder.

I knew he had come after me and his actions were concerning. I hadn't said anything but I couldn't be sure how much of Adam's statement he overheard. But, no matter what, I knew I was going to regret my actions later.

Adam appeared surprised by Tobias' sudden appearance. I wasn't. It was all part of his need to control everything about me. If I were alone, he could care less what I was doing but he could not allow me to be in anyone else's company without him present.

"Tobias," Adam stated when my husband stood beside him. "Tonight, when we stop, I believe you and I should pray together. We must discuss many things about our mission," the man continued as he placed his hand on Tobias' arm and began walking away.

I watched the scene unfold and remained hidden until they had placed some distance between us.

If I'd thought there had been any way I could have survived on my own, I would have run then. I understood that Adam thought he was offering help but what he was doing was making my life a little harder.

When I returned to the waiting wagon, Tobias and Adam looked as if they were in prayer. So, I stayed silent and climbed to my seat.

"Thank you for praying with me, Tobias," Adam said, patting my husband on the back before mounting his waiting pony. "We will be stopping by a water hole soon. While Wilma is cooking and we are planning our mission, why don't you take a nice relaxing bath, Faith?" he asked when he looked back at us.

The man was being polite and caring but he was really beginning to get on my nerves. The more he showed me kindness, the harder the evening was going to be for me.

"If that is what she wants," Tobias agreed, sounding as if he didn't mean a word of what he said.

After sitting beside me, he kept his eyes forward and stayed silent until we neared the water hole.

"I don't need to bathe," I offered, hoping he hadn't been simmering in his anger. And if he hadn't been, I certainly didn't want to change that fact.

"No," he said, shaking his head. "You're gonna bathe. And when you walk to Wilma, to ask for soap, you are gonna tell her I need to see her later. You hear me?" he asked angrily.

I was shocked and momentarily conflicted by his order but knew Wilma was really my only hope of calming Tobias. So I didn't hesitate too long before agreeing to my husband's terms.

As soon as we stopped, Adam met us and offered me his hand. "I believe the rest will do you some good. You seem to be enjoying nature. And that is a good thing."

I bit my lip and prayed the man would stop being so thoughtful. I didn't have much experience with flirting or courting. Still, I absolutely did not feel as if Adam was interested in anything other than my happiness. Unfortunately, I was sure Tobias didn't see the man's kindness the same way.

"It is beautiful," I agreed before looking at Tobias. "Are you sure?" I asked meekly.

He rolled his eyes, rubbed the bridge of his nose, and looked at the sky before answering me. "Remember, Wilma has the soap you will be needing."

I nodded and walked directly toward the woman whom I should have seen as my rival.

Wilma looked shocked and scared as I approached her. That information confused me for a bit and then I realized she was afraid that I might tell her husband what I knew. I probably should have but couldn't. I needed the woman as a buffer and even if I knew that was not the right thing to do, I was going to continue to do so as long as I could.

I tried to communicate to her that I was no threat and slowed my pace, stopping a few steps from her.

She was still looking from me to Howard, who was occupied with pulling the cookware from the wagon.

"I just came to ask for the use of some soap," I informed her as I resumed taking small steps closer. "And Tobias would very much like to see you tonight," I whispered.

Relief washed through her and she smiled before walking to the wagon and bringing me back a bar of soap. "Thank you," she said quietly. "And I have no idea why you are not angry about our relationship but thank you for everything."

I didn't know what to say so I stayed silent. I wanted to ask her why Tobias didn't treat her badly. But I couldn't. Maybe I was afraid the problem didn't emanate from my husband.

Was there something fundamentally flawed in me? Was it my fault I was abused? The questions were weighty and depressing. And I wanted to enjoy the peace of a bath so I shoved all the bad thoughts from my mind, undressed to my underclothes, and walked into the crisp, refreshing water.

While I was enjoying the water and its surroundings, I blocked everything else from my mind.

Being helpful to my husband's carnal affair may not have been the right thing to do, but doing so gave me a good chance at sleeping soundly that night.

# Chapter Seven

Lone Crow was so fixated on the woman that the tall, thin, white man surprised him when he spoke again.

The man turned and looked back at the woman while speaking. "That is my wife and the other woman is Howard's wife. Her name is Wilma ..."

The short, stocky man interrupted, stepped in front of the man who was talking, and smiled before holding his hand out to Lone Crow. "I am called Adam. And this is Tobias."

Lone Crow hated the thin man immediately but the man who just introduced the pair was different. There was a genuineness to him that Lone Crow had never encountered before. Still, he had no intention of shaking the stranger's hand.

The Warrior shook his head and kept his hands by his side before speaking to the Chief. "Pathkiller this is Adam and that," he said, pointing at the thin man who appeared to be angered at the shorter man's actions, "he is called Tobias. One of the women is called Wilma and the other man is called Howard. What do you want me to say to them?"

"I do not like the thin one," Pathkiller stated, looking at his uninvited company. "The woman with the flame hair..." the Chief stopped talking and focused on the thin, discontented man. "She carries the same look in her eyes as you did when you were young."

Lone Crow didn't respond to the Chief's keen insight but he did once again look to the woman.

The tall, thin man cleared his throat and also turned back to look at his wife.

The woman was oblivious to the attention she was garnering.

She was sitting with her elbows on her knees, watching some children playing. Her hair fell from its bindings and brushed her face with each gentle gust of wind.

As badly as Lone Crow wanted to convince himself he had been mistaken, he could not. He was sure the woman was the girl he had fallen in love with.

Many emotions swirled inside him but he hid them all and forced himself to concentrate on his task.

"Who is she?" Pathkiller asked, pulling Lone Crow from his thoughts.

Lone Crow looked at the man standing in front of him. "Pathkiller would like to know who the other woman is." He explained, forcing himself to stay attentive to the man called Adam.

"That is Faith. She is married to Tobias." He answered, acting as if he weren't through speaking.

Pathkiller raised his hand to stop the conversation from continuing. "Tell them the women stay here. The men can follow us," the Chief stated, sounding bored with the discussion thus far.

Lone Crow did as he was instructed and fully expected the men to agree. So, when the thin one, Tobias, objected, he looked to Adam.

"He is a very intense person," the man quickly made excuses for Tobias' behavior.

Lone Crow gritted his teeth and explained what was happening to Pathkiller.

"They either stay or you all go. It is simply the way of our people," he interpreted before taking a step back and crossing his arms in front of his chest.

The Chief was not telling the truth but Lone Crow was not about to question Pathkiller's statement.

Adam turned to Tobias and spoke in hushed tones before apologizing and making a few more excuses for the behavior.

Lone Crow was doing his best to stay focused but the woman continued to demand his attention.

"We appreciate your hospitality," Adam assured the Warrior. "And we will not cause you any more grief. Can I just go and tell the others what is happening?" he asked with reverence in his tone.

Lone Crow nodded his agreement to the proposal before explaining his actions to Pathkiller.

Adam smiled gratefully before grabbing the other man and turning him around.

Lone Crow couldn't hear what was being said but he wasn't as interested as he should have been.

"Do you know that woman?" Pathkiller asked as soon as the visitors were out of earshot.

Lone Crow was again mentally willing the woman to look his way when he heard the Chief's inquiry.

"Why are you asking me that?"

It was a valid question. Lone Crow may have been forced to live among the white people for two years but in that time, he had only truly known three people. The odds were against him running into any of them in his village.

He thought he had been able to hide the rushing, heavy emotions he was experiencing and was angered at the thought he had not.

"She is a delicate, beautiful woman. A woman who makes you want to protect her," Pathkiller answered.

The Chief's reply had not satisfied Lone Crow's question and he found he couldn't allow the query to go unanswered.

"Why did you ask me that?" He repeated, turning to face the man.

"As I said, she has the look you carried. And I forget just how many whites are here. I suppose it would be impossible. But I find I must ask, do all the adult men mistreat the women and children?"

Lone Crow had no idea. In his experience, they had. But he hoped the practice of beating on anyone smaller and weaker was not normal.

Before Lone Crow could form an answer that wasn't full of anger and hate, the men returned with the third one in tow. Pathkiller nodded his head and they began walking to the council house.

The meeting was longer than Lone Crow was comfortable with and in the end, all that was accomplished was the council gave the visitors permission to sit at the large fire and read from the book they held in such high regard.

Lone Crow was on the verge of speaking his views on being expected to interpret when Pathkiller informed the men that no one would understand what they were saying. Still, he had no problem allowing them to speak.

"Thank you," Lone Crow spoke while the three white men murmured about the last piece of information.

"I am more interested in what they are trading than in their stories. Now, inform them that they are welcome to join the fire tonight. We have other matters to speak about. Can you return them to their wagons?" Pathkiller asked after making his decision about the rest of his day.

"We brought plenty of food. Can we share with you?" Adam questioned after conferring with the other men.

Before answering the question, Pathkiller asked Lone Crow if the white man's food was good. Lone Crow had to think before he answered. As strange as it was, he couldn't remember one meal he'd eaten when he was living with them.

"Make sure they eat it first," he replied without answering the question.

The Warrior hadn't expected to speak the words and wasn't sure why he did. But he suddenly felt untrusting of the men. The town may have been on speaking and trading terms with his people but they had been the same when his village was burned and he was taken.

Lone Crow had asked why his village was raided when he first met Father Silas. The answer he received made little sense but it was the only one he'd ever heard. His family and friends had been killed and his life had been dramatically altered because of a cow. The animal had walked away from one of the ranches that dotted the outskirts of the town. It wondered near the village and his people had eaten it. It may not have been the most honest thing to do but no one should have died over the incident. Instead of the town's people asking to meet with the Chief to discuss the issue, the men of the town banded together and attacked the village, killing everyone. When the men were finished with their brutal, unspeakable acts, Lone Crow was the only person from his village to survive.

Because of the barbaric act, there hadn't been a genuine peace between the peoples in many years. They weren't openly fighting but the Cherokee were growing more distrustful with each incident. Whether it be big or small.

"Tell them we will share a meal and they can speak all they like. I want to trade tomorrow and then they can leave," Pathkiller stated as he stood and walked from the dwelling.

Lone Crow did not want to escort the men back to the wagons. What he truly wanted was a few minutes alone.

The men did not frighten him. They held no sway over him. He was a grown man and feeling more confident with each passing moment but he did not enjoy their company and was apprehensive about walking them back.

His fear had nothing to do with the men or his safety. He was sure he was in no danger from the visitors. His fear was only because he would have to face the woman called Faith.

The white men sat and watched as the house quickly emptied while Lone Crow attempted to fight his demons.

"Did Pathkiller agree to break bread with us?" Adam inquired after a lengthy silence.

Lone Crow snapped out of his mind and stood. "Yes. I am to return you to your wagons and we will meet when the sun sets," he informed the small group.

"Thank you for this opportunity," Adam said, walking beside Lone Crow as the two others fell in step behind.

Lone Crow shook his head but found he couldn't remain silent. "Why are you people here? How were you planning on communicating? There is no way you knew someone would be able to interpret for you."

The Warrior hadn't planned on speaking so much but suddenly, the answer to his question was important.

"Oh, well, you see, I can speak the language well enough. You are doing a wonderful job, by the way," the man called Adam replied, with no malice in his tone.

Adam's statement was by no means a threatening one but the knowledge stopped the Warrior in his tracks. "How did you learn our tongue?" he asked in Cherokee to assure the men following would not understand.

While he awaited an answer, he mentally scanned his memory to ensure he hadn't spoken anything that could be taken as a threat.

Adam smiled and gestured for Lone Crow to continue to walk before looking over his shoulder at his friends. "Not many people know this, but my mother was Cherokee. They," he said, pointing at the men following behind, "are too ignorant to accept that. As are many men," he added, slipping into rough Cherokee as they walked.

Lone Crow was shocked by the information but understood Adam's desire to keep his lineage hidden.

"What do they really want?" Lone Crow asked, feeling comfortable with the man.

"Only to enlighten the people to the Lord," he answered with sincerely thick in his voice.

"What is wrong with the Great Creator?" Lone Crow asked, keeping his opinion and knowledge of Adam's God to himself.

Adam smiled. "Come and listen to the stories," he offered. "And the food we plan to share is not poison," he added with amusement in his voice. "But, I do understand your concerns."

Before Lone Crow could explain himself or ask why the man believed in the white man's God, Adam turned the tables on him.

"How did you come to speak English so well?"

Lone Crow may have been feeling strangely comfortable with the man but he was not going to share any part of his childhood with him.

"A trader," he lied.

"Well, I would very much like to talk more later, Lone Crow," Adam stated.

"I will be leaving after I inform Pathkiller that my talent is no longer needed. And I am going to do that as soon as you are back at your wagons," Lone Crow informed the man.

That was precisely what he planned on doing. The more space he could put between the party and himself, the better.

Again, he wasn't frightened of the men. He would suggest that Pathkiller have one of the warriors watch their movements but he didn't view them as a physical threat. The Warrior was experiencing a wide range of emotions, from terror to excitement. The cause was simple. The path the rest of his life would take hung in the balance. Everything would change if, in fact, the woman he was nearing with each step was his Faith.

## Chapter Eight

Tobias maintained a bright outlook the next morning and into the afternoon.

I didn't speak. I simply enjoyed the silence and my surroundings.

My husband had not spoken a word to me since I returned from bathing. And then when the silence was finally broken, it was only to ask if I had talked to Wilma.

The guilt I felt burdened with for helping my husband commit a sin lessened when the man returned to a calm state as soon as I answered him.

I wanted to know how much longer we would be traveling but dared not inquire.

"Tobias," Adam spoke as he rode up next to the wagon. "Faith," he greeted, removing his hat and nodding. "The village is there," he continued, pointing off to the North.

"So, what's going to happen?" Tobias asked, sounding slightly apprehensive.

I sat in silence and internally enjoyed his discomfort.

"They have been sent word. They know we are arriving. In fact, I am sure they know where we are now. There is no need for concern. This is a friendly, peaceful village."

Tobias grumbled and again, I found his concern enjoyable.

If he wasn't sure what he was walking into, then why were we there? Did the man never think before acting? I had many questions and opinions but I kept them to myself. Adam didn't seem to agree, though, and his reaction dampened my spirits considerably.

"We are on a Godly mission. We will be safe," Adam continued, employing the tone one would when talking to a very young child.

It was challenging not to smile even if I did know Adam's attitude would lead to some form of punishment later.

We were the lead wagon that day so after Adam leaned in to pat Tobias on the leg, he stopped moving and waited for the others.

"I don't like him," Tobias informed me.

"I know you don't," I replied, biting the inside of my cheek.

I knew his anger would affect me no matter what else transpired through the day and if he thought for a moment I was pleased with his reaction, it would only make it worse.

"I've been givin' some thought to our predicament," he said, sounding as if he were choosing his words carefully.

The tone he was using was not one I was familiar with and that knowledge scared me even more.

Had he planned on leaving me with the Indians? Or worse? Was Adam's presence the only reason I wasn't dead already? The questions running through my brain caused my heartbeat to quicken and my palms to sweat.

After taking a deep breath, I turned to him. "Our predicament?" I asked shakily.

When Tobias saw how frightened I was, he smiled. "One of these men may take a shine to ya. Maybe that is what you are hoping for. I mean, considering one of them killed your father. You wanted that to happen, didn't you? He couldn't teach you to behave any better than I can," he began berating me and only stopped to shake his head and wipe his face with his hand before continuing. "If Howard and Adam weren't here, I might do just that. In fact, I might ask one of those men to take you. Christ, Faith, you are just about useless."

I had heard the same thing for years but the words still hurt me and it was challenging to keep the tears at bay.

"I will try to behave better," I offered, immediately hating myself for not being stronger.

"I don't think we are good together," Tobias informed me.

He wasn't wrong but I knew whatever he was planning was not going to be in my best interest. My husband was not a man who considered my feelings when making decisions. So he absolutely did not worry about how I would react to anything. I knew I didn't matter. And I was beginning to believe I was becoming an impediment instead of a housekeeper he could beat whenever the impulse struck. It was the first time I actively feared for my life. He wasn't hitting me or kicking me but he was scaring me more than he had in a long time.

"I just need to think on this," he decided, looking ahead.

I didn't like his new mood one little bit but had no idea what I could do to change it.

Thankfully, Adam again rode up beside us before steering the horses to the left.

"Faith?" he asked. "You look like you might cry. Are you alright?"

"She was sneezing a minute ago," Tobias spoke for me.

Adam didn't appear to believe my husband but didn't argue. What he did do was stay by our side until the flat-roofed homes began to come into view.

I had no idea what a Cherokee village should look like but was pleasantly surprised to find it appeared nicely set up.

Buildings, what I assumed were homes, lined an open, center path and the large area in the middle of town had several children running around and chasing one another. The village seemed to be 'alive' and thriving. Contentment and happiness filled the space. The smell was pleasant and the scent of cooking meat filled the air. Most of the animals were gathered in an open area not far from the center of the village. There were no fences or ropes to contain them. They just grazed easily on their own, satisfied with what they had.

"There are a lot of them," Tobias spoke almost under his breath.

Again his worry didn't faze me.

"There are more of us," Adam informed him before sliding from his horse and halting the wagons at the outskirts of the camp.

"I can see more than five of them from here," Tobias corrected in his best condescending voice.

"We are in their home. I was speaking of the Americans in general. We far outnumber these people. Now let us go meet the men who are coming to greet us," Adam suggested when he noticed two men walking toward the wagons.

Tobias jumped from the seat and I watched as the Native men neared.

My vision was blurred by the unshed tears so I didn't maintain my attempted focus on the greeting party. Instead, I turned and watched the children playing in the center of the village.

I continued to try to keep my mind from the threat Tobias had left me with and enjoyed listening to the joy the young were exhibiting. I didn't envy them for being so free and happy but wished just a slice of my childhood could have been half as carefree.

Once we were told to stay with the wagons, I crawled into the back and curled up in my bedding.

Tobias hadn't bothered with me the night before but I still hadn't achieved a sleep-filled evening.

The tossing and turning were because I was foolish enough to entertain the idea that we might be walking into Moses' home.

After my marriage, I didn't allow myself to wonder or worry about the boy. At first, I was angry with him for leaving me. But as I grew older, I understood he thought my life would be better once my father was dead. He was doing what he thought was best for me. And although I had accepted that fact, there was still a small part of me that was angry with him. For six months, I sat at my aunt's window with some clothing and food packed, waiting for Moses to come and get me.

We had made such plans when we were younger. He promised he would take me to his people and that we could be happy. No one would beat us or force us to do anything we didn't want to. His life sounded wonderful to my young ears. But when I remembered he had been ripped from his family and thrown into mine, I wondered how long his people would be happy and carefree.

Watching from atop the bench of the wagon, my heart was glad to see the children still played.

While I lay in the back of the wagon, I tried to concentrate on their laughter.

My peace was interrupted almost immediately when Wilma called for me from the outside of the wagon.

I took a deep breath and attempted to ready myself for whichever way the impending conversation was going to go.

"Don't these people scare you?" she asked as she backed away while I exited the wagon.

"No," I answered honestly. "Why? Do they frighten you? They seem to be going about their day. No one is even looking at us. I am more worried about me right now."

I let the last bit of my statement slip from my tongue before I could stop it.

Wilma looked shocked by my reply but I wasn't sure which part shook her so I stayed silent and began unpacking the kitchen supplies.

"Why are you worried about yourself?" she asked hurriedly as she fell in step behind me. "Oh," she continued, sounding as if she had attained some sort of clarity. "Is it because an Indian boy killed your Pa?"

I stopped what I was doing and slowly turned to face her. "That boy saved my life," I informed her quickly.

I was not one to share stories or even speak to many people and was having trouble understanding why I was so freely sharing things I knew I shouldn't, with the woman sleeping with my husband.

Wilma looked more confused than before. "How did he do that? Your Pa was the town Reverend. How could he be saving you from anything? I still can't believe the townsfolk couldn't find him. I guess it doesn't matter much, though. I'm sure he didn't live long on his own in the elements. I'm sorry, I am just going on and on. So, how did the boy save you?"

Since it was more challenging for me to want to be in the woman's company than it was for her to be in mine, I returned to my work setting up the cooking vessels.

"Well?" she pressed gently.

"Wilma, you have been in the town as long as me. I am sure you heard the gossip. Now I think our time is best served starting a small fire and beginning to prepare the meal. Don't you?" I asked as sweetly as I could manage.

The woman did not seem special but I was quickly learning she was extremely nosey. It was not a quality that Tobias abided. So I still couldn't understand why Tobias treated her with love instead of pain. I was also keenly aware that if Tobias returned and it appeared Wilma and I were getting friendly, he would be angry. And after being threatened with abandonment, I wanted to keep my husband as happy as possible.

"I know this is in no way what anyone could call normal," Wilma continued speaking but thankfully, she began helping. "But I don't think I can continue to see Tobias."

Her tone was flat but when I heard her declaration, I stopped moving.

If she broke things off with Tobias, I knew my life was going to be a new level of hell. But I did not want her to have to endure the treatment I did either. Even so, I should have been all for her ceasing her affair with my husband. But whether it was sinful or not, I wasn't.

She had made my life a small bit easier and I didn't want to lose the buffer she provided.

"Why?" I asked, only after I was sure my feelings wouldn't bleed through.

Wilma made a noise that assured me she was grateful that I asked. "Nothing can come of it. We are both married to other people. I know you don't mind but if Howard learned the truth, he would try to kill Tobias. And I am with child."

Wilma had time to digest everything she'd just informed me of but it took me a minute.

I rubbed my forehead in disbelief and confusion and anger. "You are carrying Tobias' child?" I asked through gritted teeth.

She reddened and looked away from me to busy herself elsewhere. "I think so. But I am not going to tell him. I just think this is for the best. Don't you?"

I was placing some of the logs on a clear spot of ground and again stopped moving.

The woman was asking for my opinion as if we were friends. "If you tell Tobias you are carrying his child, he will not let you go," I warned against my better judgment.

She again looked shocked by my reply. "I said I wasn't going to," she snapped before retreating to the cover of her wagon.

I wasn't about to ask her to continue speaking to me so I finished my work. By the time I saw the men returning, the pit was aflame and I was just beginning to make some biscuits.

I stood and watched as the four men walked closer.

The sun was obstructing my view so after calling to Wilma to alert her to the men's return, I placed my hands above my eyes to get a better look.

Adam was walking in the lead with a man I couldn't get a good look at. He was definitely a Cherokee but as hard as I tried, I couldn't focus on the man.

Tobias and Howard were walking closely behind and neither man looked pleased nor enthused.

I repeated my call to Wilma with a little more enthusiasm.

"I'm coming," she complained as she slowly made her way to my side.

"Who is that with them? Isn't he the same one who met us?" she asked, squinting into the distance.

"I think so. But they don't look happy," I shared, continuing to try to get a closer look at the man accompanying the group.

"I'm sure it will be fine," she surmised happily.

When I realized that Tobias would be angry that I was standing there gawking at the men, I returned to my perch on the ground and turned my attention back to the biscuit dough.

"We need water," Wilma informed me as she moved to stand behind me. "Do you think there is water close by?"

"Tell the men when they return," I suggested, taking my anxiety out on the dough.

"You seem nervous. I'm sure we are safe," she offered as she walked to meet the group.

I didn't bother to look up when I heard the men talking. I didn't think anything they were speaking about had anything to do with me so I continued my task.

"And this is Faith," I heard Adam say. "She and Tobias are man and wife," he continued.

I still kept my head down.

Tobias grabbed my arm angrily and pulled me to my feet.

Before I was standing, both Adam and the Native were beside Tobias, pulling his grip from my arm.

"You have no business telling me how to treat my wife," Tobias told Adam before turning to the other man. "And from the looks of the scars on your back, you know how to take a disciplining. So this is none of your business."

My eyes were still closed but I heard Tobias clearly and cringed from embarrassment at his behavior.

"It was my fault," I began making excuses for my husband but still kept my eyes closed.

"Tobias," I heard Adam speak. "Let us take a walk and pray," he suggested as he pulled Tobias away.

"I can't leave her with that Indian," he argued, sounding as if his anger was cooling slightly.

I was still standing with my eyes closed and quickly wrapped my arms around myself in an effort to self soothe.

"Faith," I heard my name.

Tears sprang to my eyes and I couldn't stop them from falling down my cheek. I knew the voice. It was him. As impossible as it was, Moses was standing beside me, calling my name.

"No, Tsisqua, this is not your fault. It is mine," he said with sadness thick in his voice.

I had endured my share of beatings and yet had never fainted until I heard Moses call me by my childhood name.

## Chapter Nine

"I am sorry to hear that," Adam said. "I was looking forward to talking more."

Adam may have been fascinating to Lone Crow but nothing was going to change his plans. He was going to leave the village but only after doing everything in his power not to face the flame-haired woman. After nearing the wagons within a few steps, and they were being greeted by the other female, Lone Crow convinced himself he was being foolish. The woman was absolutely being abused but there was nothing he could do about it. He held no power to force the man called Tobias to stop mistreating his wife. In fact, he wasn't sure that wasn't the normal behavior of the white men. Plain and simple, it was horrible and he felt for the woman but it was none of his business. The woman had more in common with his Faith than just a name. But entertaining the thought that she was his Faith, his Tsisqua, was ridiculous.

The men stopped walking when the woman spoke. "I was wondering if there was water nearby?" she asked, avoiding looking at Lone Crow.

The Warrior could tell she was frightened of him.

Adam smiled at Lone Crow. "We stopped at a nice waterhole earlier. Is that the closest source of water?" he asked before standing aside and waiting for Tobias and Howard to move.

They didn't. They stood beside Adam and Lone Crow and waited for an answer.

"It is," Lone Crow answered. "But we will share our water with you. Give me your container and I will have someone return it full," he offered, hoping his contact with the people was coming to an end.

"You don't have to do that. Wilma and I will go with you and fill the water," Tobias offered quickly. "That way, Howard and Adam can work on the sermon," he added just as rapidly.

"Where are my manners?" Adam spoke, breaking the strange tension. "This is Wilma," he introduced. "She is Howard's wife. And this is Faith," he continued pointing at the woman who was doing her best to be ignored. "She and Tobias are man and wife."

Lone Crow nodded but didn't allow his gaze to linger on the woman.

Before the Warrior could say his goodbyes, the man called Tobias grabbed the woman and forced her to a standing posture, clearly causing her pain.

Lone Crow knew the moment he saw her face. It was the same face, carrying the same expression that he had seen many times when he was young. There was no denying it any longer.

He moved to her side before giving his action any thought but was relieved when he saw Adam had done the same.

It took all of the strength Lone Crow possessed not to beat Tobias. Only seconds earlier, he had convinced himself that whatever was happening was none of his business and yet, seeing Faith changed everything.

Lone Crow watched as the woman blamed herself and Adam took the man away.

He did not suppress the thin smile that crossed his face when he heard Tobias say he couldn't leave Faith with him.

As soon as the pair walked away and Wilma and Howard placed some distance from the uncomfortable scene, Lone Crow walked closer to the woman.

She had grown even more beautiful over the years. And yet she was still a delicate little bird. She still exuded the fear and need for protection that she had when they were young.

Lone Crow wanted to reach out to her, needed to take her in his arms and tell her he was there and he would do everything in his power to make her life better. It was beyond obvious that he hadn't improved her life by killing Silas. She was still experiencing the same abuse. And with that realization, guilt flooded his body.

She was standing with her eyes closed and had begun to wrap her arms around herself. She had done the same thing when she was young and he knew she was doing her best to control her emotions.

Lone Crow knew there was nothing he could do about Faith's situation at that very moment. And he also knew the smart thing to do would be to just back away from the scene.

But he didn't do the smart thing. He walked close enough to whisper in her ear. "No, Tsisqua, this is not your fault. It is mine."

He meant his declaration to the core. But, he hadn't considered revealing himself to her would cause her to pass out.

She would have hit the ground if he hadn't acted quickly. As soon as she was in his arms, he looked to the other people. They were almost cowering near the fire with a look of terror on their faces.

"She may be unwell," Lone Crow explained, doing his best to hide his anger at the pair's inactiveness.

"I'd leave her where she is, if I were you," Howard spoke quietly before turning his attention to his wife.

The woman only nodded her head.

Lone Crow was not about to place Faith in the dirt and walk away. No matter what the others thought of the idea. It was disrespectful. Understanding that the only woman whom he'd ever loved was treated in such a way made it difficult not to carry her away and end the life of the man responsible for her pain.

He stood, still holding the limp woman in his arms, and headed to the wagon.

Faith stirred in his arms. "Moses?" she asked weakly.

The name she mumbled caused his step to catch. He couldn't decide if it was best for her to be unsure of his identity or not. Lone Crow had every intention of speaking to her at length. But the time was not optimal and he worried that if she knew it was him beyond a doubt, it would cause her more pain and concern.

"No. My name is Lone Crow," he corrected gently.

"No," she argued, still speaking as if she were in a dream. "You called me Tsisqua. You have to be him."

"No. I am Lone Crow," he repeated before gently placing her in the rear of the wagon.

It wasn't her bed but he knew taking a white woman and placing her in bed was something that would cause bloodshed. And he wasn't quite ready to kill the man called Tobias just yet. He was sure he would have to do it eventually but he wanted to know the story and have a plan in place for Faith. He would not make the same mistake again. He would not leave her in the hands of another abuser.

"I think you have done enough. The poor girl is gonna pay for this as is. If he thinks you, of all people, had your hands on her, she is really gonna get beat," the man called Howard stated as he walked beside Lone Crow.

It was challenging not to show his anger but he knew Howard was not the person doling out the punishment. The man was not innocent; he was a coward and should have helped Faith earlier. But the time was not right for Lone Crow to air his opinions. What the man was saying was truthful. The white men had no problem marrying Native women but a white woman and a male Native was just not acceptable and more than likely held a death sentence for both. If the whites couldn't locate him, they would absolutely take their anger out on his entire village.

"Why do you allow this kind of treatment?" Lone Crow asked as he backed away from the wagon.

"There ain't much we can do. He is the Reverend, after all. I mean, we all feel sorry for the little thing. Still, it really is none of our business," the man began making excuses for his appalling behavior.

Nothing Lone Crow could have said would have done any good so he shook his head and turned away from the man.

"Are we still breaking bread together?" Howard asked as Lone Crow began walking away.

"Unless that man touches that woman again. If he does, then you will be expelled from our village," Lone Crow answered without turning back.

He wasn't sure his statement would hold true. The Warrior had little sway over the decisions his people made but he thought he had a good chance of convincing them to drive the whites back home.

Lone Crow needed time to think. He knew he couldn't do much of anything as long as the party was visiting his village. If he took action at all, his people would surely be blamed for it. If he waited for the group to return to the city, he could follow and help Faith there. It wouldn't be too difficult to travel in the shadows. No one expected an Indian to be walking through the town. It just didn't happen unless they were invited to talk of giving up a few more miles of the land for a new settlement. And that was happening more frequently. But even invited Natives were gone by nightfall. If he did choose that plan, Tobias' death still had to appear to be accidental. Learning that he too was a man of God didn't mean much to Lone Crow but he knew it did to the people of the church. And if they believed the man was murdered, it would make things more difficult for Faith. She may even be blamed for it and hung in the town square. That was not the outcome he wanted. Lone Crow went in search of his father for guidance. He was unable to decide what his next move should be.

It wasn't like him to reach out to anyone but he hadn't felt so limited in options since he'd fled the city when he was young.

His plan to alert Pathkiller to his impending absence was forgotten as he walked toward the pony herd.

Otter was a man who spent the better part of his day combing and working with his impressive pack, so he was always easy to locate.

"Father," Lone Crow spoke as soon as he saw Otter.

Otter stopped what he was doing and smiled at his son. "It is not often that you come in search of me. What is it I can help you with?"

"I want to kill the man called Tobias," Lone Crow stated, feeling it vital that he get to the point.

Otter's look was a mixture of concern and sad acceptance. "If you kill him, they will come after us," he stated the obvious.

"I know," Lone Crow replied as he began rubbing down one of his father's ponies. "I know the woman," he admitted, not stopping what he was doing.

Informing his adopted father about more of his childhood was not without difficulties but he found that petting the animal somehow made it a little less trying.

"Pathkiller told me that he thought you might," Otter informed his son gently. "Please continue," he added, moving closer to his son.

Lone Crow was again disappointed that he hadn't hidden his feelings better but didn't dwell on it. Instead, he attempted to tell his father the story he had kept to himself for the last ten years.

After Lone Crow spoke at length, he paused and allowed both Otter and himself to digest the whole of the story. It was Lone Crow's past but he had never spoken so in-depth about it and as he sat and waited for Otter to nod his head, he realized he felt better for doing it. He felt stronger and even more determined to do what he had to; save Faith.

Otter nodded and moved to embrace his son.

"Thank you for everything you've done for me. I feel better for having told you about the past. But I must ask what you would do?" Lone Crow asked as he gently broke the embrace.

"How do grown men get away with beating their children?" Otter asked, still looking as if he was coming to terms with everything he heard. "I knew you had been beaten and treated poorly. But I had no idea the depths of the man's barbarity. And I do understand why you killed the man. But now that I know, I want you to leave this place. Just until the white people are gone." He suggested earnestly.

"I cannot leave her again. No one but Faith knows what happened. I imagine the others assume the Indian boy called Moses killed Father Silas. There is no way they can know that boy was me," Lone Crow began arguing his point.

"But the woman knows. Can you be so sure she doesn't blame you for the situation she is in now?" Otter asked, using a tone that he rarely did with Lone Crow.

"She did call me Moses," Lone Crow admitted, not being pleased to learn Otter was making sense.

Faith had been unconscious. But if she happened to wake and alert the others to his identity, they would surely arrest him and possibly take their anger out on everyone in the village.

He did not want to leave but if it was to protect the people who saved him from pain and likely death, he would.

But he was not going to allow Faith to believe he didn't care. He had to convince her he was going to help even if he wasn't sure how.

## Chapter Ten

When I woke, my brain began firing on all cylinders. My heart rate was rapid, I was shaking, and I was in a strange state of arguing with myself.

Was Moses close by? Or had I imagined the whole thing? I was pretty sure the man who carried me told me his name. The fuzz in my brain receded and I remembered he said he was called Lone Crow. I hoped that if the man was really my Moses, he would admit it. But he had called me by the name Moses had and I couldn't completely convince myself that was coincidental.

Persuading myself that Moses was close and would help me was a stretch even if the man had called me by my childhood name. I knew the word meant bird because Moses said that was what I reminded him of. In my hopeless, confused state, I quickly accepted the fact that I really did appear to be nothing more than an injured bird.

Lone Crow couldn't possibly be Moses. If he was, I was sure he wouldn't leave me once again. I was sure he would have taken me to safety and worried about any repercussions later. He owed me that much, didn't he?

He had promised me my life would get better when he left. And he had lied. Before I could bring myself to the verge of tears once again, I heard Wilma's voice.

"Adam and Tobias are returning," she said loud enough to alert me.

Her actions were appreciated and I planned on thanking her as soon as possible.

I sat up slowly and wiped my face with the hem of my apron. After quickly attempting to tame my unruly hair, I slowly exited the wagon.

My legs were weak and it took a minute for me to be sure I wouldn't fall.

As soon as I felt steady, I noticed that the anger Tobias was carrying seemed to have eased. I was pleased to think he was calmer but knew I would still be punished later.

"Has anyone gone for water?" Adam asked in his normal cheerful voice.

I looked at Wilma and Howard.

Wilma was standing over a large cooking pot and Howard was sitting on a blanket reading his Bible. They both shook their heads in unison and avoiding looking at me.

Again I was grateful for their actions but couldn't help but wonder why their attitude changed.

"Tobias," Adam spoke again once he and my husband were standing around the fire.

I was making my way to join the group after mentally wiping away all my foolish wants and thoughts. The man, Lone Crow, was not Moses and I was not going to get a chance at a better life. And there was still the very real possibility that Tobias planned on killing me or abandoning me on the way home. Adam was definitely a buffer for those plans but as soon as I stopped wishing for the impossible, all the dark thoughts began consuming me again. By the time I arrived at the fireside, I was sweating and it was hard to get a good, deep breath.

"I hope you didn't upset our meeting because of your anger," Adam continued, with no annoyance in his voice.

"It wasn't all my fault," Tobias began making excuses but Adam held his hand up to silence my husband and looked at me. "Did Lone Crow say anything before he left?"

I knew better than to answer. There was no reply that wouldn't end in angering Tobias.

"Well," Howard joined the conversation, sounding as if he was hesitant to do so. "He did say, and remember it was him saying it, he said if that man touches that woman again, we will be driven from the village."

I didn't remember hearing the man speak those words. So maybe I had dreamt the few words we spoke. Accepting how silly my wish was, made it easier to abandon.

"Tobias has his anger under control and we will have no more trouble," Adam assured. "Faith, would you like to join me in search of some water?" he offered as he walked to my side.

Tobias hadn't looked at me since he returned and I really was unsure of how to respond.

I cleared my throat. "Tobias?" I asked sheepishly.

My husband seemed startled by my voice. "Yeah," he said dismissively, waving his hand as he continued to look into the distance. "Do what you want."

I very rarely heard that tone. Tobias always had strong opinions on everything. So, I wasn't sure what the smartest thing to do would be.

"Faith," Adam said gently. "Come. We will chat as we walk," he urged, gesturing for me to walk ahead of him.

My feet refused to move when he suggested we talk. It was the last thing I should be doing if I wanted to ease Tobias' anger. He had warned me against doing the very thing Adam was advocating. And yet, my husband still seemed to be a million miles away.

When I looked at Wilma and Howard, I noticed they hadn't stopped what they were doing. But Wilma had glanced at Tobias with question several times. Howard only looked up from his reading to inform Adam about Lone Crow's words. As soon as the man said his piece, he went back to reading.

"No," I replied, walking back toward the fire. "I will stay. I am needed to cook if we are still going to share a meal."

Adam smiled sadly and moved back to my side. "The walk will do you good," he insisted carefully. "Come," he repeated.

"Tobias," I spoke quickly, wishing, for the first time in our marriage, for him to act like himself.

"Just go," my husband said, seeming to slowly return to himself.

Since I was pretty sure Adam didn't think Tobias' treatment of me earlier was a first-time event, I knew our relationship would be a topic that wouldn't be easily avoided. And I really just wanted to go back to finishing the biscuits and go to bed. I desperately needed to decide how much credence to give my darker thoughts. If the possibility of my death was real, then I needed to calmly plan a way to escape. And I couldn't do that if I was walking with Adam, trying to keep the subject to something that wouldn't better my chances of pushing Tobias over the edge.

"I am sure we will not be long. I assumed Lone Crow would bring the water but it seems he was put off by our behavior," Adam surmised, loud enough for the others to hear as we began walking down the well-worn path.

My response to his uncalled-for comment was a sigh. But I fell in step beside Adam, keeping my head down and my attention on the path.

"He will not hurt you again," Adam stated as he slowed his gait and reached for my arm.

I yanked my arm away and stopped walking. "How dare you?!" I asked in a screamed whisper.

Adam looked as if I had slapped him across the face and I was honestly having trouble understanding where my question came from.

"I appreciate you are upset," Adam admitted, sounding very much like he didn't and was just attempting to placate me.

I remained unmoving and placed one hand on my hip before speaking to his last statement. "How can you possibly understand why I am upset? Have you lived my life?"

The decibel level of my angry queries was low but I was sure Adam was beginning to understand just how angry I was.

I still wasn't sure where all the anger came from or why I was directing it toward a person who was only trying to lessen my pain. His actions may have been doing the exact opposite but I was sure he wasn't adding to my problems on purpose.

Adam removed his hat and wiped his forehead as he quickly glanced around the village. "Has no one tried to help you before?" he asked, confusion thick in his tone.

I knew the man had no idea he was scratching a raw nerve by asking a simple question, but he was.

Tears welled in my eyes and I quickly wiped them away before balling my hands into fists and releasing them. After blowing an errant hair from my face, I took several deep breaths and gave my answer some thought.

Did it matter if I answered his query honestly? Would it change anything? Nothing was going to change anything. I was where I was because I was where I was. It was my lot in life and I had more to worry about than me telling the man a story I was sure he already knew.

"One person tried to help me, a long time ago," I finally answered.

When the words left my mouth, I began crying almost uncontrollably.

Adam moved to bridge the gap between us but I quickly raised my hand to keep him at a distance before closing my eyes and willing myself to get a grip on my emotions.

I knew if I didn't, I would attract the attention of the people milling around nearby.

"This is difficult for me, for some reason," I informed the concerned looking man before again lifting my apron and wiping my face. "Perhaps we can just get the water and not speak?" I suggested, hopefully, as I attempted to smile.

Adam looked disappointed but undeterred. "I am sorry. Of course, I heard the stories," he admitted before beginning to walk again. "Did Father Silas mistreat you as well?"

"The last person who tried to help me didn't do such a great job either," I answered before looking from the ground and seeing the man I was sure was the Chief walking toward us with a warm smile on his face.

"We will speak more later," Adam said out of the side of his mouth as he turned his attention to the Chief and smiled his customary charismatic grin. "Pathkiller, this is Faith and we are in search of some water," Adam explained in a language I didn't understand.

Pathkiller looked both impressed and surprised to learn Adam could communicate with him.

I was shocked as well but also thankful we would be able to communicate.

The Chief nodded and offered to take the vessels Adam was holding. Adam smiled gratefully and handed them to the man.

Pathkiller turned and we followed him to a home that was larger than the others. He stopped next to the front of the door and removed the wooden lid from a barrel of water before filling the vessels.

I stood several steps removed from the pair and continued to try to calm my frightened, angry mind.

Adam and Pathkiller spoke for several minutes and I was left to occupy my time. So, instead of worrying about the future, I turned my attention back toward the still frolicking children.

"The Chief hasn't seen Lone Crow so he had no idea we had a problem. The meal is on and I would very much like it if you would partake in the readings," Adam informed me as soon as we were on our way back to our small campsite.

"I was planning on getting some rest," I argued weakly, glad that he hadn't continued to ask about my childhood.

"Have you no interest in the way the Cherokee live?" he continued to talk.

As normal as his questions were, they weren't meant in malice, and yet everything out of his mouth elicited raw emotions and memories.

I remembered listening to Moses talk about his people. The longer he was separated from them, the less he spoke. But he made the scenes come alive when he would talk about the hunting and the Warriors going off to fight with another Nation. I remembered the way his face would light up when telling me about the women and children. He once told me that the women owned the property. I hadn't believed him at the time but hoped he was telling the truth because I thought their homes were beautiful. It was comforting thinking a woman had something of theirs that no one could take.

"I know more about the people than you think," I stated, again shocking myself with my openness.

"Was the boy you grew up with a Cherokee?" he asked, sounding interested in my slip.

"I think so," I lied as I began walking faster.

I never thought I would have chosen Tobias' company over anyone's. But the more I spoke, the more trouble I was causing for myself. As it was, I would have to tell Tobias everything we spoke of. I had to speak the truth because I didn't know if I could trust Adam, as badly as I wanted to.

"You know, anything we talk about will go no further," he offered when he caught up with me.

"You think you know everything already and I'm sure all you have done is make my life worse. I realize you are only trying to help and I appreciate that. I really do," I explained as quickly as I could without slowing the pace.

"But," Adam said, waiting for the rest of my sentiment.

"I have other things to concern myself with," I answered before again casting my gaze to the ground.

"I want to hear your story and I plan on gaining your trust enough for you to tell me," Adam informed before walking toward the fire.

His statement sounded like a threat, even though I was pretty sure he hadn't meant it that way.

## Chapter Eleven

After giving Otter's advice some thought, Lone Crow decided to inform Pathkiller of his decision.

Over the years, the Warrior had often wondered if Faith harbored hatred toward him but never considered what her anger could cost.

He had lived through the devastation of a village once and could not, would not, be the reason his family was killed again.

The only option he had was to seek the solace he enjoyed and leave the poor woman to her fate. And yet, even after accepting that leaving was really his only option, he was torn.

Faith had every right to be angry with him, hate him even. But the Faith he knew would never want to cause anyone else to suffer. She had saved him from enduring severe beatings several times. Lone Crow was sure the girl couldn't have changed that much. Even after all Father Silas had put her through, she still insisted Lone Crow not speak the hatred he felt. Faith's heart was pure and he wasn't ready to believe that had changed.

Still, if there was the slightest chance that his mere presence could bring death to his family, he had to err on the side of caution.

Pathkiller was walking toward the council house when Lone Crow spotted him.

"The man, Adam, speaks our language," the Chief informed Lone Crow, in lieu of a greeting. "Where have you been? I expected you to return. I had to fetch the water for the visitors."

Lone Crow couldn't miss the small amount of aggravation in Pathkiller's voice.

"I was aware of that. I did not return immediately because I had to speak to my father. If you have a moment, I would like to speak to you," Lone Crow explained, hoping he could stand firm in his decision.

The thought of explaining his situation to Pathkiller caused him anxiety but he knew it had to be done. He may well have already endangered the village so the Chief deserved to know the story. And if the Warrior had his way, it would be the last time he would tell the tale.

"Come, sit," Pathkiller invited the Warrior inside.

The fire never went out in the dwelling but the flames were non-existent; only hot embers remained.

Before sitting, Pathkiller added a few logs from the nearby pile.

Lone Crow was doing everything in his power to exhibit patience but was still fidgety.

"The woman, the flame-haired woman," Pathkiller began speaking before sitting.

Lone Crow wanted to interrupt but knew he had to give the Chief respect.

"Are they all so frightened?" the Chief asked as he took a seat next to Lone Crow.

"No," Lone Crow answered after clearing his throat. "I don't believe so. Her name is Faith and she is the reason I have come to speak to you," the Warrior added in hopes that his admission would keep the conversation on track.

Pathkiller looked at Lone Crow with his eyebrows raised. "Tell me," he urged, looking interested in the story.

Lone Crow condensed the tale because of the time restrictions and because he quickly learned it wasn't any easier to speak about it the second time. He told Pathkiller the bare necessities about his childhood and then waited while the Chief digested the tale.

"I am sorry you had to endure that kind of treatment," Pathkiller said with a raw honesty in his voice. "I am sorry that woman must endure the same treatment," he added before pulling his pipe from his bag and filling it. "But I think you have made the right decision. If you get involved or if they do realize who you are, the least they will do is kill you. The worst is they will begin a war that will be difficult to win. I do not want either one of those things."

Lone Crow remained silent and took the pipe when it was passed.

"I will promise you this," the Chief offered. "I will ensure she is not mistreated while they are here."

Lone Crow knew the man was attempting to ease some of the guilt the Warrior was experiencing. But there was not much Pathkiller could do.

Still, he appreciated the Chief's offer. "I wish... no, wish is not a strong enough word for what I am feeling. I need to speak to her and at least attempt to help her," Lone Crow admitted, feeling his statement deeply.

"Adam speaks our tongue so I will speak to him when the meeting is taking place. How does he know our language?" the Chief asked, sounding reluctant to brush aside Lone Crow's problems.

Lone Crow knew the man had many things to consider and many hats to wear and didn't begrudge Pathkiller one bit. The question was an important one and no one else could answer it.

"It is not known amongst the white people but Adam's mother was Aniyunwiya."

Lone Crow stopped talking when he saw the shock on Pathkiller's face. "I understand his reluctance to admit who he is but why does he want us to listen to talk of the white man's God?"

The question was a logical one but Lone Crow did not have the answer. "You should ask him. I get the feeling he wants to learn more about his people. I also believe he will help Faith if he can. He seems to be genuine. Now, I must go, or I will talk myself out of it," Lone Crow stated as he slowly stood and turned toward the doorway.

"Did you love the girl?" Pathkiller asked.

The question stopped the Warrior in his tracks.

A lump formed in his throat and his muscles tightened. "I will always love her," he answered, honestly.

Although he had arrived at that conclusion years earlier, he had never vocalized the words. It was painful.

"Then I am sorry, Lone Crow. I will send Otter after you when they have gone. You have grown into a good man. And this may be a painful turn in your life, it may also be what you need to continue to grow."

Lone Crow turned to the Chief and smiled. "You are most probably right but this is still one of the hardest things I've ever done," he admitted defeatedly.

"I do understand. And your people thank you. Decisions that lead to change are never easy ones." Pathkiller stated as he stood and walked beside Lone Crow.

Lone Crow nodded his head when Pathkiller patted him on the back. "I will do what I can to protect her," he repeated, dismissing Lone Crow in a gentle fashion.

"Thank you," the Warrior said, meaning the words to his core.

Gathering his belongings never took more than a few minutes because of his habitual absences but he found himself packing more than he needed. The action was a conscious one. The Warrior was still toying with the idea of following the wagons as they rode back to town. The fact of the matter was, Lone Crow was sure of very few things at present. Except for the fact that he wanted to be alone.

And yet, it was proving much more challenging to leave Faith for a second time.

When he found his favorite pony, he saw his father was still working nearby.

Instead of leaving the man's company with the customary nod, he felt the need to inform Otter where he planned on staying.

"Pathkiller will send you for me when the wagons leave," he informed his father. "I will be near the fast water."

"You are doing the right thing," Otter stated, pulling Lone Crow into an embrace. "I will do anything I can to help."

"Thank you," Lone Crow replied, embracing his father tightly before placing space between the two. "Do not hesitate to find me."

Otter smiled and nodded. "I hope you find some peace, my son."

Lone Crow wanted the same but didn't think he would attain any level of peace until he did what he could for Faith.

"I will do my best," Lone Crow spoke as he backed away from his father.

The fast water was not far from the waterhole where he'd seen Faith just a day before. Over the years, he'd spent much time there. It was the place he went when he suffered his darker moods.

His mind relaxed for the first time since leaving when he began to hear the rushing waters.

From his favorite spot, he could see the calm waters which fed the rapids. It was a cool, clear pool and, as it flowed into the rocky rapids, its smooth surface became tormented and sloshy. The water seemed to fight with angry abandon as it flowed across the rocks toward the deep, turbulent pond on the other end. Across the unsettled water were tall trees, wild grasses, and colorful flowers, all showing off their best coverings, almost as far as he could see. His place was the defining line between the comfortable meadows and the steep hillside. And it was a place he had always felt safe and secure.

Lone Crow continued to sing a song in his mind to block all the weighty issues he knew he would eventually have to face. The song he sang was not the one Faith had taught him, it was one his father would sing to calm the Warrior when he was plagued with night terrors.

After setting up a makeshift camp, he lit a small fire and ate some of the dried meat he'd packed. He would not allow any questioning thoughts to enter his mind until he was ready to think his next move through. And he did not want to do that until he was comfortable and even then, he found himself attempting to put the plan off. A small part of his brain would not allow any other outcome but his death. That conclusion did not dissuade him in the slightest. Saving Faith, really saving her, would be worth his life.

But he still couldn't decide the best way to go about it. Or even a way to help her that wouldn't cause repercussions for the village. He had been seen by the very man he wanted dead. Whoever came after him would know where to begin looking and not care if he was or wasn't there. They would be out for blood and his family would pay the price of the heroic action he took as a child.

While Lone Crow was gradually allowing the critical items to run through his mind, he slowly realized his favorite spot was a reflection of him. The stark difference between the flora and fauna on one side of the river and the steep, unforgiving cliffs on the other. The rushing, destructive waters fighting with the calm. The water and cliffs represented his hatred and anger and the calm beauty was Faith. And as sad as it was, the raging water never conceded. Still, he was not going to rest until he had a plan. The longer he sat and watched the water, the surer he became that he wouldn't be able to plan anything until he spoke to Faith. He was willing enough to accept any reception he received but he needed to know what she wanted, if anything.

It was a terrible idea and he knew the odds of him being able to speak to the woman were slim at best but he felt so strongly about it that he stomped out the fire and began riding back toward the village.

It would be nearing the middle of the night when he arrived but he hoped Tobias and Wilma were together again. It would give him the chance to speak to Faith without any chance that he would be caught.

He needed to know she wanted his help. Needed to know she didn't hate him. Needed to know what she desired.

Chapter Twelve

As soon as Adam and I were back in our small camp, I separated myself as much as possible and went back to working the dough for the biscuits.

I did not look at anyone. My head was down and I was more unsettled than I had been before we left.

"Tobias asked me to meet him tonight," Wilma whispered as she neared me.

That news was not what I wanted to hear. If Wilma broke it off with Tobias before we returned home, I was sure it would only serve to slim my odds of survival.

But in an effort to not let the woman know just how much was at stake, I scanned the area quickly before replying to her statement.

The men were all gathered near our wagon. Adam was talking and Howard was hanging on his every word. Tobias looked as if he had returned to himself, an angry scowl adorned his face.

"I'm afraid he is going to start hitting me," she admitted before I could gather the courage to speak.

Several emotions ran through me when I heard her announcement. But before speaking, I once again looked Tobias' way.

"He might if you tell him you don't want to see him again," I voiced barely above a whisper.

I knew why I said it. It was merely an act of self-preservation. But that didn't make it right. And in my defense, I wasn't sure I was lying. After quickly convincing myself I was helping her as well as me, the knot in my stomach eased slightly.

Wilma took a step backward and a deep intake of breath involuntarily filled her lungs.

The sad truth of the matter was, she had never before considered he would turn his anger on her.

"What have I done?" she asked in horror.

I knew the tone and understood her fear. I also knew if I didn't try to calm the woman, we would draw unwanted attention.

"Move back to the pot," I urged as I stood and walked toward the flames.

She followed but was clearly having trouble not breaking down into tears.

"He has never hurt you before," I began, talking from the side of my mouth while I kept a watch on the men. "I understand you wanting to leave the relationship but wish you would wait to tell him until we are back home."

"I have never given him a reason to hurt me," she whimpered.

I noticed her hands shaking when she stirred the stew. And in her short rebuttal, I understood that she was of the mind that I deserved the treatment I received from my husband. I wanted to inform her she was wrong but knew it wasn't the time or place. Still, I was hurt and angry.

"If you like, I will help you. But you have to wait," I urged.

"Why? He is less likely to touch me if we are surrounded by people," she reasoned weakly.

Her assumption only served to anger me more. It showed just how little she thought of me and just how much she thought of herself. But I still needed her help.

"Because Tobias might kill me if you do," I answered, biting the side of my cheek in an attempt to stop the tears from pooling in my eyes.

"He wouldn't take it that far," she argued, sounding more concerned by the second.

"They are coming back," I informed her. "Please wait until we return," I begged, hating myself for doing so.

"I will try," she decided, before smiling and welcoming the men back to the fire.

"Faith, have you decided to join us?" Adam asked, looking at me across the flames.

My stomach began aching and sweat broke out on the bridge of my nose when I heard the question.

I immediately looked at Tobias for a sign on how to respond.

Honestly, I wanted to crawl in the wagon and sleep. When I slept, my world was peaceful. But before I could enjoy my slumber, I had to work on my plan of survival.

"Tobias," I said cautiously.

My husband was watching Wilma when I spoke his name. He cleared his throat and turned to me.

The look on his face was unusual. He didn't seem to be angry, he appeared to be battling with regret. And that frightened me further because I had no way of knowing what he was regretting.

"What?" he asked before forcing himself to smile when he realized the others were close and watching him.

"Would it be alright if I stayed here? I have a headache and would like to get some sleep," I explained softly.

"You aren't gonna be able to sleep. I'm sure there is gonna be drumming and singing," he stated, looking at those gathered before rubbing his forehead, exhaling deeply, and rolling his eyes. "Stay if ya want."

He might not have been pleased with his decision but I was practically gleeful. "Maybe Wilma should stay with you," he added carefully, again looking to the men for their agreement. "I mean, we don't want to tempt these poor men."

It was a flimsy reason and neither of the men seemed to be of the same mind.

"Wilma will be sitting next to me," Howard said, joining the conversation as he placed his arm around his wife's waist and pulled her close.

Tobias turned away from the scene and I noticed he was angry about the pair's closeness. I couldn't be sure, but I thought Adam saw it too.

"Tobias, these people have allowed us to visit and spread the word of God. They are no threat to us," Adam chided. "Faith, if you are not accompanying us, I would like to pray with you before you retire."

I may not have thought God answered, or even listened to, my prayers but wasn't about to stop someone else from trying.

"She needs to finish the biscuits," Tobias asserted before walking back to the wagon and pulling out the case of blankets we brought to trade. "The other box is in Howard's wagon," he stated as he placed the box near the front of the wagon before pulling our only wooden stool to the fire and taking a seat.

Wilma wiggled from Howard's grasp and walked to the box of pans and cooking utensils.

I had no idea what the men planned to trade for the items but thought the only reason the Natives were being so patient with us was because we had things they wanted and nothing more.

I moved in what felt like slow motion. When the food was ready and the boxes had been laid out, the rest of the group took a minute to smooth their clothing and hair then began making their way to the big fire near the center of the small village.

"You are gonna pay for making Wilma scared of me," Tobias seethed as he leaned down to whisper in my ear before smiling.

Adam must have seen the reaction I couldn't hide and gestured for the others to walk ahead.

I saw Tobias turn and watch as Adam walked toward me.

I bowed my head and tried to walk around the man.

"He will not hurt you while we are here; as long as *I* am here," he assured me.

I shook my head and made my way to the security of the wagon, thankful that Adam seemed to forget about praying with me.

I sat and cried until the sun set and the moon fought to shine through the gathering storm clouds.

Doing so hadn't helped me decide on what to do but it had exhausted me.

When the talk from the fire quieted, the drumming and chanting began. The rhythm and song touched my heart. Tobias had warned me that the noise would keep me from sleeping but I found the sound both soothing and heartbreaking. Instead of continuing to cry or allow my fears to drive me crazy, I embraced the beautiful music and fell, happily, sound asleep.

The dreams that followed weren't nightmares. They were scenes from my childhood but ones that I considered happy. As I slept, my mind replayed all the times Moses and I talked. The dreams were overwhelmingly enjoyable; until they turned dark and I watched as the boy walked away from me and everything we had planned together.

When I woke, the sounds of the drumming were still present and the heat of the evening had turned to a chilly, breezy night. And yet I was sweating and felt as if I needed just a little bit of fresh air.

I pulled the blanket around me loosely and stumbled through the back opening.

As soon as my brain began waking, I considered going back inside. But the drumming was too much of a draw so I walked to the front and sat on the hard, wooden bench.

I was sure I couldn't be seen but because of the light from the burning flames, I had a front-row seat to members of the village as they sang and danced. The sight warmed my soul. And I was saddened to think I would never hear the music again.

I stayed entranced until the music ceased and the murmured talking began again. When the drumming stopped, I felt it in my soul. It was a sound I never knew I enjoyed but would always remember the beauty of how it made me feel.

Knowing I was pressing my luck by going outside after asking to stay because of a headache, I slowly got down from the front of the wagon and went in search of a canteen.

After taking a drink and a deep lungful of pure, clean air, I walked to the back of the wagon.

While hiking my leg to take the first big step, I felt a large strong hand press heavily over my mouth.

I screamed and kicked but it did no good.

"Shh," the voice urged tenderly. "If you do not quiet down, I will be punished, and so will these people."

I had no idea who was manhandling me but his calmness was strangely contagious. I may have been a little calmer but still wasn't happy with being held so tightly, so I continued to squirm but ceased calling out.

"I am going to remove my hand," the man continued to employ docile tones. "Do not scream, Tsisqua. I know I did not save you the first time but I plan to rectify that now."

While the man was talking, he removed his hand from my mouth and turned me to face him.

I don't know how I had missed it before. As impossible as it seemed, Moses was standing in front of me, holding me up.

"You said you weren't Moses," I accused tearfully.

"I am sorry," he said, sounding as if he had never meant a statement more.

"How?" I asked.

There was much I had to say and many questions to ask but I was still in shock and didn't know if I still hated him or not.

"I know you have many questions. We do not have much time. If they find out who I am, they will surely kill me. And I will gladly face death but only when I am sure you are out of danger."

I knew he was speaking. I was watching his mouth move. But I could hear nothing.

It felt as if I were in another dream. Had I ever woken up? Was this just what I wanted so badly to happen?

"Faith," he said, pulling me into his strong, protective arms.

Because of the life I lived, my defense mechanism was to push people away and even cower when someone reached for me. But I fell into Moses' embrace without a thought.

When my arms went around his neck, I could feel the welts he still carried from my father's beating and the tears that had been threatening to fall began to do so in earnest.

Moses stood tall and gently rocked me. "Shh," he soothed. "I thought you hated me," he admitted sounding as if he were close to tears himself.

"I did," I admitted, holding him tighter.

As soon as I realized being in his arms caused me to completely calm, I pushed him away.

He looked hurt but understanding at the same time.

"Are you going to help me? I mean, really help me?" I asked, quickly falling into the hysterics that had been threatening since we left town.

Moses pulled me back into his arms and picked me up before placing me back in the wagon.

"I do not know what I am going to do," he spoke in a whisper before scanning the area quickly. "But I will not allow you to continue to be punished. All I needed to know was that you needed my help. And now that I know, I will do everything in my power to leave you in a better place this time," he vowed.

While he answered my question, I watched him. He was an extremely handsome man. His hair was shorter than the other Cherokee I had seen but it still laid well past his shoulders. His features had hardened with age but he wore it well. His eyes had changed and I was glad of that. Gone was the frightened child. The man I was watching so closely was a fully grown man and my only hope of happiness.

## Chapter Thirteen

Lone Crow rode his pony in silence while repeatedly questioning if he was doing the right thing by going to Faith.

He knew his plan could go sideways very quickly. And if it did, there were more lives at stake than his own. And yet, he still didn't turn back.

It was not easy to admit that saving Faith was worth putting others in danger. Especially since he had no idea how she was going to react when he told her who he really was.

Even if revealing his true identity to her did cause his death, he was going to do it. The fear he was experiencing was not about the outcome of the visit, he was feeling anxious about Faith's reaction. But whether Faith be overjoyed or full of hate, Lone Crow still felt driven to help her. His hope was that she understood he hadn't imagined she would continue to be mistreated. The guilt of knowing he had done nothing but free himself from a terrible situation by killing Silas was one of the reasons he so was so willingly riding into the unknown. The other reason; he loved her. He had loved her since she intervened in his first 'disciplining.' The longer the two were separated, the easier it was to tuck her away in a special place in his mind. But she was always in his heart.

There had been other women. Women he should have been able to settle down with. But it was difficult for him to trust or be unguarded. Accepting that his issues were his own and the women who sought his attention were not to blame wasn't enough to make him want to keep putting time into them.

His personality was guarded and quiet but he never hesitated to help others when they were in need. He just preferred being on his own and away from others. It was only when he was alone that he could meditate and try to accept that his past didn't define his future. It had been a slow, arduous, soul-searching journey. One that he often thought would never end. But when he faced Adam and Tobias, he was able to put closure on the past. That is, until he saw Faith. Then he knew he wouldn't have closure until he helped her.

The Warrior was feeling confident and yet knew he wouldn't be able to continue to grow if he didn't face the woman he loved. He had accepted the fact that he would be alone but had never wished that fate for Faith. But as he stopped his pony and slid from her back, he wondered if Faith being alone wouldn't be for the best. She may grow lonely but at least she would be left in peace and not worry every moment of every day that she was doing something wrong.

His trepidation turned to anger when he thought about the treatment she'd been forced to endure. But all emotions forsake him when he saw Faith walking from the front of the wagon and taking a drink. The Warrior found he couldn't take his eyes from her as he slipped from his pony's back and patted her side.

Her hair had fallen from its constraint and several strands fell across her face and cascaded over her shoulder.

She had grown into a breathtaking beauty even while she lived in the darkness. Before Lone Crow reached for her, he wondered just how much more beautiful she would be if she had sunshine and happiness in her life.

The look of fear and exhaustion was gone and she appeared to be almost peaceful.

When he reached to restrain her, he knew he needed to be gentle. The last thing he wanted was to frighten her more than necessary.

As soon as she was in his arms, he began shaking with anxiety but was convinced she couldn't possibly tell because she was fighting too much.

Once she heard his statement, he knew he had her attention and held on to hope that she would not cry out.

The drumming had stopped and Lone Crow knew time was limited. But even after explaining what he needed from her, he found he didn't want to leave.

Hearing Faith admit she had carried hate for him hurt his heart even if he understood her emotions. It was a situation he planned on righting.

He was aware the men were saying their goodnights to the others when he promised he would not leave her any longer than necessary. He even admitted he had no plan, just a promise.

"I will return tomorrow if I can," he spoke as he began backing away from the scene.

The look of disappointment and despair Faith was exhibiting caused him to slow his departure.

"He is going to meet with Wilma tonight," she offered in a panicked whisper before sliding from the back of the wagon.

"Hold," Lone Crow ordered gently as he raised his hand in front of himself. "They are returning. Get in the wagon. If there is a way we can speak more tonight, I will come back. If not, I will search you out tomorrow."

Understanding and disappointment graced her face as she climbed back in. Her attempt was hampered only because she never took her eyes off of Lone Crow.

"It is so hard to let you leave me," she admitted, attempting to control her quivering lower lip.

Her statement tore at Lone Crow's heart. But he knew he had to leave.

"It is," he agreed as he slipped into the darkness and waited.

The men seemed in good spirits when they returned.

Lone Crow watched as Adam said his goodnights to everyone gathered and disappeared behind the other couple's wagon with his bedroll.

Howard sat by the fire and waited for Wilma to pour him a drink.

Wilma nervously busied herself while Tobias paced a line back and forth alongside his and Faith's wagon.

Lone Crow decided if Tobias climbed into the wagon, he would return to his spot and wait until the next night.

If Tobias and Wilma did try to escape for some private time, he still wasn't sure he should chance seeking Faith out for a second time. And yet, he remained crouched in the tall grass and bided his time.

It wasn't long before he saw Wilma talking to her husband. Howard nodded his head and stood in what looked like preparation to follow his wife.

The woman smiled and kissed the man on the cheek before pointing to the wagon and saying a few more words. Howard climbed into the wagon without much argument and Wilma waited until the man was gone before she too disappeared behind the wagon.

Lone Crow was sure they would be interrupted if Adam was alerted to their presence and again tried to convince himself to leave.

Tobias looked inside his wagon and then took the long way around the small camp before heading in the same direction as Wilma had taken.

When Lone Crow saw the man leave, he began backing up. It was challenging to do so but he had no idea how Adam would react to the pair. And if there was trouble, he needed to be far away.

After two small steps, he heard the grass behind him crack under the weight of something (or someone).

He ceased moving and searched for the source of the noise.

"Lone Crow?" he heard Adam's voice whisper.

The Warrior's muscles tensed and self-disappointment slammed into him.

He was caught and needed to quickly think of a reason he was lurking around their camp.

"Adam," he greeted reluctantly and a little angrily.

"What are you doing here?" he asked as he moved closer to Lone Crow and crouched beside him.

"I was looking in on the woman," Lone Crow answered after deciding that sticking to the facts was the best thing to do.

"I am doing the same. Why were you not at the meeting?" he continued the conversation, keeping the volume of his voice low.

"Because I am not in the village much. If you are watching out for her, I will leave," the Warrior offered, wondering just how much he could trust Adam.

He was pretty sure the man would not die for Faith so Adam couldn't possibly be much help. Still, the man's concern brought a new emotion to light. Lone Crow was angry. His throat was dry, and a knot had formed in his stomach. He was jealous of Adam's attentiveness and concern for Faith. Jealous and angry. If the man had underlying feelings for Faith, why hadn't he helped her before? He wasn't sure why he felt so strongly about Adam not being a part of Faith's future but he did. And the Warrior found it extremely difficult not to inform the man of that much.

If the circumstances of their conversation had been any different, he would have. But he was going to have the discussion with Adam as soon as possible. Faith did not need a half breed any more than she needed him. She needed to be loved and comforted by her own people.

"Will we see you before we leave?" Adam asked, unaware of the simmering anger Lone Crow was feeling.

"Yes. Come to the water hole tomorrow before dusk. We will be able to speak then," Lone Crow said, looking forward to setting the man straight.

"I won't let anything happen to her," Adam informed the Warrior, sounding resolute in his declaration.

Again, Lone Crow wanted to ask why he hadn't helped earlier but knew he needed to return to his spot and attempt to plan just how he was going to save Faith and not bring fire down upon his village.

"Tomorrow," Lone Crow spoke in a tone that sounded more like a threat than a promise.

Adam looked shocked but remained smiling. "Is Tobias inside the wagon?" he asked before Lone Crow moved far.

"No," Lone Crow answered, continuing to back away. "He is with the other woman. They were walking in the direction you took. So, I thought you would discover them and they would be back by now," he informed the man, surprised he was so willing to give Adam information but not accept his help with Faith.

"Then I shall return and make sure they know I have seen them," Adam decided, smiling a wicked grin.

Lone Crow was finding it difficult to hate Adam as much as he wanted to. But he couldn't leave without reminding the preacher of his only job, keeping Faith safe.

"Do not let your actions cause Faith any pain," he warned.

"Why do you care so much about her? I mean, I know she is beautiful and has the ability to make you want to protect her but she is a white woman," Adam continued their whispered conversation while moving closer to Lone Crow.

There was no way Lone Crow was going to continue to speak the truth with Adam.

"As you said, she needs to be protected," he answered, turning away from the man.

"But she is just a white woman," Adam pointed out, sounding as if was growing concerned that Lone Crow might be developing feelings for the woman.

"She is much more than that," Lone Crow corrected before disappearing into the grass.

He knew he hadn't needed to leave the man with questions. In fact, it was definitely not in his best interest but he couldn't help himself.

He knew he couldn't stay and protect Faith forever but he didn't want Adam doing it either.

## Chapter Fourteen

I was shaking and overcome with a deep sense of hopefulness and the familiar feelings of abandonment as I watched Moses backing away from me.

He had changed so much but I could still see a small part of the boy I knew in his eyes.

I desperately wanted to follow him. Seeing him, touching him, talking to him again was more than I dared ask for. And yet he had returned to my life and for the briefest of blissful moments, I saw an escape.

He promised me he would help me and I believed him. I again reminded myself he had never done anything to cause me pain. But the nagging hatred was not completely silenced.

Hatred may have been too intense of a word. The more my brain adjusted to the new information, the more I thought the strong feelings were more doubt and disappointment.

I believed Moses was going to do everything he could to help me, just as he had the first time he saved me. But he'd had to kill my abuser the first time and I did not want more blood on his hands because of me. No matter how many times I ran scenarios through my mind, Tobias' death was the one constant.

There was no way he would let me leave him without a fight. My husband may have found a woman who brought out the tender side of him but unless both of them were suddenly widowed, there was no way they could be together. It just wasn't done. So, it boiled down to me dying or Tobias dying. It was a fact that I easily understood but still didn't know if I wanted Moses involved.

My nerves were calmed just by knowing he was near. However, I didn't want my comfort to cause him to be hurt physically or mentally. He appeared to be strong and confident, two things I would never be. But instead of envying the fact his life had gotten better, I wanted him to stay healthy and happy. While I sat in the back of the wagon and listened to the muffled talking from my traveling companions, I slowly came to realize I wanted Moses' happiness more than I wanted my own. The drowsiness I was experiencing before had gone, and I found myself not being able to sit still.

I could hear Tobias grumbling outside the wagon and therefore did everything in my power to stay silent and keep my movements limited to my bouncing legs.

When I heard his footsteps approaching, I quickly laid down and closed my eyes.

"She better not be scared of me, Faith. I am on edge as is," he whispered his hate-filled threat before quickly turning around.

As soon as I was sure he was far enough away to not see me, I moved to the back of the wagon and scanned the area.

It was dark and the fire had all but gone out so the moon was the only light I had. It was overcast and rolls of thunder could be heard in the distance so the moon was not much help.

My heart rate sped up when I saw the grass moving just a few steps from me but my excitement waned when it stopped.

I still hadn't decided what I wanted from Moses but couldn't quell the elation I was experiencing.

Instead of backing away, I jumped down and cautiously started walking toward where the grass had moved.

"Do you want me to accompany you?"

Howard's voice startled me and I quickly tried to hide the fact that I thought I was being sneaky.

I stood from my crouched posture and turned to look at the man.

He was climbing from the wagon as he awaited my answer.

"Oh, no. But thank you," I answered, doing my best to keep my voice down.

I didn't want to alarm Tobias or frighten Moses.

"I'm waiting on Wilma. Can you go check on her?" He continued our conversation as he sat down and stirred the dying embers.

I absolutely did *not* want to go check on Wilma but knew I couldn't share my hesitation with Howard. Instead, I nodded and smiled weakly.

"Which direction did she go in?" I asked, walking toward him slowly.

"She went that way. I'm sure she is fine. I just worry. We are in the middle of nowhere," he answered, making excuses for his concern. "I would go but she said she was having female difficulties and ..." he continued, clearly fighting with the notion of going and looking for her himself.

I knew that idea was even worse than me interrupting Wilma and Tobias.

"I will go. Please do not wake Tobias," I added before taking a few steps backward from the man.

I didn't know why I added the request about my husband. But I did know it was best if Howard believed he was sleeping and not romping with the man's wife.

"No," he answered, lowering his decibel level and casting his glance at our wagon before turning back to me. "I am sorry about how he treats you."

I smiled and nodded my head before turning my back on the man.

I did appreciate his words but words did little.

Before taking too many steps, I decided that the more noise I made, the better. So I began humming and stamping my feet as I moved deeper into the tree line.

I was still startled and ultimately disappointed when Adam reached for my arm.

I yanked back and took a step away from the man as soon as I realized he wasn't Moses.

Adam appeared disappointed by my reaction but didn't immediately voice his emotions. Instead, he placed his finger in front of his mouth in an attempt to remind me to be quiet. I wasn't sure why he wanted me to stop making noise. He didn't know Tobias was with Wilma or even that Wilma had left the camp so I was curious to his concern.

"Why do you want me to be quiet?" I whispered, still keeping my distance from the man. "Aren't there wild animals near?"

Adam looked taken aback by my questioning. I was usually extraordinarily meek and yet Adam seemed to bear the weight of my misplaced anger. I couldn't explain why that was but I knew it wasn't his fault. So I quickly decided to try to stop being so short with him. After all, he seemed genuine in his concern for me, even if he wouldn't do anything to stop my treatment. The only person I could count on was me. And after reaching that conclusion, I was determined to be strong enough to inform Moses of my decision the next time we spoke.

"If you are quiet, they won't hear you," he explained with patience in his voice. "What are you doing?"

I rubbed the bridge of my nose and sighed before answering him. "I am looking for Wilma," I stated a little louder than necessary.

Adam scanned the area when I answered. "Why?"

"Howard was worried and I said I would check on her."

Once again, I spoke louder than needed. I was hoping that Wilma or Tobias heard me and did the decent thing; arrive back at the camp, separately. And if they were smart, Tobias would stay hidden until Howard was back in the wagon. But I didn't know if the two ever thought their actions through.

"I am here," Wilma spoke up, sounding winded.

I relaxed and smiled. "See, I am sure we are fine now," I said, doing my best to dismiss Adam politely.

"Wilma," I greeted as I took a step toward the woman.

The night was dark enough that I was sure Adam couldn't see she was buttoning her dress as she walked.

"Howard was concerned so instead of having him wake Tobias, I offered to come check on you," I explained loud enough for both Adam and Tobias to hear. I did not want my husband taking his anger out on me. Especially after the day I'd had. I experienced hope for the first time in as long as I could remember and I was not planning on allowing Tobias to take that from me. And from the looks of Wilma, she hadn't told my husband of her plan to call it quits.

"Oh," she said, still having trouble catching her breath. "I certainly did not mean to cause worry. Thank you. I just needed a little time to myself," she continued explaining when Adam made his presence known.

Her voice didn't reflect the shock she experienced when she saw the man but her face did.

"I was just walking the perimeter to ensure no animals were near and check on the horses," Adam explained his appearance easily enough. "Next time you need privacy, take Faith with you. It is much safer that way," he added with a smile and a tip of his hat. "I am going back to sleep. Goodnight, ladies."

As soon as Adam began walking away, both Wilma and I let out a breath.

"Thank you," she said, sounding as if she meant the words. "And Tobias should be fine for the next few days. I will not tell him until we are home," she continued quietly.

I wanted to thank her but couldn't seem to form the words. It was what I wanted and had asked her to do but the victory still seemed bittersweet.

"Where is he?" I whispered as we neared the camp.

"I am sure he will be close to your wagon. I hope he heard your warning about Howard," she spoke in hushed tones but picked up her pace. "How would I explain that?"

The thought was clearly worrying her and I couldn't say I blamed her. If I didn't care about others, I would have told the man long ago. But again, telling him that his wife was having an affair with my husband would only result in bloodshed. Tobias was the only one I truly had a quarrel with.

"I'm sure Tobias can handle that situation," I answered, hoping I wasn't giving my husband too much credit.

I was thankful to see Howard had stoked the fire and was pacing back and forth beside his wagon.

Even if Tobias hadn't been sneaky, Howard wouldn't have seen him so that gave me hope that my night would be one of peacefulness.

The look of relief on his face when he saw Wilma was one I knew, even if I had never been the recipient of such an expression. He was glad his wife was unharmed and thankful to me for bringing her to him.

I smiled and backed away from the reunion before slowing my step and again looking out into the grass. I knew I wouldn't see Moses again that night but still had hopes he would be able to speak to me the next day. It was all that occupied my mind.

In all the years Tobias and I had been married, I couldn't remember one other time that I looked forward to waking in the morning.

"I'm gonna sleep out under the stars tonight," Tobias' voice startled me.

He was leaning against the side of the wagon hidden from the fire and actually appeared to be happy.

I knew his happiness wouldn't last long but also knew that was something I needed to keep to myself. The trip home would be less arduous for me. Just because my fear of being thrown from the wagon had dulled, I still knew both my marriage and my life had to change.

"Fine," I said as I climbed back in the wagon.

"Thank you, Faith," he mumbled into the side of the canvas covering.

It was another first. Tobias had never thanked me for anything. And as easy as the words were to say, they still meant a lot. I might have allowed myself to believe everything would work out fine, maybe I had been overreacting to the situation and Tobias' affair.

But I was too jaded. I knew as well as Wilma that their relationship had to end. I would still need a plan of escape. Wilma's cooperation had only given me more time to think of what to do.

"I said, thank you, Faith," he repeated, sounding less appreciative than the first time.

"You are welcome, Tobias," I answered, forcing myself to sound sincere. "Sleep well."

I listened as he walked toward the back of the wagon.

I should have been trying to plan out my future but instead, I laid in the bed and tried to rehearse the conversation I was going to have with Moses when I saw him again. The thought that I might not see him tried to take hold but I wouldn't allow it. I was going to speak to my friend. There was just no other outcome I could accept.

Moses filled my mind even when I knew it wasn't smart. I was still sure I didn't need his help but I needed to sit and talk to him.

I wanted him to tell me about his life and his family. I wanted to simply sit and talk like we had when we were young.

When I'd pushed those memories to the back of my mind years earlier, it had been a form of self-preservation. I had no hope of seeing the boy again and very little hope that he had survived on his own.

He had, and I needed to know how he survived more than I needed to plan my future. As I fell into a deep slumber, I smiled. It was again a first.

## Chapter Fifteen

Instead of returning to his secluded spot, Lone Crow retrieved his pony and left her amongst the other horses.

Since he felt confident Faith was not going to inform the others in her party of his identity, he felt drawn to stay close.

His decision was not without liability. He was sure enough in himself that he willingly risked the repercussions. Still, before returning to his home for the night, he walked in the direction of Pathkiller's house, knowing his decision did affect others. He also knew he would need to explain his presence to his father.

The Warrior was relieved when he saw Pathkiller standing outside his doorway, speaking to another member of the village.

Pathkiller looked up from his conversation and smiled his customary greeting. The Chief's grin turned to a look of concern and he quickly dismissed the man he had been speaking to.

"Why are you here?" the Chief asked as he gestured for Lone Crow to approach him.

Lone Crow walked closer while still considering just how much of an answer he was willing to give the man.

"Well?" the Chief asked when Lone Crow stayed mute.

"I believe it is safe for me to be here," he answered, trying not to sound the slightest bit uncertain in his answer.

There were many ways his presence could be dangerous but he still believed his actions were relatively safe.

Pathkiller raised his eyebrows in question. "What has changed?" he asked as he crossed his arms in front of his chest.

Lone Crow looked back at the wagons before continuing his explanation. He believed Faith would keep his secret. And he was sure he left no signs of his presence. Adam had seen him, but again, he was confident the reasons he gave the man were good ones and felt he left Adam with no question of his sincerity and intent.

Seconds earlier, he had been convinced he was not actually putting his family in danger. But as he stood in front of Pathkiller, he found himself second-guessing his decision.

Faith was important to him and he had already reconciled the fact that she was more important than him, but he was still unsure of his choice.

"I spoke to her," Lone Crow divulged, barely above a whisper.

"You did what?" the Chief asked, his tone was a mixture of anger and shock.

"I couldn't help myself," Lone Crow explained quickly.

There had been few times in his life that Lone Crow felt like he was in the wrong, or worried about disappointing anyone. So he was having trouble not walking away from the conversation and returning to his isolated spot.

"Since there is no gunfire and no white people running around yelling, I will assume the talk went well? It was not wise for you to take that chance, though."

Pathkiller kept his chastising subdued but Lone Crow knew he had disappointed the man. The Warrior quickly learned it left a bad taste in his mouth.

"I know it was chancy," he admitted before preparing to tell the man all the reasons he couldn't do the smart thing. "I have to help her. She saved me when we were small and I thought I'd repaid the favor but I didn't. I must free her this time."

While he was explaining his actions, he felt himself growing more adamant with each word.

Pathkiller placed his hand on Lone Crow's shoulder. The Warrior fought the normal reaction to pull away and stood his ground.

"If that is how you feel, then we will meet about this in the morning," he decided before patting Lone Crow's shoulder. It was the Leader's way of showing the Warrior he was finished talking.

Lone Crow nodded his head and turned to locate his father.

Otter had the same questions about Lone Crow's appearance and after the queries were answered, the two sat around the small fire that burned in the center of Otter's home.

"Son," the man began after clearing his throat and giving himself time to think his next statement through. "This is not like you. You are not one to act without thinking. In fact, overthinking is your one flaw. I do understand your desire to help this woman ..."

"Faith," Lone Crow interrupted as he loaded his pipe. He knew he was going to have to listen to his father's thoughts on his bold action but found he did not like the way Otter spoke of her without using her name. "Sorry, Father," he mumbled. "Please continue."

Otter squinted his eyes at his son before continuing. "I understand your desire to help ... Faith. But I do not see a way to do so without it causing, at the very least, your death."

Lone Crow understood Otter's concern and did not have a good response, so he took a long draw from the pipe before handing it to his father.

"Do you?" Otter asked before taking the pipe from Lone Crow.

"Not yet," he answered honestly.

"Do the others know about her treatment?" Otter continued, passing the pipe back to Lone Crow.

"They do," the Warrior answered. "But they do nothing. It is much like when I was young. The people had to know how the Father was treating us but no one did anything. I believe the man, Adam, would like to help her but he is no good for her either," Lone Crow stopped talking when he realized he was saying more than he was comfortable with.

But it was too late. Otter appeared to be quite interested in hearing more about the man called Adam.

"Then let him do the dirty work," Otter suggested. "Why do you believe you have a say in who she is with?" he asked with no malice in his tone.

Lone Crow was taken aback by his father's question. "I ... will not see her with another abuser," he stated as he stood up and began pacing the length of the dirt floor.

"And you believe Adam will treat her badly?" Otter continued his interrogation before taking another pull from the pipe.

"No. I don't believe he would. But he is not white and if the townspeople ever learned of his true lineage, Faith would be treated as an outcast," Lone Crow explained, finding it difficult to keep his voice at an acceptable level.

Before Otter could offer more questions or words of advice, the sounds of horses and warriors quickly leaving the camp caused both the men to look outside.

Pathkiller was on his best pony in front of the opening. He looked tired but excited at the same time.

The familiar adrenaline began flowing through Lone Crow's body until he remembered he was needed there. For the first time since he had been fighting alongside the village warriors, he wasn't filled with the unbridled desire to join them. He did not want to leave Faith.

"The Shawnee have stolen some of the herd," the Chief stated. "Will you ride with us?"

Lone Crow was truly torn.

"I will watch the white people," Otter offered, patting Lone Crow on the back.

"Come, Lone Crow," Pathkiller urged excitedly. "It will take your mind from your troubles."

Lone Crow nodded his head. "Do not lose sight of her, Father. Please," he implored before he ran to fetch his pony.

The next few hours were intense and blood-filled. The Cherokee Warriors regained the pony herd and lost only one man with another two nursing only minor injuries.

The fighting was fierce and fast and Lone Crow fought with the same enthusiasm as always. And yet he didn't hoop and celebrate like the others as they rode back to the village. As soon as the battle was finished, his mind returned to the troubles he'd left behind.

"Lone Crow, I do not believe we will meet until later. Everyone is weary from the fight and the visitors plan to leave early tomorrow morning so we have to say our goodbyes. I will tell the men to plan for our meeting at midday. I am sorry it will not happen before then. The fight was unexpected but I believe they will not come back for some time," Pathkiller informed him as he rode beside the Warrior.

Lone Crow understood Pathkiller's decision and reasons for it but still wanted to be free to continue with his plan and have the members of the village agree. And he wanted to accomplish that before the party left.

He was tired and in need of some sleep but he still wanted to speak to Adam further and was determined to find a way to inform Faith of his plan. That meant he needed to have one, and as it was, he still didn't.

Lone Crow knew he was capable of shooting Tobias and riding away. The simple act would solve most of Faith's troubles. But again, his actions would definitely circle back to the village. The party had just visited and if an attack happened, as unlikely as that was, any repercussions would leave no one in the village alive.

Lone Crow had no hatred toward the other members of the party and did not see a reason to possibly cause an all-out war with the white people. So the simplest solution was not the most prudent one.

He was battle-weary and decided to sleep a few hours before thinking on it again. He stretched out on the floor of his father's home and hoped when he did meet with Adam, the man would have some ideas of his own.

Lone Crow had not been asleep for long when he was awoken by the sound of a scuffle. He sat up quickly, reached for his bow and quiver and walked to the doorway.

The noise he heard seemed to be coming from Tobias. Adam was standing between Pathkiller and Faith's husband.

Lone Crow felt the anger rise and before he could stop himself, he walked to the scene, with his weapon still in his hand.

"What is happening?" he asked, not bothering to mask his aggravation.

Adam looked like he was on the verge of punching the white man. But Tobias was still yelling about the trade being bad.

Lone Crow wasn't privy to the trade so he had no idea what was going on but the more Tobias complained, the more he looked forward to beating him. Shooting the man was too easy. Lone Crow wanted the man to feel some of the pain he had inflicted on Faith before he left the earth.

The Warrior took a step from the men and looked at Pathkiller. The Chief appeared bored by the theatrics but Lone Crow could see the simmering anger in the Leader's eyes.

Adam finally managed to push Tobias away. "Stop this. The trinkets they traded are not false idols. You know nothing about these people. What you *are* doing is undoing all the good we have done. Get the wagons ready. We are leaving!"

Tobias looked like he wanted a fight and Lone Crow was finding it extremely difficult not to acquiesce to the man's wishes.

Adam turned back to Pathkiller and Lone Crow. "I am sorry this happened. He is not a good man and we, well they, are not all like him," he apologized and made excuses for the poor behavior.

Pathkiller shook his head. "You are welcome back but they are not. We will have no more white 'holy' men in our village," he decided using his authoritative voice.

Adam nodded his head and removed his hat before reaching his hand out to the Chief. "I am sorry. You do know I am a Holy man, right?" he asked, employing a tone that sounded as if he were attempting to cool the emotions.

Lone Crow did not want the people to stay but he felt a panic set in when he realized just how adversely the departure could affect Faith.

"Adam," Lone Crow spoke as he grabbed the man's arm to stop him from walking away.

Pathkiller looked both confused and concerned by the Warrior's action.

"We need to speak before you depart," he said, trying to hide his panic.

"I will send two warriors to watch the others as they pack to leave," the Chief offered before walking away.

It was clear that Adam was no happier than Lone Crow about the sudden change of plans.

"I will do whatever it takes to keep Tobias away from Faith," the man offered as he wiped his brow before replacing his hat. "And I am sorry for the misunderstanding."

Lone Crow wanted to believe the man but couldn't quite force himself. So, he stood facing Adam while gnashing his teeth and flaring his nostrils.

"Why is this white woman so important to you?" Adam asked after a lengthy and awkward silence. "You have to know if you get involved in this mess, it will end badly. And not just for you. You have your village to concern yourself with."

Lone Crow knew many things. Mostly things he couldn't do. So, he knew Adam's opinion was correct. Still, he was going to do something. Even if he had no idea how or what, yet.

Before answering the man, he attempted to quell the jealousy from rising and tainting both his mind and words. "If she were important to you, you would have helped her by now."

Lone Crow took a step back and crossed his arms in front of his chest before widening his stance slightly.

A look of anger crossed Adam's face but was quickly replaced by one of calm and sereneness. "I have just become acquainted with Faith and I promise you I will not allow her treatment to continue."

"You cannot believe that you can give her the life she deserves. You know they will turn on you if they learn who you really are," Lone Crow objected.

He was doing his best to remain calm but Adam was saying all the wrong things and acting as if he were falling for Faith.

Lone Crow was not willing to allow that mistake to happen.

Before Lone Crow could begin explaining why Adam's plan for the future was a terrible one, they were interrupted by a warrior informing them that the wagons were ready.

"I appreciate your concern but the woman will be fine," Adam assured, returning to his typical attitude before waving at all those milling around their dwellings.

Lone Crow did not move from the spot and watched as the first wagon began moving away from the camp. Tobias' face was set in anger and Faith looked frightened.

He watched as Adam rode beside her before taking the lead.

Faith looked at him with a sadness and desperation that tugged at the Warrior's heart.

After ensuring Tobias wasn't looking, Lone Crow mouthed the words. "We will talk tonight."

Faith smiled and blinked until tears fell down her cheek.

## Chapter Sixteen

My sleep was interrupted by the sounds of riders leaving the camp. For reasons I couldn't explain, I felt a panic run through my body.

Instead of leaving the wagon through the back, I climbed onto the bench and tried to see what was happening.

Men were on their horses. Some had paint on their faces while others looked as if they had just woken. Women were standing outside the homes, lovingly telling the men goodbye and chanting.

I scanned the area quickly, hoping to be able to locate Moses.

I saw the Chief riding atop his pony but the darkness limited the view.

"What is going on?" I heard Tobias ask as he walked toward me.

His voice was still husky from sleep and he was rubbing his eyes as he sat beside me.

I involuntarily tensed and sat up straighter, all while scooting away as sneakily as possible.

"I don't know," I answered honestly.

"Somethings got them all fired up. But look at their weapons. About half of them still carry a bow and arrow. A gun is so much more efficient when it comes to killing."

I rolled my eyes and kept looking straight ahead. There was no reason for me to purposely upset Tobias so I remained quiet. My opinion on the matter was, the Natives had been doing just fine without them until we introduced guns to the new land.

But I was relieved when everyone began waking and asking the same questions as Tobias. And even with Adam usually making my life more difficult, I was pleased to see him walk beside Tobias and lean against the wagon.

"From what I can tell, the Shawnee snuck into the pasture land and stole a bunch of their ponies," the man informed us without being questioned.

My heart felt as if it literally missed a beat when Adam's words sunk in. I was frightened for Moses but quickly attempted to calm my concern by reminding myself it was his way of life and he appeared to be confident in his skills.

Still, I must have made a noise because Tobias grabbed my arm.

"They aren't coming for us," he stated, still digging his fingers into my flesh while watching Wilma being held tenderly by Howard.

The words were ones that should have been spoken in calming tones. Tobias wasn't fooling anyone. He wasn't the slightest bit concerned about the Cherokee people. He was too concerned with his lover's husband's protective stance to care about anything else.

"Tobias," Adam spoke and my husband's grip only got tighter.

I was biting the bottom of my lip and desperately trying not to show the pain I was experiencing.

"Since we are awake, why don't we fetch some water from the waterhole and then go through the items we received in trade? Howard?" Adam continued, moving more out in the open when he called for Howard. "Would you like to come with us?" he offered.

Tobias released me but did not agree to Adam's plan before leaning closer. "Do not upset her," he warned, before moving to the end of the seat and jumping down.

"Will they be alright?" Howard asked.

"The Warriors are all leaving. I am sure they will be fine while we get a head start on tomorrow," Adam assured before stopping and looking at me. "I will keep them busy for a few hours."

I smiled a weak thankful smile at his statement because I wasn't sure what response was required.

Again, I thought the man was attempting to ease my suffering but in my experience, putting Tobias off usually ended in more pain. I understood Adam wasn't privy to that information but what he was doing was angering Tobias more. My husband bruising my upper arm was painful but it was mild compared to what he was capable of.

"What shall we do?" Wilma asked, pulling me from my thoughts.

I turned and looked at the woman. She was stirring the embers of the fire while yawning widely.

"If you are sleepy, then go back to bed," I suggested as evenly as possible.

She was helping me, in a way, but she still wasn't my favorite person. Not to mention, I was sure we had already said almost everything we needed to.

Wilma looked pleased with my suggestion and dropped the stick she had been using to waken the fire. "Are you sure?"

"I am sure. I will probably go back to bed soon," I answered, looking from her to the village.

The men had ridden away and most of the gathered women were slowly returning to their homes. Others visited calmly as they walked the central lane of the village.

The dust the ponies kicked up had settled and there was a low hanging fog that gave the village an almost magical look.

The chill in the air forced me to lean backward and grab my thick quilt. After wrapping the blanket around myself, I slowly moved to the edge of the wooden seat and jumped.

I wanted to walk around the village. I felt as if I had to. The fluffy low hanging cloud called to me.

I was also fully aware that doing so could cause me both pain and embarrassment. It was not like me to want to do anything out of the ordinary. I didn't even go to the general store without Tobias. And yet, I still couldn't talk myself out of taking those steps.

My feet crunched the lightly frosted grass as I slowly began walking toward the open area where I'd seen the children playing.

They had been so happy and carefree that I wanted to soak up their energy. The village, and the people who called it home, touched me on a level I didn't know existed. The drumming and chanting had soothed me and the openness of their joy broke my heart while lifting it up at the same time. I was both happy and overcome with sadness as I sat on the cold ground and looked up at the cloudy sky.

Even the sky was clearer. The stars I could see through the clouds were numerous and all seemed to twinkle.

"Osiyo," an older man spoke softly.

As soon as I heard his voice, I immediately stood from my relaxed position.

He smiled, shook his head and gestured for me to sit back down.

I was nervous and thinking about running until he sat across from me and again motioned for me to do the same.

I smiled what I was sure was an awkward grin and slowly returned to a seated posture.

"Hello," I greeted nervously after clearing my throat.

"Hillow," he repeated with a genuine smile still covering his face.

The man appeared to be pleased with himself and I couldn't stop smiling back at him and repeating the greeting once again.

"Hillow," he repeated, sounding even more impressed with himself after voicing the word a second time.

I had no idea who the man was or why he came to sit by me but I hadn't been so happy about sharing an experience with someone else in a very long time - since the last time Moses and I talked and planned a future that would never be, to be precise.

"Faith," I stated as I pointed to myself.

It wasn't the first time I tried to communicate with a Cherokee so I was sure I remembered some words but still spoke my name in English.

Instead of searching my memory, I pointed at him and asked. "You?"

His smile seemed only to deepen and he rocked as he laughed.

"Tsiya," he said slowly.

I was preparing to keep engaging the man when he scanned the area before standing and returning his attention to me.

I didn't know what he heard but I stood up too.

He nodded his head and pointed back to the wagon. The smile was still there but not as bright as it had been a second earlier.

I got the feeling he was trying to tell me to go back but was doing his best not to panic me.

He had no idea who I was or what my life was like but he was gentle and kind. He seemed to not want to worry me, he just wanted me to go back.

"Thank you," I spoke as I quickly made my way back to the campsite.

I had just reached the side of the wagon when I heard the men talking.

My new friend had saved me from doing a lot of explaining and I was grateful for that.

"Where's Wilma?" Tobias asked as he scanned the site.

Howard and Adam both looked at him with confusion.

Adam's expression was mixed with aggravation but Howard was genuinely puzzled by Tobias' concern for someone other than me.

Since I was the only one with the answer Tobias wanted, I cleared my throat, pulled the quilt tighter and walked to the gathered men.

"She is sleeping. I said I would watch," I offered, smiling at Howard.

"If ya worried about your own wife a little more, it might be better," the man mumbled as he broke from the others and walked toward his wagon.

When Howard walked beside me, he reached to pat me on the back but I quickly dodged his contact.

He looked sad, I looked apologetic, and Tobias looked angry. Adam walked in the direction of our wagon, shaking his head, and from what I could hear, he was cussing under his breath.

"Tobias," he called when he reached his destination. "Help me pull the box of stuff from the back before Faith goes back to sleep," he directed in a stern voice.

"I will pull our box out," Howard offered as he grabbed for the big wooden container that practically blocked any easy access to the inside of the wagon.

"Thank you, Howard. If ya want to go to bed, go ahead," Adam offered when he pointed to the box in the back of our wagon and waited for Tobias to help lift it out.

I was enjoying watching my husband quietly do as he was told but again worried Adam might have overstepped his bounds.

"Try to get some sleep," Adam suggested when the box and both men were free of the wagon. "Let's drag it to the fire. I will go get the other one and we will start the flames again."

Tobias' jaw was tight but he did as he was told without argument.

"Did you talk to her?" he asked in a whisper before following Adam.

"No. She said she was tired," I answered, not looking him in the eye.

After making myself comfortable, sleep came easily enough. I wasn't smiling but I wasn't terrified either. Nothing about Tobias had changed so I attributed my calmness to the area and the people.

Before I fell into a slumber, I heard the shouts and yelps coming from the village. I slid my body so that I could see what was happening.

The Warriors had returned and they seemed pleased with the outcome of whatever had taken place.

I squinted and tried to locate Moses. I didn't fear that he might not have returned but I still wanted to see him. Between the dust and the people's movement, I returned to my bed, disappointed.

Once back in my sleeping world, I was plagued with dreams. Dreams of the future, visions of me being dragged through the town and thrown into the jail. I tried to wake but was forced to continue to watch the unfolding scenes. The townspeople, people who I had known my whole life, were spitting on me and calling me horrible names. They were the same people who turned a blind eye to the way I had been treated my whole life. So I was not only experiencing the sheer terror of the situation; I was confused and deeply hurt. I attempted to pull from my abductors but couldn't break free, nor could I wake. I saw the gallows at the exact same time I heard Tobias yelling.

His voice yanked me from the dream and before I knew it, I was sitting up and moving to see what had angered the man.

The chilly wind instantly cooled my sweat-soaked body. The dream was something I planned on examining but I needed first to understand why Tobias was throwing such a fit.

Tobias was shaking his head and looking both disgusted and livid at an object he was holding. His expression was one I had witnessed before and knew nothing good was going to come of his mood.

I stayed where I was and watched as Adam did almost everything in his power, except punching the man, to stop Tobias from continuing to rant.

I did hear the words 'false idol' once or twice but still had no idea what he was talking about.

It wasn't long before Wilma and Howard were climbing from their wagon and some of the Natives who were still awake began closing the gap between us.

They had no look of anger on their faces. The people of the village were simply curious as to why my husband was

122 Elizabeth Anne Porter

behaving like a spoiled child. I understood their confusion but still didn't approach my husband. Instead, I traveled back through the wagon and retook the seat at the front. From there, I had an unobstructed view of both my husband and the group nearing us.

I watched as the man who first met with us closed the gap and spoke to Adam before walking away.

Adam appeared to be experiencing mixed emotions. He had lost his customary calm sereneness and it looked very much like he wanted to deck my husband. I won't lie, I did enjoy the thought. The images even ran through my mind several times.

Adam placed himself in between the Native and Tobias but they still moved further into the village and my husband was still repeating himself over and over.

Tobias' mood was enough to force me to consider getting involved. Doing so probably would do no good and assuredly cause me to pay a price but I did not want him making trouble with the people I felt most at home around.

So I bit my bottom lip and decided to stop watching the scene. As I turned away, I saw Moses join the group. Instead of continuing my retreat, I stayed and watched.

Watching Moses gave me a sense of pride and happiness. It was clear the man had been able to overcome his childhood and go on to lead a full life. That understanding was just another reason why I couldn't take his help. Whatever ended up happening with my marriage and future had to be by my hands. Even if that meant I would be hanged. The dream did try to resurface but I pushed back and continued to watch Moses in action.

As soon as I heard Adam declare that we were leaving, I ducked back inside and waited.

"We are leaving. Pack our stuff," Tobias sneered into the canvas as he walked by.

I jumped down and did as he asked while Wilma and Howard hurriedly packed their belongings.

"What is the matter with Tobias?" Howard asked.

"I wish I knew," I answered before returning to the wagon and waiting on the horses.

Tobias was so angry he couldn't seem to voice words and I knew there was little Adam could do to calm him. Especially because it looked to me that Adam was doing the most to continue to anger my husband. I knew we were waiting on the man and the last time I had seen him, he was close to Moses so I desperately longed to look up but knew better. The submissive, hunched over state I chose to take was my best choice of posture.

As soon as I felt the animals begin to move, I risked looking in Moses' direction.

If it was the last time I would see him, I wanted to remember him as the strong man he was and not the frightened child I'd known so well.

When I saw the determination in his features, my breath caught in my throat and when he promised we would talk again, I couldn't stop the tears from flowing down my cheeks.

## Chapter Seventeen

Lone Crow meant what he vowed. He would speak to Faith later and there was nothing that would stop him.

All he was lacking was a plan to help her. And he was sure after sleeping a few more hours, his head would be clear enough to think of one.

"We leave again at dusk," Pathkiller informed him when the dust settled and they were free of their visitors.

Lone Crow looked at the Chief in question. "I am going after her," he stated. "Are you planning on accompanying me?"

Pathkiller had little sleep so he immediately showed Lone Crow he was not in the mood for levity on any level.

"The council will finalize the plans. But we are going to repay the Shawnee for their arrogance. They will be horse-less tonight."

Lone Crow understood the feud with the Shawnee took precedence in his Leader's eyes but it meant nothing when compared to Faith's needs.

"I will follow the wagons," he informed Pathkiller gently. "You have no real need for me. And I feel that if I do not do something for Faith, I cannot move on. My mind would not be in the battle."

Pathkiller grumbled before nodding his head. "You are always needed but I understand. Do not do anything to bring more white people to our village. Give your plan thought before acting," the Chief warned before walking away and leaving Lone Crow to his thoughts.

Pathkiller was right. He had to think and plan. But only after sleep.

When Lone Crow woke, the village was again preparing to pray for the departing warriors. He wasn't accompanying the men but did quickly stand and walk to his door to show his support.

The sun was beginning to lower in the cloudless sky and the warmth still held the chill at bay. It was a welcome change and a sure sign that summer was doing its best to hold on. The ripe corn festival would be coming up soon and he wanted to have his mission accomplished by then. That meant he had two weeks to change Faith's future and return to his life. The job wouldn't have been so challenging if he had a plan.

After eating and washing, he gathered his still packed bags and headed off to retrieve his pony.

"Lone Crow," Otter greeted when he saw his son.

Lone Crow wasn't surprised by his father's presence but he was shocked to see the man was combing the Warrior's horse.

"I knew you had made up your mind when you stayed behind," Otter said, in lieu of a greeting.

Lone Crow nodded and stood next to his father.

"I still do not know of a way I can help. But I may have to follow the wagons back to the town," he admitted as he gently moved Otter's hands from his pony's back.

Otter looked alarmed by Lone Crow's information. "I do not believe that would be the best solution," he cautioned. "Have you thought to ask if you could trade for her?"

Lone Crow was taken aback by his father's suggestion but couldn't dismiss the notion as quickly as he would have liked. Was it possible that the man thought so little of his wife? Even if he did, Lone Crow knew the others in the party would not allow such a trade. Faith was not an object. She was a person. An extremely important person. Even if she voiced no objection to the idea, bringing her to his village was not something that was done. His people would take her in and teach Faith their ways but he was sure such an action would draw the attention of the military. Doing so also didn't give Faith the house and life she surely desired. After considering his father's idea, he decided it was not a terrible one, just another he didn't believe was an option.

"I do not believe the others would allow such a strange proposition," he answered, not wanting in any way to belittle his father's idea. "But I do appreciate the suggestion. I plan to be back in time for the festival. If I am not, do not worry. I may not ever return. But I will see Faith has every opportunity to spend the rest of her life in peace."

"She is so frightened," Otter asserted. "Hillow," he said, smiling at his son. "I sat with her while you were gone."

"You what? When?" Lone Crow asked after placing the bags across his pony's back. "How could you sit with her? And how did she have time to teach you a word?"

Lone Crow desperately needed to hear the answer so instead of mounting his horse, he stood his ground beside Otter.

"She walked to the playing grounds and sat down. The men were away so I went and sat beside her," Otter answered, smiling. "She was afraid and then at peace. I told her what I am called and she told me what she is called and then she said, 'hillow.' I say it well. The white man words are not so difficult," he continued to explain.

Lone Crow did not know how to react to the news. His father was not one to take unnecessary chances so he didn't think the meeting of the two would change anything. But he did find himself interested in what Otter thought of Faith, aside from the fact that the woman was frightened and frail.

"What was she doing walking around the village?" Lone Crow continued his gentle interrogation. "She didn't run when she saw you?"

Otter smiled and expressed his understanding to Lone Crow. "I believe she was going to until I showed her I meant her no harm. What is it you called her?" Otter answered while he moved to another horse and began combing his mane before braiding it.

Lone Crow knew his father well enough to know the man was delaying his departure on purpose. The two could have spoken about the meeting the last time they talked. The Warrior didn't know what his father's reasons were but he also didn't attempt to speed the conversation along.

"I called her Faith unless we were alone and then I called her Bird," he answered. "I am eased to know you did not add to her constant state of fear."

"She is much like a bird. You selected a fitting name. Why don't you come back to the house and we can eat before you leave?" Otter suggested.

"Why are you delaying me?"

There was no anger or aggravation in the Warrior's voice. It was merely a question he needed to be answered even after deciding it was best to stay quiet on the subject. The Warrior found it impossible to remain silent and respectful. He suddenly needed to know the reason for his father's tactics.

"What is the rush?" Otter answered with a smile on his face.

"I need to assure the man does not take his anger out on Faith again. You had to see how mad he was when they left," Lone Crow answered, doing his best to keep his voice even.

"The other man, Adam, will not allow that. You said as much before you decided he was no better than you for the woman. They will most probably stop at the water hole. It is not far and you can get there in short time. If we spend some time together, maybe we can think of a plan to accomplish your goal," Otter answered, after thinking his reasoning through before responding.

"The other man is another issue I will need to deal with. I believe he has feelings for her and he is no better than ..." Lone Crow stopped talking when he realized two things.

The first was he was repeating himself entirely too much and the second was he'd accepted his feelings for Faith. He loved her. That was the brutal and sad truth. It had been Faith since he walked away from her the last time. She was who he thought of when he woke and she was the last thing he thought about when he fell asleep. Since reuniting with her, the feelings were harder to fight. He wanted to hold her in his arms and remove her fears. He wanted to soothe her when she was scared and laugh with her like they had when they were young.

Just as quickly as he acknowledged the depths of his feelings for the woman, he understood his desires were all a dream.

The best he could do for her was set her free from Tobias and wish her well. He didn't have any say if she did choose to start a new life with Adam. His jealousy would have to take a back seat to whatever was best for Faith. It was not an easy fact to digest and he knew it would be difficult to let go, but he would do it.

"What is wrong with Adam?" Otter asked, waiting for Lone Crow to follow.

The Warrior was not going to speak about Adam any longer. The topic angered him and until he could learn to control that feeling, he needed to not think about the man.

"I have eaten and plan to be waiting when the wagons stop for the night," Lone Crow replied, avoiding answering his father's last query and mounting his pony.

Otter smiled and nodded but Lone Crow could see the unease in his father's eyes.

"I am concerned that all this will take you back to the dark place you were in when I found you," Otter expressed as he walked back to stand beside Lone Crow's pony.

Before Lone Crow could react to his father's statement, Otter continued.

"I do not want you to lose who you have grown to be," he admitted, looking serious.

Lone Crow appreciated his father's words and concerns. The Warrior did not want to lose himself either but didn't see how he could. He had stood up to the men and the fear he'd carried for years was gone. But anger and resentment took its place easily enough.

"I will be fine," Lone Crow stated as he looked down at Otter. "Your concern means the world to me. But I will do as I must. I will be back in time for the festival," he said, smiling a confident grin before gently nudging his horse forward.

Otter nodded his understanding as Lone Crow's pony walked past him.

"Before you go," Otter spoke louder to ensure his son would hear.

Lone Crow stopped and turned his ride to face his father.

"After you answer my question, I will let you go in peace," he offered, again smiling easily as he walked to meet Lone Crow.

The Warrior held no malice toward his father. He knew the old man was doing his best to keep him safe. But his stalling tactics had done nothing more than delay his departure. And the quicker he left, the quicker he could decide on a plan.

"Then ask, Father," the Warrior suggested gently.

"Adam will not cause her pain. So what is wrong with Adam being her savior?"

Lone Crow had just accepted that the end result could be just that. But he still wasn't happy about it and still didn't want to talk about the troublesome man.

He clenched his jaw and looked to the sky before answering Otter. "Adam is not me," he replied before turning his pony and pushing the animal into a gallop.

## Chapter Eighteen

We rode in silence except for the occasional grumbles and mumbles Tobias spewed.

I knew it would be tricky to avoid his wrath but thought I still had a chance of having to deal with nothing more than a whispered, hate-filled, outburst. Tobias didn't care for Adam but he still seemed to want to impress the man. The reason evaded me but it was helpful so I didn't want to question it further.

Any other time I would have been panicked and anxious to get my punishment over with. My mind would have been full of worry. But it wasn't. It was occupied with the promise that Moses would find me and we would be able to talk one final time. The thought truly excited me. I was actually looking forward to it. And was determined not to let anything or anyone change my mood.

It had been a warm day and we left without taking the time needed to pack appropriately so it wasn't surprising when Adam suggested we stop at the waterhole. The idea sounded wonderful because I had been given some privacy the first time we stopped there. So I didn't think I would have a problem separating from the group again.

My plan seemed to be coming together quite nicely so I continued to ignore the various unhappy sounds that emanated from my husband and tried to replay some of the happier conversations Moses and I shared years earlier.

We had been woefully naïve. But I believed him when he said he would take me with him. Believed that his people would accept me and that the townsfolk would just allow me to disappear. As an adult, remembering the conversations didn't bring me the joy I longed for. They made me a little sad and angry. The plan would have never worked and I doubted if the two of us would have made it to the outskirts of town. I was sure Moses would have been killed even at his young age. He had killed a man. The people of the town wouldn't have cared about the two of us enough to even ask for our side of the story. They couldn't have disbelieved our story but they wouldn't have cared either. So, in the end, Moses did the right thing. The only thing that allowed him to live a full life. When the discovery washed over me, the last sliver of anger I held toward the man disappeared. If Moses was able to experience a life free of constant fear and hopelessness, that was enough for me. I was happy for him. A little envious, but pleased.

While I was reliving snippets of my past, an idea came to me that was hard to ignore. I had toyed with the idea earlier in the trip but wasn't the slightest bit comfortable with the possible outcomes.

I could simply run away when everyone was sleeping. The act itself was simple enough. I could pack some food and an extra dress and just walk away.

The obstacles were what concerned me. Could I hide from the others when they came in search of me? How long would they continue to try to find me? And if they did locate me, I knew there would be no stopping Tobias' wrath. If they gave up and went home, which was the best possible outcome, what would I do next?

I couldn't live off the land. There were hungry, wild animals everywhere and I would have no way of protecting myself. I considered running to the village we just left. Moses was there and the people made me feel such peacefulness. It was tempting. No, temping was not a strong enough word. The thought momentarily overtook my brain.

Moses promised we would talk later and I could ask him to wait and take me back to his village. And we could live and laugh and be happy. And then, reality reared its ugly head again.

The village was the first place Tobias and the others would look. Would it still cause trouble for the people even if I wasn't there? Would my running somehow cause pain to Moses?

The short-lived joy I was experiencing was ebbing and my leg was beginning to bounce. Was there nothing I could do? Before abandoning the only real chance I thought I had of leaving Tobias, I considered delaying my escape until we were closer to the town. All was not lost but I was disappointed that I couldn't run right away. Putting off running would also diminish my chances of survival. There were many things I could have worried about but since I was determined to not go down that particular rabbit hole, I nursed the excitement I was feeling about talking to Moses.

"Those people can't be helped," Tobias stated, yanking me from my thoughts.

"Sorry?" I asked sheepishly. "You did your best," I added quickly in hopes of not adding to his ire.

"Why do you suppose that one spoke English so well?" he asked as he wiped the sweat from his brow before leaning to retrieve the canteen.

His anger appeared to have lessened. His question didn't appear to have any underlying malice. But it still caused my heart to skip a beat.

My mouth went dry but I swallowed a few times and attempted to answer my husband's question. Before I could, he continued his line of queries.

"And why does Adam speak theirs?"

The second question was asked with a hint of irritation.

I wanted to ask him why he hadn't thought about the language disparity before, but knew that was not going to help me one bit.

"Aren't there trappers mixed with the Cherokee?" I asked innocently.

"You think both men had trappers for fathers?" Tobias questioned, squinting at me.

I knew I was pushing my boundaries but I was not going to allow Tobias to continue playing connect the dots or continue to question anything about Moses. But Adam speaking Cherokee was a question I wondered about too.

"Have you asked Adam about his parents?" I asked.

The man was riding beside Howard and Wilma's wagon. The vehicle was too noisy and too far ahead for me to hear what was being said. Still, Adam and Howard seemed to be enjoying an easy conversation.

"No. I assumed he was a son of a preacher. I will ask him when we stop. And what about those marks on that one's back?"

I bit my bottom lip and took a deep breath. I had no idea what I could say in response without it either angering him or angering me.

"Well?" Tobias asked as he elbowed me in the side.

The breath left my body and I had to hold to the bench to stop from falling.

The ever-present tears clouded my vision but I turned to look him in the eye.

"Maybe his father was like mine?" I asked as I rubbed my side gently.

Tobias shook his head. "No. Your father was only trying to do the same as me. There is an evil in you. And I gotta tell you, Faith, I am getting tired of trying."

I was struck silent and breathless when I heard his statement.

My father repeated the sentiment every time he beat me. I was evil. There was a time in my life when I did wonder if there weren't something wrong with me. But I never raised my voice, never disobeyed, and rarely thought for myself.

Internally I did all the things I wanted to. I screamed, questioned, and fought back. But my external actions were a different matter altogether. I was a doormat and that was something I was growing weary of. But self-preservation prevailed and I stayed silent as I looked at my folded hands in my lap. I cleaned, cooked, did chores, and stayed quiet. I was a middling woman but I couldn't accept the thought that I was evil.

"What am I gonna do with you?" he asked, sounding as if he expected an answer.

I was not inclined to do as he wished so was thankful to see Adam had stopped his horse and was waiting for our wagon.

Tobias' grumbled but still plastered a smile to his face when he saw the man waiting for us.

"Can I go to the back?" I asked, hoping Tobias would think my attendance wasn't necessary.

I might have been taking advantage of Adam's presence but I did not want to continue listening to Tobias' questions or his thoughts about me.

Tobias nodded and centered his attention on Adam.

After sliding to the back, I began to tidy the wagon left in disarray from the hasty departure then sat in my bedding. No matter how hard I tried to recreate the excitement I was enjoying earlier, I couldn't. Even the notion of seeing Moses again couldn't lift my spirits.

It seemed every time I looked forward to anything or began to believe in myself, I fell back into a dark place with the slightest word.

I didn't enjoy thinking I could have been the problem. Maybe there was something wrong with me. And perhaps I was unlovable. They were not pleasant possibilities to consider but it wasn't the first time I'd pondered those very things.

I felt the wagon lurch.

"Are we here already?" I asked, quickly climbing back to the seat.

The sun was nestling into the horizon and casting colors onto the sky in the most gorgeous way. I had never seen such a sunset. I must have been in the back of the wagon for hours and felt less sure of myself than when I had ventured back there.

But the sunset was an awesome sight and I was glad I didn't miss it.

"Yeah," Tobias answered. "While you are unloading the back, tell Wilma I want to see her," he added as he steered the wagon to a full stop.

The only thing I was sure of was that Moses and I were going to talk if he showed up. Not even Tobias was going to stop that from happening.

"After my chores are done," I suggested gently. "I would like to bathe," I added hopefully.

"Yeah, after you've done your duties. I don't care. Just make sure Wilma knows I want to talk to her."

I nodded and took another long look at the sunset before returning to the back and gathering the cooking utensils.

I made beans, bacon, and biscuits for dinner, informed Wilma that Tobias wanted to see her after everyone was sleeping, and went through the motions until the dishes were all sitting on a linen used as a table cloth.

"Would you like some help?" Adam asked as he leaned down to help me secure the load.

Tobias and Howard were sitting on wooden stools by the fire in awkward silence. Both had their bibles in their hands but neither looked as if they were reading.

Wilma was beating the bedding and looking pensive. And Adam was being helpful by asking to aid me.

I took the dish laden cloth from his grip and smiled gratefully.

"Thank you for the offer. But I think you could help me more by speaking to Tobias while I am gone. After I clean the dishes, I plan to bathe. I won't be long but I do think he needs some guidance about how he reacted today."

I had not intended on begging the man but hadn't ruled that eventuality out either. I needed to be alone so that I could speak to Moses. And I was not prepared to allow any other outcome.

Adam looked a little wounded by my suggestion but quickly smiled and nodded his head. "I will do that," he agreed before leaning closer to me and whispering. "I brought some wine along. I will see that Tobias drinks enough that he will not be a bother to you tonight. Enjoy your bath."

I watched as he walked back toward the men and shook my head. I admired the plan but didn't think Tobias would partake much. My husband already had plans. And he was not a man who embraced changing anything easily.

The water hole was not far from where the wagons were parked but I heard the frogs singing before I saw the water.

The moon was not full but the sky was cloudless and it was light enough to see. A large tree sat at the edge of the water and took on an ominous posture in the darkness.

I remembered the place had been peaceful and beautiful when I was there before and was a little shocked by the change the night brought.

But I was not afraid. I was anxious to see Moses and disappointed when he didn't immediately show himself. Instead of allowing the thought that he wasn't coming to root in my brain, I quickly cleaned the utensils before stripping down to my underwear and walking into the cool, clear water.

The night was chilly but the water still maintained its warmth. After ducking my head under the water and slinging my hair back over my head, I heard movement at the edge of the water. Before turning, I said a prayer, asking that the intruder be Moses.

"Tsisqua," he said softly.

I began walking toward him as soon as my name left his lips.

By the time I reached the water's edge, he had dislodged the utensils and was holding up the linen for me to cover with.

It was a small sweet gesture that brought happy tears to my eyes. No one, not my father, not my husband, had ever shown me such a kindness.

"I'm so glad you're here," I said, doing my best to stop my teeth from chattering.

"I will light a small fire," he offered.

"No. I will be fine. Just sit and talk to me," I suggested as I sat in the cool dirt.

He smiled and sat next to me. "I will help you. But for now, I would just like to look at you."

I smiled and felt a blush cover my cheeks. "I do not need your help. And it is good to see you too," I replied.

He looked hurt and angry when he heard my declaration. "You are going to stay with the man? He will kill you one day. And I cannot allow that to happen."

"I cannot allow my actions to cause you or your people any pain. I plan on running," I divulged, scanning the area as I did.

I still wasn't feeling confident in my plan but attempted to sound as if I were. I wanted to sit and speak to the man and then convince him to go back to his life.

"Running?" he asked, cautiously reaching for my chin.

We had cuddled and soothed each other many times when we were young but I was still surprised at my reaction. I didn't attempt to distance myself. I did the opposite. I moved closer to him.

"Yes. I will leave before we return to town. It is best if I do not run when we are so close to your home." I answered as I scanned his deep brown eyes.

"They will find you," he stated, smiling and letting go of my chin. "Where will you go?"

I kept my head up and still looked him in the eyes. The tears threatened to fall but I willed them to stop. I wanted him to believe I would be fine. Even if I wasn't sure I would be. It was the only plan I had. It had to somehow work. And if I stayed with Tobias, he *would* kill me one day. So death was acceptable. And if I were to be eaten by an animal, it would be a better death than at the hands of my cruel husband.

"I will go to the next town," I answered after ensuring my voice wouldn't break. "We don't have long. I have missed you," I admitted.

"You have never entirely left my thoughts," he confessed. "Are you sure the next town will not give you back to your husband?" Moses asked, not hiding his anger when he spoke of Tobias.

I did not want to talk about the future. I wanted to just be in is company. "If they act as if they are going to fetch Tobias, I will go to the next town. Please tell me how it is to be free," I suggested, not being able to stop my voice from catching.

I didn't realize just how sad my request was until I saw the expression on Moses' handsome face.

"I am sorry," he declared, employing a heartbreaking tone. "I should have taken you with me."

I reached for his arm and pulled him into a hug. "You did not know," I whispered into his neck. "It would have not ended well either way. And this way, I can live through you. If you will just tell me what it is like," I urged, doing my best not to sob openly.

Moses enveloped me in his strong, protective arms and pulled me closer to him.

I was still wrapped in the thin linen but the heat his body was giving off instantly warmed me. The feel of his heartbeat was comforting on a level I had forgotten I could attain.

For one beautiful moment, I was indeed at peace. And then I felt Moses' muscles tense before he quickly placed space between us and scanned the area.

He stopped looking and homed in on one spot as he reached back and pulled his bow and arrow from the sling he wore across his back.

I pulled the sheet closer to my body and began curling into myself.

"You will be safe," Moses whispered as he slowly drew the string of the bow taut.

"There is no need for that," Adam said as he stood and revealed himself.

I was shocked but could tell Moses was angered by his appearance.

## Chapter Nineteen

By the time Lone Crow reached a spot close to the pond, he had made up his mind to follow the wagons back to town. The plan was not without fault nor was it guaranteed to solve all Faith's troubles. But it was the only idea that lessened the chance that his actions would return to his people. And something had to be done.

He was going to follow behind and once Faith was home, he planned on killing Tobias. The Warrior accepted the dangers of such a bold move and was willing to accept that he most probably would be hanged for his crime. The only regret he had was that he hadn't shown Otter more appreciation. But he was sure his adopted father would be fine. Lone Crow's death would be enough to calm the white men. There would be no need to take out their anger on other Natives.

The last decision he needed to address was when and if he should inform Faith of his plan. Would telling her do any more than add to her worry? Would including her only cause more anxiety? Would Faith try to stop him from killing her husband? It was apparent she wasn't happy. But being miserable did not mean she was willing to allow Lone Crow to kill the man. Would she trust him if all he told her was that he had a plan and would see it through?

While slowly realizing he could only guess at all the answers, he found a place to stay hidden and watched as Faith cleaned the items before walking into the water.

She was wearing several layers of thin, white material that clung to her when the wind blew. Before she fully submerged herself under the water, Lone Crow saw a small exposed part of her back.

The scars were pink against her white skin. He had never seen his own wounds and was shocked when he saw the scars Faith bore. He was deeply distressed when he realized there were many more welts under her clothing. Some were his fault. They were there because he hadn't done a better job of protecting her.

Before he moved closer, he calmed his anger and tried to settle his nerves. He hadn't felt the level of stress he was presently enduring since his first battle.

He spoke her name and she turned. She looked excited and flushed by his presence. And he found himself actually questioning why they couldn't be together. He knew there would be no other woman for him and thought Faith felt love for him. The reasons they couldn't, were too numerous to count so he smiled and picked up the cloth to cover her.

When she informed him she didn't need or want his help, it stung his ego. But holding her in his arms made everything just a little easier. What was challenging was finding the strength to break their contact. He had no choice. Someone was nearing them and no matter who it was, they were risking their lives.

Lone Crow kept his aim true and his bowstring tight even after Adam showed himself and tried to calm the situation by smiling.

The man had seen too much and if Faith hadn't been so very fragile, he would have killed the man and sent Faith back to the wagons with a story. From what he had seen, he didn't believe anyone would go to considerable trouble to locate the man. It would be a disappearance that was easier to explain than Faith's or Tobias'.

Adam was smiling but the look on his face had changed. It was a look Lone Crow knew well. Adam loved Faith and had just found a way to have the woman. There was no way Adam hadn't seen their embrace.

"Does he know about me?" Lone Crow whispered.

Faith was shaking and sniffing but she shook her head.

"He has seen too much and he must die," Lone Crow decided.

"No," Faith spoke above a whisper as she reached for Lone Crow's leg.

"I think I understand what this is," Adam began, standing still with his arms above his head. "You were concerned because you are the boy who got away."

"What do you want?" Faith asked as she slumped into the dirt in a submissive position.

Lone Crow dropped his weapon and moved to wrap his arms around Faith before attempting to right her.

"Do not beg the man," he ordered gently. "Sit up and we will hear him out."

Faith sniffed, nodded, and sat beside Lone Crow.

Adam hadn't moved but was failing to exhibit the normal emotion for a man in his position. He was looking pleased with himself and not the slightest bit concerned that his life was hanging in the balance.

"I came to tell you that Tobias will be passed out soon. But finding the two of you like this is fortuitous. You," he said, lowering one hand and pointing at Lone Crow.

The Warrior fought the overpowering desire to pick his weapon up and end the man.

"Lone Crow is the boy who killed your father," he stated with absolutely no question in his voice. "And that is why you care."

Lone Crow's muscles tensed and he felt Faith grip his leg tighter.

"So," he continued, before gesturing for permission to move.

Lone Crow growled and Faith nodded her head. She looked frightened again and holding her close to him wasn't what he should have been doing. Lone Crow should have been denying Adams assertions. But since Adam had already learned their secret, Lone Crow couldn't force himself to push her away.

As soon as he felt her body touch his, she seemed to breathe a little easier.

Adam looked touched by the two but gone was the smile and serenity Lone Crow was familiar with. The man was planning his next step and Lone Crow was confident he was going to regret not killing the man.

"I told both of you I would protect Faith. I will. And I will never lay a hand on her in anger. The two of you have a wonderful story but you are no longer children. You know there is no way you can continue to see each other," he continued, walking a circle around the pair.

Faith's breathing was no longer sporadic but Lone Crow could still feel the fear emanating off of her as Adam spoke.

"Get to the point. But remember I know much about you as well," Lone Crow warned in a menacing tone.

"That may be true but what I know carries a death sentence and you are a known Indian. They will not believe you. This doesn't have to be ugly. Leave her now and leave her to me," Adam offered, stopping in front of Lone Crow.

Faith leaned into the Warrior and then turned to look at him. "I will not be the cause of your death," she stressed, doing her best not to fall into hysterics. "Go. Forget me. But enjoy life, laugh and love."

Adam looked crushed by Faith's words of love. "I will strive to make you happy," he assured her, doing his best to get the woman to look at him.

"I will not leave you," Lone Crow promised, holding her tighter and meaning every word.

"You must," Faith declared, gently pushing Lone Crow away. "Lone Crow, you aren't Moses anymore. But I will always be Faith. I will be fine. Adam seems to have a plan."

Lone Crow could tell Faith was unsure about her new reality but instead of concerning herself with her future, she was thinking about his.

It was no time to fight with her. He knew he needed to do as she asked and walk away. The jealousy he felt toward Adam was gone. Faith didn't love him any more than she loved anyone. But the man did have information. Information that would ensure Lone Crow couldn't help Faith. Because no matter what she said, he was going to be there for her. Until she told him she didn't love him, he would do everything in his power to make her life easier.

Faith was right. He wasn't Moses any longer but she didn't have to continue to be Faith. She could begin a new life as Tsisqua. Why he hadn't simply offered the impossible when he had the chance was beyond him. Because suddenly, he was sure it was the right way. As challenging as it was, he planned on leaving as Faith asked but only to speak to Pathkiller before acting. The Chief had to agree with him. He wouldn't accept anything else.

"I will go," Lone Crow stated before hugging Faith again and gently helping her stand beside him. "Adam. You remember who drew first blood."

The Warrior heard Faith's sharp intake of breath at his warning before she grabbed his arm.

"Lone Crow, you have done everything you could. I will miss you," she said, wiping the tears from her face.

He wanted to kiss them away, wanted to sweep her away, wanted to confess his love for her. But he didn't. He simply nodded and smiled bravely before focusing his attention back to Adam.

"I know this isn't ideal but like I said, she will be safe and maybe even happy after a time," Adam offered.

His tone carried no pride, just satisfaction. It was an emotion Lone Crow was familiar with but the man hadn't seen the last of him.

Adams uninvited interruption did nothing to change the destined outcome, it only served to delay it.

"You are making a mistake," Lone Crow informed the man before pulling Faith back to him and whispering in her ear. "This is not over."

She looked up at him and smiled weakly. "It has to be. Go and be happy, please. If you stay, it will only break my heart," she explained as she pushed from the embrace took a step back.

"I didn't want it to come to this," Adam began explaining. "I just want what is best for Faith," he offered, clearly looking for agreement from either Faith or Lone Crow.

"How do you plan on dealing with Tobias?" Faith asked as she grabbed for Lone Crow's hand.

The gesture was one she had performed many times but never did it carry such meaning. She did not want him to leave her. No matter what she was saying. She was showing him she still wasn't ready to lose him.

"Can I say goodbye to my friend?" she asked in a meek voice that angered Lone Crow to his core.

Adam nodded his head at the same time as Tobias yelled for the two.

"We are coming. Just helping gather the kettle," Adam hollered back. "You don't have time. Go. She will be fine."

Adam reached for Faith and she avoided his attempt. "Go. I will never forget you," she said, pushing the Warrior away.

Lone Crow was going to do as she ordered but planned on talking to her the next evening. He was not giving up on her yet.

"We will meet again," the Warrior promised as he placed his hand over his heart when he began backing away.

"It won't be so bad," he heard Adam inform Faith.

She was still watching Lone Crow move away.

Just before he turned his back on the two, he saw Faith smile and mouth the words he never thought he would hear.

"I love you."

He stumbled when he turned but nothing mattered. She loved him and that was all he needed to know. They had a chance. She would be free the next night, as long as the Chief agreed.

He rode back to his village at a break-neck speed, all the while rehearsing his speech and praying there was a way.

## Chapter Twenty

I never expected my reunion with Moses to end the way it did. Nor did I expect to tell him how I really felt. The only reason I was able to mouth the words was because I was sure he was walking away from me for the last time. It was what I asked him to do even if deep down, I didn't mean it. I wanted him safe and as soon as Adam figured out the relationship Moses and I shared, I knew the only way to ensure his safety was to tell the man I loved to go.

Adam had come across as a good man but as he was hurrying me along, I again questioned my ability to tell the difference between a good man and a bad one.

Oh, he had made it clear he wouldn't hurt me but I wasn't sure he would be able to keep his word. Tobias had started beating me the night of our wedding but before that, he hadn't shown much emotion at all. So, I wasn't sure Adam wouldn't change. And again, I wasn't totally convinced that my treatment wasn't my own fault somehow. And maybe most troubling of all, I wasn't attracted to Adam any more than I was Tobias. That issue might not have reared its ugly head if I hadn't felt the butterflies and warmth course through my body when Moses held me. I enjoyed the strange feelings and very much wanted to experience them again. But knew that wasn't my lot in life. My lot was to follow Adam back to the camp and pretend he hadn't just told me I was going to be his or concern myself with how he planned to go about achieving that outcome. On top of that, I had to do everything in my power to not appear as heartbroken as I was. I had to pretend as if I had just bathed and nothing more.

Nothing changed. But it had. And I didn't know if I would ever get over watching Moses walk away the second time.

He had promised to return but I didn't think he would. He was smarter than that. Moses might have, but he was Lone Crow now and Lone Crow knew how to survive without me.

It felt as I was moving in slow motion but I walked to my clothes, dropped the cloth I was using as a blanket, got dressed, and walked back to the ever-smiling man.

Adam looked away while I dressed and I understood his reasons for doing that. He was attempting to show me that he was a gentleman. It wasn't working. A gentleman would not have threatened the only man I would ever love. All my senses seemed to dull and nothing was as vibrant as before. My hope for the impossible was gone. But I knew there would be plenty of time to dwell on my mistakes and feel sorry for myself later. So, I buried all my emotions and kept my head down as Adam and I walked side by side back to the others.

"I'm sorry," Adam whispered. "I thought he was drunk."

I was destroyed and fighting with overpowering sadness but still walked with the man until I heard his apology. It was misplaced. He was sorry Tobias wasn't drunk and not because he'd just made me send away the only man I truly loved.

He had run away the only man I wanted to spend time with. I'd had every intention of sending Moses away myself. But it would have been on my terms and in my time. Adam was still clearly under the impression that he was helping me. He wasn't. His plans were putting a cramp on mine, though. I knew I couldn't run if Adam was watching me. He wasn't Tobias. My husband was frightened by anything he didn't understand so I assumed he would give up looking after one half-hearted searching day. I wasn't sure why but I didn't think Adam would be frightened by the land.

When I stopped, Adam did as well before turning back to me and looking confused.

"I won't let him hurt you," he repeated.

"He is going to see Wilma tonight. So, he wasn't going to hurt me either way," I informed him, allowing the slightest bit of irritation to creep into my tone.

It was the first time I embraced some of the anger that was always overshadowed by fear.

"I care for you, Faith," he began explaining as he again reached to touch my arm.

I pulled away and looked at the ground.

"I won't ever hurt you. Now, shall we? While Tobias and Wilma are together, we will speak of our future. How does that sound?" he asked while he waited for me to continue walking.

"I would very much like to hear that," I agreed.

Adam smiled and we walked back to the camp in silence.

I was curious about the man's plan. I had thought of a way to escape for days and still wasn't sure my idea would work so I was growing more interested to know what Adam was suggesting. And I thought if I kept my mind busy, I wouldn't have time to mourn Moses.

"Then we will meet at the fire," he stated as he walked back toward his waiting horse.

"I will be sleeping behind Tobias' wagon tonight," he addressed those gathered.

I knew it was his attempt to give my husband and his lover a chance to rendezvous. But wasn't sure Tobias wouldn't suspect the same thing. That was the one thing that would guarantee my night was full of pain.

"Sleep where ya want to. I'm turning in myself. I thought I'd sleep out here tonight too," Tobias informed everyone as he stood and wobbled slightly.

His speech was a tad slurred but other than that, he seemed to be aware enough.

After hearing his declaration and observing his lack of coordination, I wasn't worried about him. He was most brutal when drunk but if he didn't plan on sleeping beside me, I could relax a little.

"Faith," he shouted.

I rolled my eyes, took a deep breath, prayed I hadn't dropped my guard too soon, and slowly turned to look at him.

"Yes, Tobias," I spoke, hoping my voice would remain steady.

"Button your dress. What have I told you about modesty?" he asked, growing angrier with each word he spewed.

I did not flinch but did chastise myself for thinking all would be well.

"I ..." I began to explain before I knew what I was going to say.

"That is my fault Tobias," Adam interrupted as he shook out his blanket.

The man was smiling and his voice was friendly enough but there was hatred in his eyes.

Tobias shook his head and looked at Adam. "How is it your fault?"

"She was dressed when I arrived and I told her she needed to hurry. Remember, I am a man of God. It was simply a time issue. Now would you like some help laying your blanket out?"

While Adam and Tobias were talking, I looked at Wilma and Howard.

Howard seemed bored and slightly discomforted by Tobias' behavior. Wilma looked as if she might be rethinking how easy it would be to get out of her relationship with my husband.

I was sure it was the first time anyone but me had been privy to a dark mood when it overtook Tobias. If I thought it would have done any good, I might have enjoyed his lack of control. But it wouldn't and I felt terrible that his behavior was making the others uncomfortable.

"Well, she knows better," Tobias declared after giving Adam's explanation some thought. "Fix yourself before you go to sleep. But throw me my bedroll first," he demanded, sounding less angry and more slurred.

I knew Tobias was more intoxicated than he was letting on and was pretty sure he wouldn't be meeting with Wilma. He would be passed out as soon as he laid down.

I did as he asked and before climbing into the wagon, I looked back at Adam.

He shook his head and scanned the area.

I knew he was telling me that he still wanted to talk and I did want to hear him out so I nodded and climbed in.

The moment I was alone, powerful emotions began slamming into me. Regret, loss, and hopelessness. Hopelessness was no stranger but the regret and loss were. I found it difficult to breathe and the more I concentrated on not breathing, the more I worried.

The thumping in my head was clearly my heartbeat and I felt as if I might pass out at any moment.

I didn't know what was happening but I didn't like it. What I wanted to do was climb out of the wagon and walk for a minute but knew that was not a possibility. I was stuck until everyone went to sleep.

After several failed attempts to calm down, I tried to convince myself that all was not lost. Maybe there was a chance I could persuade Adam that he didn't want me. The only thing that had changed was the length of time I got to spend with Moses. And I was still unhappy about that but didn't think that fact would ever change. No matter what I did or what I considered, my nerves were still raw.

And yet when I heard Tobias moan and fall to the ground, the sound didn't alarm me because he was inebriated and he usually passed out when he was in that state.

The next few things I heard did worry me. But I didn't move. I stayed curled up on my makeshift bed and tried to force my brain to interpret the sounds I was hearing differently.

There were whooshes and gurgling noises and footsteps.

I was afraid to look outside but as soon as most of the noises dulled, I began to peek out the front. If I were careful and used the blankets, I thought there was a chance that I wouldn't be seen.

And then Wilma screamed a bloodcurdling shriek and I once again froze.

It wasn't but a moment before I was being dragged from the safety of the wagon and thrown to the ground beside a still weeping Wilma.

I was frightened but the tears wouldn't form. Until I saw what all the noise was.

Tobias, Adam, and Howard were all dead. Arrows protruded from various areas of their bodies. They were gone and we were on our own. And the men who attacked our wagons seemed to be debating on our fate while they untethered the horses and ransacked our supply bags.

One of them squatted before us and seemed to be considering our fate.

"Don't kill us," Wilma cried in between hiccups.

It was clear the man had no idea what Wilma said, nor did her request even seem to register.

The man stood and walked to the other two before again speaking.

"We are going to die," Wilma wailed. "I'm with child."

I understood her terror. I was sure whatever happened next was going to be painful, if not a death sentence. But I still couldn't gather the courage to fight it. I maintained my ingrained defeated posture and reached to touch Wilma on the leg.

She stopped blubbering and looked at me.

"Say your prayers," I whispered, trying to show her I was strong even if I didn't think there was any way out of our predicament alive.

I didn't know much about the relationship between our town and the close Native peoples. There had been a strained peace for years. Cattle and the occasional horse would come up missing and the important men of our town would travel to the nearest village. When they returned, we would have no more trouble for months. But I had never heard of a Native killing white men before. I was quite sure it was a risky thing to do - maybe even war inducing. So I was sure they were going to kill us too. If the whole party were dead, it would be harder to prove who killed them.

"I don't want to die," she whimpered, before falling into a heap on the ground.

"Death is not the worst thing that can happen to us," I said, forcing myself to sit up straighter.

"Oh, God," she moaned before beginning to bawl once more.

I hadn't meant to make her cry more or add to her pain. My statement was the truth. There were times in my life when I would have welcomed death. And since the future I was handed wasn't what I expected, I was willing to accept I was enduring my final moments easily enough.

I was still visibly shaking but gone was my submissive posture. I was watching the men and had no plans of looking away.

It wasn't like me but I wanted to be free for a few minutes to think on my own.

The men had untethered the horses and seemed pleased with Adam's. After much back and forth, the older one took the reins and mounted his pony.

The two younger men packed the sacks they had stolen and talked amongst themselves, almost like we weren't there.

It was strange behavior.

One of the men stopped smiling and turned serious before he walked to Wilma and gently threw her over his shoulder.

Wilma screamed and kicked and then fell still. I hoped she had only passed out.

I was left with the last man and he didn't seem inclined to leave or try to communicate with me.

Since I was doing everything in my power to maintain what looked like a backbone, remaining silent was not conducive to that. What it did do was give me time to look at the man who treated me so very cruelly over the years.

He was lying on his stomach and he was facing me.

The look on his face was a mixture of sheer terror and surprise. I knew I should be saddened by his passing but I couldn't force myself to feel that way. I was relieved he was gone and maybe even resentful that he'd felt little pain as he passed.

I did feel sadness at the loss of Howard and Adam. There was no reason for them to die. They had been good men as far as I could surmise.

The Native looked over everything one final time and then stood in front of me.

My life had taught me to avoid his glare but I forced myself to look him in the eyes.

His look of disapproval and disgust changed to one of curiosity. He made a gesture for me to stand and waited while I did as he asked.

Once I was standing, he walked around me and stopped after making a complete circle.

I tried to stop my body from trembling and kept my chin up.

"Mkwa," he said, pointing to himself and then to me.

I didn't know what he said but was sure he was introducing himself.

He seemed more curious than hate-filled and I wasn't sure what that meant for my future. I had readily accepted my death and was mildly angered it wasn't going to happen yet.

"Mkwa," he repeated a little more dramatically before again pointing at me.

I swallowed and then cleared my throat before answering the man. "Tsisqua," I answered, meeker than I was pleased with.

Recognition crossed his face, followed by a smile and look of satisfaction.

I knew we couldn't communicate but it seemed as if he understood my name. I wasn't sure if that was a good thing or not but he seemed pleased.

He bridged the gap between the two of us and bent to reach for my legs.

I instinctively backed up. He looked up at me, shook his head, and again reached for me. Once I was in his arms, I hung there like a sack of flour. I had no idea what to expect but didn't really care either.

## Chapter Twenty-One

Lone Crow hadn't allowed himself to consider Pathkiller would fight him on his plan to bring Faith home. But he still slowed his gait before stopping in front of the council house.

His argument had been rehearsed and he was sure of his words. Before announcing his presence, he found himself recognizing just how much he was asking from his Leader. He was prepared to ask the man whose job it was to protect the village, to allow a white woman to join the ranks. An act that would absolutely end in disaster if anyone found her. The Warrior still clung to hope that there was a way and took a deep breath before asking for admittance.

"Come," the voice from inside stated.

Lone Crow walked in and stopped just inside to allow his eyes a chance to acclimate to the darkened room.

Otter smiled but looked concerned at his son's sudden reappearance and Pathkiller shared his expression.

There were four men in the house when he entered and before he'd sat down, two had said their goodbyes.

"Why are you back so soon?" Pathkiller asked as he added another chunk of wood to the fire.

"I have a request," Lone Crow stated, thinking it was best to express his desire as quickly as possible.

Both men sat in silence while Lone Crow laid out his plan.

"And, I do know the risks involved in allowing this to happen. You have to know I would do nothing to harm our

156 Elizabeth Anne Porter

people," the Warrior added before taking a breath and waiting for a response.

"I am sorry, Lone Crow."

Pathkiller apologized and Lone Crow found it nearly impossible not to interrupt.

"What you are asking simply cannot be done."

There was no joy in the Leader's voice when he spoke his decision.

"What happened with the other man? I know you do not care for him but you said he would not harm the woman, Faith. Perhaps that is the best solution," Otter suggested, joining the conversation.

"He knows who I am," Lone Crow admitted before he could stop himself.

It was a development that he had purposely omitted when he stated his case for bringing Faith to the village. But only because he knew Adam added to the risk.

"But, I can handle him," the Warrior added quickly.

"No. I am sorry. If you chose to rescue the woman and want to be with her, you cannot bring her here. You are a valued member of our band and we would miss you and your strengths if you choose to leave us. But what you are asking is too much," Pathkiller explained gently.

It was apparent the Chief was not happy with his ruling. And some part of Lone Crow understood the decision. But he still planned to give Faith the opportunity to be with him.

It wouldn't be an easy life but he was sure they could stay hidden from the white soldiers and most anyone else who traveled the wilderness.

"Son, I wish things were different," Otter offered as he stood and walked beside Lone Crow before taking a seat. "You must decide what is more important."

Lone Crow did not care for his father's choice of words.

"You and my people are important. I do not choose to leave you," he stated sadly. "But Faith is important, and if she will have me, I will not leave her side again."

"Where do you plan to go?" Pathkiller asked, his tone devoid of anger.

"I do not know," Lone Crow admitted. "But I will do all I can to give her a happy life," he vowed before standing. "I will pack my belongings and leave."

The words were not easy to express. He would miss his father and members of the village. He would never hunt or battle with his brothers again. If Faith accepted his offer, it would be only them. There would be no support system and the land would be their lives. He was sure enough of himself to know it was doable. It would take time for Faith to adjust to that way of life. And he couldn't help but be disappointed that the women of his village would not be able to teach her about their ways. But he understood why things were the way they were and couldn't leave without voicing his love and appreciation to the two men.

"You have given me the chance to grow and live and be free and I will never be able to thank you enough. I do not know when we will see each other again, or even if we will, but I want you to know I will never forget you," he declared before turning to the doorway.

"I wish you luck and prosperity, Lone Crow," Pathkiller said, turning his attention back to the flames.

"I will help you," Otter offered as he stood and nodded at Pathkiller. "You must find a way to let me know where you settle for the winter," he continued talking as he walked beside his son.

"I will do my best. Thank you, Father."

Lone Crow felt a deep sense of sorrow when he heard the tone of his father's voice. The pair might not have had many long conversations but Otter had silently and carefully taught Lone Crow how to be a man. And Lone Crow would miss his father's guidance.

"Maybe I will ride to the camp with you," Otter offered as they neared Lone Crow's home.

The Warrior stopped walking and reached to embrace his father. "I would like that," he mumbled before breaking their contact.

Otter smiled warmly and clapped his hands together. "I will go pack some necessities and meet you at the corral."

Lone Crow hadn't given a thought to how the battle with the Shawnee went until Otter mentioned the corral.

"Did we make the Shawnee pony free?" he asked before Otter could turn.

"No," the old man answered before smiling wickedly. "But they have very few. This back and forth will not end anytime soon so we will need to be extra watchful."

Lone Crow agreed with his father's opinion. "We will be. I am eager to get back to her. And yet, I am frightened she will not want me. Because, Father, if she does not, I will still see that she is free of her abuser."

"It sounds like you were the only human who ever treated her with kindness. She is still broken but patience and love will help her begin to mend. We will talk more as we travel," Otter decided, looking excited about traveling with his son.

"Meet you at the corral," Lone Crow agreed before walking into his home.

His abode was not special. It was like all others in that his sleeping pallet was close to the fire. The walls were thick and bare. Others hung beadwork and baskets but Lone Crow didn't stay in the home long enough to add any personal touches. The most he did was sleep and leave for a battle in the morning. He did keep food and water in containers near the door but his packs were always full and ready for him to leave.

While he looked at his home for the last time, he wondered if creating a life with Faith in the wilderness would be harder than he anticipated. Would his need to be alone simply go away because she was near and needed him? It was an important issue to try to figure out but he crammed it to the back of his mind and said goodbye to his home.

Before walking out, he saw Pathkiller's outline in his doorway.

"This is for your woman," the Chief stated as he held his hand out.

He was holding a small, beautifully beaded bag. At the center was a yellow bird.

Lone Crow was overwhelmed by the action and found he couldn't voice his appreciation right away.

"I wish there were more I could do. This has been in my family for a time. I thought it might be something your woman would like. I do hope we will see each other again. I have grown used to counting on you. When the soldiers come, and make no mistake, they will, we will pray that they do not act before they ask. We will delay them as long as possible. It is a risk we will take and in doing so, it may slow them from looking for you," Pathkiller explained before handing the bag to Lone Crow and turning away. "Be happy, my friend."

Lone Crow held the bag tightly and took a moment to accept the gratefulness he was experiencing. There was no way to be entirely sure he wasn't causing problems for his village. Pathkiller was correct. The soldiers would surely come looking for Faith. When the reality finally hit him, he decided he would do whatever he had to, to make it look as if Faith just walked away. He still wasn't sure how that would work but it was the best option he had. The soldiers would still come but they may be calmer if they weren't informed the white woman had been taken by an Indian.

He was leaving his family but he was doing so to start a new one with Faith. So he only hoped the joy with her would overshadow the grief of losing the others. It was strange that he felt so strongly he was doing the right thing when Faith was near but he found himself second-guessing that when she wasn't.

He jogged to the corral and was pleased to see Otter was already astride his pony and waiting.

Lone Crow put the small bag into his waist and placed the packs across his pony's back before mounting.

"You look deep in thought," Otter shared when Lone Crow rode beside him.

"I am confused," Lone Crow admitted. "I do not know what the right thing to do is."

"I believe in life, we are faced with easy decisions and difficult ones. The more important, the more thought is needed. And as I have said numerous times, Son, you are one who overthinks. The problem with that is, love and right rarely run the same course. Love is an emotion even stronger than hate. I know you feel strongly for the... Bird, but are those feelings love or protectiveness?"

Otter rarely gave lectures so Lone Crow was surprised by his father's speech. But the old man had raised valid points.

"I do want to protect her," the Warrior agreed. "And I understand your question about my feelings. I have known her longer than anyone. And I think I knew I loved her when she stopped Father Silas from killing me the first time."

Otter made an unhappy noise. "Does she feel the same about you?"

That question was just as valid but harder to answer.

The pair rode in silence while Lone Crow thought about his answer.

"She stops shaking when I hold her, she does not shy away from me when I reach for her, and she did say the words when she told me to go," he finally replied.

Otter looked shocked by his son's answer. "She told you to leave her? Why?"

It was another part of the story he had omitted when he was talking to Pathkiller.

"Adam caught us holding one another. And he knows who I am. He threatened to tell the others if I didn't leave. Faith told me to leave too. I am sure she didn't mean it."

The more Lone Crow explained, the less sure of himself he was.

"I suppose we will learn the answers to these unanswered questions soon enough," Otter stated soothingly. "How do you plan to get her away from the others?"

Again Otter was asking questions the Warrior didn't have answers for.

All Lone Crow was concerned with was asking Faith to run with him. It was ten years too late but he was consumed with the possiblilties.

"I believe I can sneak in. The only person who concerns me is Adam. He may sleep lighter and be more aware of his surroundings. I do not look to kill the man but if he gets in the way, I will."

The Warrior grew angry when he spoke about the troublesome man. Adam had drawn first blood and Lone Crow would have no trouble taking his life. But again, he wanted to put Faith through the least amount of stress possible. He did not want her first memory of their new life together to be one of bloodshed and death. There was also the consideration of making it appear that the act was not perpetrated by a Native.

"I see the tops of the wagons," Otter pointed as he rose from the back of his horse to get a better look.

Lone Crow mirrored his father's movements.

The darkness had crept in and taken full hold. Lone Crow could see that there was no fire and could hear the sounds of a murder of crow overhead. Something was wrong. Without a word, the men urged the ponies into a full run.

## Chapter Twenty-Two

I was still scared but not abnormally so. Wilma was making enough noises and pleas for the both of us and they were going unanswered so when the man placed me on his horse and climbed on the animal behind me, I cringed as little as possible.

The two men talked non-stop as we rode in the darkness. Wilma continued to beg until she seemed to get on their nerves and the man quickly gagged her. From then on, I could hear her sniffing but nothing more. The two men continued to talk and although I hadn't a clue what they were saying, their manner was relaxed and friendly. I was beginning to wonder if I was going to be killed, after all. And as strange as it was, I felt a twinge of sadness at the thought I might be kept alive. I had very little hope that life with a Native who hadn't known me from childhood and quite possibly saw me as an enemy to his people, would be any different from the life I was used to. And then I found myself wondering if they were going to make me someone's wife. That thought caused my heart to skip several beats and my stomach hurt. I did not want that. I was willing to do as I was told and even work for the people but was not going to be thrown into another marriage without love and trust. And the only person I felt that way about I had sent away. So, before I felt the slowing of the pony, I managed to allow myself to feel almost as distraught as Wilma. Of course, I internalized my worries because it was ingrained in me. In my experience, the more I cried and fought, the worse my treatment was. I did understand Wilma's fear and planned on trying to help her if given the opportunity.

The village was not unlike the Cherokee's. There were fields and two long houses. The only difference I could see was the homes were rounded at the top and looked like a half-circle. And I could not see a cleared space with seating. It was more alike than different and yet the peaceful feeling I'd experienced in Moses' camp was absent. I was still tensed and worried.

The man sitting behind me leaned close to my ear and said something. He spoke slowly and a little louder than necessary but I still failed to understand.

I moved away from him and nodded my head. "I don't understand you," I explained, doing everything in my power to not allow the words to catch in my throat.

He said a few more words, sounding as if he was displeased with my answer. Then I heard the one word I knew. He said my name.

"Yes," I said, pointing to myself. "Tsisqua."

He looked confused and shook his head before sliding from the horses back and grabbing me down.

I didn't fall on my face but wasn't ready for his action so I hit the ground with a thud. Wilma was treated the same and when she raised her head, I could see a line of blood flowing from her nose.

"Do not fight them," I offered, barely above a whisper.

She mumbled something but because of her gag, I couldn't understand.

I tried to smile in hopes of giving the poor woman some reassurance. It was a challenging feat because I wasn't sure just how bad things were going to get.

My hope was that someone in the village would know how to speak English. If so, I was sure we could straighten out any misunderstanding before a war broke out. It was asking a lot but I was getting more desperate by the minute.

The man who threw me to the ground grabbed me up and pulled me to a standing posture.

I tried to help as much as I could but since I had never ridden a horse that long, it took a second for my legs to awaken.

It was becoming more evident by the second that the man was not as pleased with me as he was when he abducted me.

Wilma fought, kicked, hit, and cried against her gag until her captor grabbed her by the hair and began dragging her toward the long houses.

People of the village had stopped what they were doing and focused their attention on Wilma and me.

I learned something about myself in that moment. I may have been meek and cowardly and did not enjoy being the center of attention. But I had a small amount of pride left. So I stood up straighter and forced a tight smile across my face before turning to Mkwa.

"Mkwa," I said, pointing at him. "Tsisqua."

He shook his head and still appeared disappointed. But he didn't throw me to the ground. He did dig his fingers into my upper arm and direct me toward the large house.

I kept my head up and looked straight ahead, doing my best to avoid noticing what the members of the village thought of me.

Once we were inside the darkened home, I was roughly pushed beside Wilma near the back wall.

I could have undone her gag and really wanted to but knew if I did, I ran the chance of making the situation worse for the both of us. So as soon as I could see her, I smiled again and patted her on the leg.

Her eyes were swollen and red, her nose was running, and she still appeared to be laboring to get a good breath.

"I am sure someone will come looking for us," I whispered as I leaned closer to her.

I wasn't sure at all but I did assume as much. We were expected back in town and the waterhole was someplace anyone looking for us would pass by. The men were dead but we weren't. I had no idea how many villages were between the town and where we were but I did know Lone Crow's was near. That realization scared me more than anything. I had sent him away to keep him safe and by no fault of my own, I still might be the cause of unnecessary bloodshed.

I didn't know if Wilma appeared to calm because of my statement or because she was growing weary. Her breathing was returning to normal and she was scanning the area slowly.

As soon as her panic subsided, I began looking around also.

At least twenty men were sitting around a large fire. The conversation was animated but not angry. Each man took a turn speaking and several looked our way as they did. I was still slightly terrified but held on to hope that they would not harm us. I didn't think there was a chance they would simply let us go but I was less concerned about being forced to be someone's wife.

We must have sat in the house for hours. Wilma fell into a distressed state of sleep and her stomach rumbled loudly. I did my best to concentrate on the men who were still deep in conversation.

The warmth of the room, the cadence of the strange voices, the darkness, all made it extremely difficult not to give in to sleep. I knew if I stood up, I would cause problems but I couldn't think of anything else to do to stay awake.

Before I was fully standing, a woman was at my side, smiling in a friendly manner.

I smiled and tried to look apologetic for my boldness.

She spoke to the men in an authoritative tone and motioned for me to sit back down.

I did as she asked and waited while she gathered water and fruit and offered them to me.

After taking them and attempting to look thankful, I leaned closer to Wilma and tried to gently wake her.

She screamed through the gag and did her best to curl up. I almost dropped the food and the men in the home all looked over at her. The woman helping me bent down and tried to reassure Wilma that there was no immediate danger.

After a few moments, the woman reached to remove the gag. She moved cautiously and kept a smile on her face.

Wilma still appeared terrified and I braced myself for an ear-piercing scream to emanate from her once she was able to voice her fear.

The woman placed her hand over Wilma's mouth as she released the ties of the gag and held her finger to her lips.

Wilma's eyes were as wide as the puffiness would allow and she slowly nodded her understanding.

Once Wilma was free, she swallowed several times, wiped her mouth, grabbed for the water, and took a long drink. Her hands were trembling and she was still experiencing hiccups because of her tears, but she wasn't screaming.

The woman spoke in calm tones and gestured for us to rise and follow her.

I didn't turn to the men when I helped Wilma stand. It appeared the woman was in charge and I was comforted in thinking so. The women in my life had never been overly helpful but they hadn't directly caused me physical pain either.

There was some talk while the woman ushered Wilma and me outside but the woman helping us seemed to be important. Not one of the men objected when we left the house.

I took a deep breath when we were once again in the open and Wilma slumped as if she were going to fall.

The woman gently held Wilma up and motioned for me to move to the other side and help.

I did as she asked and we walked into one of the huts.

The room was not as small as it appeared from the outside.

A fire pit sat at the center and cooking utensils laid close by. There were rugs and skins on the floor and rolled up bedding against the walls. Drying herbs hung from the ceiling and a few large clay pots were placed against other parts of the wall.

There was room for the three of us in the dwelling but if another person were present, it would have felt crowded. But it still had a feeling of a home instead of somewhere where one only sleeps.

After walking us inside, she pointed to the ground and expected us to sit close to the fire.

We did and remained silent as we watched her stoke the flames before grabbing some fresh herbs and plants from one clay pot and placing them in another with water.

She looked up from her task and said a few words. I still had no clue what she was saying but thought she might be trying to teach us words.

"What are they going to do with us?" Wilma asked, clearly still in a state of near hysterics.

I smiled, employing a bravery I didn't feel and turned to her. "I have no idea," I answered honestly. "But I think we are better off here than with the men."

It was the truth but I knew Wilma wanted more. She wanted me to tell her all would be well. It was something I couldn't do even if I longed to be able to.

The woman stopped stirring and looked at us before placing her hand on her chest and speaking. "Wii'si," she said slowly before pointing to me.

I considered telling her my given name since the name Moses' had given me caused such a strange reaction from the man who abducted me but I didn't. I straightened my back, patted Wilma on the leg again and spoke.

"Wii'si," I repeated, hoping I was pronouncing it correctly.

The woman smiled and nodded her head.

I took a deep breath and spoke the name I loved. "Tsisqua."

The name invoked the same response from Wii'si as it had from my captor. I thought it was one of understanding and only wished I could say more.

"You, Tsisqua, me Wii'si," she said, smiling broadly.

"Can you talk to her?" Wilma asked, suddenly sounding hopeful. "I don't even want to know how. But tell her to let us go."

"No," I answered sadly. "I can't understand her. I only know that word."

Wilma looked dejected and again slumped.

"I am sorry," I spoke to both of the women.

I was. I was so wrapped up in disappointment that I failed to hear the English words the woman had used.

"You, Aniyunwïya?" She asked hopefully.

The word was one I had never heard before but was pretty sure it didn't mean white, so I shook my head and sighed deeply. "I am white. Do you speak English?"

She shook her head and held up her hand to demonstrate that she spoke little.

It was disappointing but I wasn't ready to give up on communicating.

"Wilma," I said, again patting my companion lightly on the leg. "White," I added, pointing to the both of us.

The woman's disappointment changed to one of concern but it was fleeting. If I hadn't been watching her so closely, I would have missed it. Her reaction did not instill any sense of security.

"Go?" I asked, pointing to the door.

"No," she answered, sounding unsure of herself.

"Why?" I asked, still soothingly patting Wilma.

I was beginning to panic more but I wanted Wilma to stay as calm as possible.

Wii'si poured the liquid into two bowls and walked toward us before offering them.

Wilma reached for the vessel and because of her shaking hands, she almost dropped it.

Wii'si smiled tenderly and held tight to it until Wilma was steadier.

"Thank you," I voiced before taking the bowl from her hand.

After blowing on the mixture and taking a sip, I smiled. I had no idea what she had brewed up but it was warm and the taste had a strange soothing affect.

She looked pleased and walked toward the doorway.

I wanted to ask why she said no but knew with her limited vocabulary, it wouldn't be easy.

"Why won't they let us go?" Wilma whispered between sips.

I kept my attention focused on Wii'si. "I don't know," I replied. "I might have made this worse," I admitted when I understood what I had done by calling myself the name Moses had given me.

She made a noise of shock and then began whimpering once again.

"Stop," I urged. "We should be fine."

I was doing my best to be calming and not add to Wilma's stress but it was difficult. I did internalize a lot but I was just as frightened and confused as she. And yet I wasn't crying and wailing. I knew neither one of those things would be of any help. But before growing too angry with the woman, I reminded myself that she was new to fear and I had lived with it all my life.

Wii'si was talking to someone and from her tone, I could tell she was disappointed. It didn't bode well for Wilma and me.

"I don't want to die," Wilma reminded me.

"Neither do I," I agreed, still keeping my attention on the woman in the entryway.

"What are they doing?" she asked.

I understood her anxiety but she wasn't helping mine. So I patted her reassuringly and stayed silent.

The scene I was watching so intently was growing sterner and more serious.

The conversation was changing so drastically that I stopped watching and began thinking of a way that Wilma and I might escape.

I had no idea where we were or where we could run to. And if we were able to get away, I had to accept that surviving was not a given. There was more to worry about than just Wilma. She was carrying a child and I knew we would need to rest. Stopping wasn't a good thing when running. But it was an option that would not be discussed until we were left alone or the whole village was sleeping. From my experience with the Cherokee camp, I couldn't be sure that ever happened. The Cherokee had jumped on their ponies and left in the middle of the night without a second thought – like it wasn't unusual.

In spite of my past prayers being ignored, I felt the need to pray. So, I sat there, rocking slightly, praying for the strength to deal with my new predicament and selfishly asked for a way to still be free and happy. I also prayed for Wilma and the child she was carrying.

"Oh, God," Wilma wailed out of nowhere.

Everyone in the vicinity stopped what they were doing and looked at her.

"They killed everyone," she sobbed, in a much lower decibel.

It was as if the realization had only just sunk in.

Wii'si dismissed the man she was speaking to and quickly walked to Wilma's side before sitting next to her and placing her arm around the wailing woman.

Wilma didn't pull away. She leaned into the woman and allowed Wii'si to calm her.

I wasn't sure what to make of the situation. It was clear that Wii'si didn't want any harm to come to us but she had said we couldn't leave when I asked. I was confused but not without some hope. The language barrier was monumental but I was sure I could make her understand we would walk away and not look back. But that would have to wait until I got a better feel of what was going to happen next.

"Sleep," Wii'si said, leaning Wilma back onto a small stack of furs.

Wilma didn't fight her. It was clear the woman was exhausted and when she quieted, I felt better.

We had ridden through the night and the sun was midway in the sky. A faint slice of light made its way into the home and traveled uninterrupted until it reached the fire.

I was tired but still too anxious to sleep.

Wii'si smiled and reached her hand out to me.

I picked up the empty bowl beside me and handed her Wilma's as well.

"Thank you," I stated when she took the vessels from my hands.

"Sleep?" she asked, pointing to another set of robes close by.

I attempted to look appreciative of her offer when I shook my head.

She carried the dirty utensils and cooking vessel to the doorway and laid them on a thin strip of material.

"Come?" she asked, looking as though she wasn't convinced her offer was a wise one.

I quickly nodded and stood up in hopes that if I moved quickly enough, she wouldn't change her mind and rescind the offer.

Before following her outside, I turned back to Wilma's sleeping form and looked at Wii'si in question.

She smiled and pointed to a man who I hadn't noticed standing to the side of her home.

I was pleased that some forms of communication were efficiently dealt with but wanted more. I wanted to be able to explain my story because I was sure my life would make her so sad she would give us a horse and send us on our way.

## Chapter Twenty-Three

Lone Crow had dealt with brutality all of his life so he was shocked to learn he was paralyzed. It was a reaction he'd never dealt with before.

Otter had dismounted from his horse's back and was quickly and carelessly searching for any survivors.

Lone Crow hadn't been able to force himself to follow his father. The Warrior was still atop his pony, in shock.

The three men were lying apart from each other and both Cherokees knew immediately who was responsible for the deaths and destruction. The fletching on the arrows identified the men as Shawnee.

The discovery was startling even if the bands were in the midst of a disagreement. Killing settlers was a step too far. Many Natives thought about doing as much, some even dreamed of giving the white men the same treatment as they received. But there were few examples of Native bands starting a fight with the white man. So, the scene was challenging to understand. And the absence of Faith and Wilma was worrying on a new level.

"We should return to the village," Otter shared as he remounted his horse and pulled his ride away from the scene.

Lone Crow was still battling paralysis, no matter how much he tried to follow his father, he couldn't.

"What is the matter with you?" Otter asked, turning his pony around.

The man didn't bother to mask his irritation with the young Warrior.

It was an emotion Otter rarely embraced but it was a sign that the pair had stumbled on to more than either one could have expected.

The Shawnee's uncharacteristic actions had almost assuredly begun a war that wouldn't be easily won. And it would not only affect the Shawnee. Their actions would affect the whole of the Native population.

"Lone Crow," Otter spoke, employing an imposing tone.

The Warrior shook his head and wiped his brow.

"What have they done?" he asked, hoping his father had a reasonable explanation.

"I do not know but we need to return and inform Pathkiller of what has taken place," Otter answered, keeping the urgency in his voice.

"I must save Faith," he uttered as he willed his mind to begin working once again. "Why would they do this?"

"We will return to the village and then after consulting with the others, we will decide what our next move will be. This rash action may force us to move the whole village. We will lose crops and people, but I do not see another choice. The white men will come for us."

Lone Crow was not used to hearing his father worried and even understood and shared his concern, but Faith was what he worried about most.

"Will they mistreat her?" he asked as he slowly turned his horse from the scene and followed behind Otter. "Of course they will. They have to kill the both of them. It is the only way," Lone Crow answered his own question, growing angrier with each word.

He wasn't sure he had the time to return to his village. He needed to storm the Shawnee encampment and rescue Faith and the other woman. He was aware that the death scene had not been discovered yet but the men who took the women weren't privy to that information. So he couldn't be sure the act hadn't already been committed. Faith could be gone. The thought caused the Warrior's heart to stop.

Faith couldn't be dead. She had not had the chance to be happy so there was no way she could be gone. As hard as his brain tried to get him to accept the probability of his worse fears, he fought back. He stubbornly clung to the slim chance that she was still alive.

"I do not have any answers for you. I understand your need, or your desire to follow the men. But we do not want to act in haste. As I said, this attack has changed everything."

The anger was gone from Otter's tone and acceptance and sadness replaced it.

"I cannot fail her again," Lone Crow declared.

"There is nothing you can do on your own if she is gone," Otter pointed out. "If she still lives, then we may be able to trade for her. But that does not change the repercussions we will face."

Lone Crow felt shame when he understood he had been selfish and not accepting of what the attack meant to his people.

"I know how you feel but we need to be wise in our reaction to this. Now come, the faster we ride, the quicker we will have a plan."

Lone Crow ran his pony at full speed and slipped from his back before the animal came to a complete stop.

Otter fell into step beside him as they neared the council house.

From the outside, it sounded as if there was a celebration going on inside. The realization saddened Lone Crow even more. He was sure they were thanking the Gods for a victory against the Shawnee. As badly as he wanted to find Faith, he was not looking forward to sharing the story.

Otter patted his son on the back and sighed before announcing them.

The loud talking and cheers ceased when a confused sounding Pathkiller welcomed them inside.

Lone Crow was anxious to begin the story and found it extremely difficult to behave while Otter took his place around the circle.

Otter was not hiding the fact that he was worried and sad, so the men stopped speaking and all looked from Lone Crow to his father.

Lone Crow sat down, looked at the ground and began taking deep breaths in hopes he would show the proper respect and allow his father to tell the story.

Those gathered displayed a myriad of emotions as Otter regaled them. Many mumbled and sighed but Pathkiller remained stonily quiet. Lone Crow could see the news was affecting the Leader.

The room fell silent when Otter finished the tale.

Lone Crow knew it was wisest to stay silent and allow the leaders and elders to decide what the next move would be, but he couldn't. He had to say something.

"We have to save the white women," he spoke in hushed but adamant tones.

Pathkiller's eyes widened and his nostrils flared. "We need to concern ourselves with what the white soldiers will do," he corrected, through gritted teeth.

Lone Crow clenched his jaw and forced himself to remain seated and calm.

"If we save the women, maybe the soldiers will not attack us," he reasoned, maintaining an even tone.

"I know you do not want to hear this but the chances they still live are slim to none. What would keeping them alive accomplish? And nothing we do will bring the men back to life." the Chief shared, calming and attempting to sound understanding to Lone Crow's plight.

"Lone Crow," Otter spoke when the Warrior found himself attempting to stand.

Lone Crow stopped moving and looked across the smoke-filled room.

"Listen to what we say. And Pathkiller," Otter continued, diverting his attention to the Leader. "Lone Crow's idea is not without merit. If we trade the horses we captured, they might be willing to unload the women, that is, if they are still alive. If we set the women free or let them loose on a road toward the town, we could clean up the scene and bury the bodies. If the women tell the townsfolk there was an accident crossing the river, there would be nothing left to search for. Give my son's idea some thought," he suggested calmly.

Low murmurs gave way to Pathkiller clearing his throat and silencing those gathered.

"Send a rider out. Ask for a meeting," he ordered before looking at Lone Crow. "You stay here. We should hear something by the morning."

Lone Crow wanted to fight the man's decision but instead reluctantly nodded his understanding and stayed seated as the room quickly emptied.

"Otter, he is your responsibility. He must stay out of this."

Lone Crow was his own man and was not accustomed to being given orders. Often things were suggested but since leaving the white man's town, he had never been told what to do. He quickly found he didn't like the experience any more than he had when he was young.

"I am my own man," he seethed as he stood.

Pathkiller was standing toe to toe with Lone Crow before he could continue talking.

"This is bigger than you. These women may be the beginning of the end. No woman is that important," Pathkiller informed Lone Crow before he walked out of the building.

Lone Crow was angry but he was also remorseful. He wanted to act out of passion instead of thinking things through. It wasn't like him and he wasn't proud of himself when he realized how he'd been behaving. And yet, his main concern was still Faith. As shameful as that was to admit.

Otter stood and walked behind Lone Crow before placing a hand on his son's shoulder.

"This is the time for patience."

Lone Crow shook his head and turned to his father. "I cannot stay here. I will follow the rider," Lone Crow began to explain.

The Warrior only stopped because Otter opened his mouth to speak. He raised his hand to his father in an attempt to make him understand he would listen to what he had to say once Lone Crow had said his piece. "I will stay hidden and will take any punishment doled out upon my return. You cannot possibly understand how important it is that I give Faith a chance at happiness."

Otter closed his mouth and waited for Lone Crow to finish. "Son," he said sadly. "If she still lives, I am sure she is praying for death. Do as Pathkiller suggested."

Lone Crow snorted. The Chief hadn't suggested anything. He had ordered it.

"I will tell him I slipped away," Lone Crow stated as he began walking toward the doorway. "If I return at all."

Otter grabbed his son and stopped the Warrior's forward movement. "You are not behaving normally. And you will not slip away from me. I may be old but I am still sharp. You are your own man and I will not follow you to your home. I trust you will do the right thing. The right thing is to do as you were asked, by the way. The rider will be back soon. Once he has met with the Chief, if the women are still alive, they will remain so. You running after her will do nothing more than muddle the trade. And we will not bother to speak of your threat. After this, there will be no way to bring the woman here. So you will stay with us and return to your ways. There is no other way. If Bird lives and is returned to her people, you will have nothing to do with it. It would be best if you did not see her at all during the trade."

Lone Crow couldn't argue with his father's statements. They were all true. Otter stated that he would not be able to see Faith again. That was the one thing he wouldn't be told how to handle.

"I have loved and respected you since the first day I saw you, Father. But I will give Faith the chance to stay with me. If the other woman wants to return to the town, she can. The story will remain the same but she will be the only survivor. I will walk away from my family for her. But if she chooses to return with

Wilma, I will not stop her. I will give her the chance to decide her future. Nothing will stop me from doing that."

Otter smiled sadly and shook his head. "You are dreaming, boy." He spoke as he grabbed Lone Crow's upper arm and pulled.

It was the first time Otter had touched him in anger and Lone Crow reacted before he could stop himself.

He pulled away and spun around in a quick movement and Otter was on the ground, flat on his back.

The look on the old man's face was one of pain but not physical pain, emotional.

Lone Crow had overreacted and he was immediately remorseful.

"I am sorry, Father. I do not know what is wrong with me," he admitted as he held his hand for Otter to take.

Otter smiled tightly and took his son's outstretched hand.

"I do. You love this woman but sometimes it does not matter how you feel. What you want to happen is impossible. But I can see by the look on your face you are still planning on tailing the rider. And as I have said, I cannot allow you to do that."

Lone Crow smiled and shook his head before pulling his hand from the embrace. "I am sorry, Father. But it seems we have come to an impasse. Thank you for everything you have done and I do hope one day you will understand why I chose Faith."

The Warrior meant what he said. Every word of it. He couldn't understand the drive to save the woman and turn his back on his family either but it was there and he meant to see it through.

Otter shook his head and looked away from Lone Crow before turning his back on his son.

Lone Crow slowly turned back toward the corral. Before he could take more than a few steps, he heard a voice in his ear.

"I will save you from yourself."

The voice wasn't Otter's. The man speaking in his ear was Pathkiller. Before Lone Crow could react or argue with the statement, he felt a pain in the back of his head. As the pain deepened, he watched as his surroundings darkened and couldn't fight it when his feet gave out.

Chapter Twenty-Four

While we were walking toward the river, I made an effort to pay attention to my new surroundings. It was an attempt to keep my spirits up and continue to cling to my flimsy plan of escape.

My companion smiled whenever we looked at each other but I was convinced she wasn't as pleased with our appearance as she had been when we first arrived. She was a pleasant woman but something in her manner had changed and it worried me a little.

Speaking in single words was not conducive to understanding much but it was all I had so as we walked, I tried to think of a way to learn as much as possible.

The walk was beautiful and the scenery breathtaking but I knew I didn't have time to enjoy my surroundings. I had to find out as much as I could and as quickly as possible.

As soon as we reached the riverbank, Wii'si pointed to the ground and began filling several water containers. I had never seen anything other than a canteen or barrel of water so I was immensely interested in the fact that she was filling a soft, thin material with liquid. I was so curious that I forgot about asking anything other than what the container was made from.

Wii'si concentrated on her task but did look back at me several times. I was pretty sure she was checking to see if I had tried to run.

Instead of backing away, I slid myself closer to the woman and gently reached to touch her arm.

When she looked at me, I pointed to the container and tried to convey the question.

"Bladder," she said after taking a moment to think of the proper word.

The thought shocked me momentarily. I hadn't been in the company of Natives for long, nor had I spoken to any at length, except Moses. But it seemed as if the people wasted much less than the townsfolk. What we couldn't eat, we threw away. And I was witnessing an excellent use for part of an animal that would have been considered waste.

Sitting in silence, I readily accepted the fact that the Native peoples were much more respectful and cognizant of the land and animals than my people. We took what we wanted from the vastness and assumed it would never be depleted. There was a balance to the way they lived that I was sure we would never find. I decided rather quickly that the Natives were better equipped and thankful for what the earth provided them.

I couldn't be sure if I was so accepting and intrigued by the people only because of Moses, but even if they did turn ugly, I respected them for being able to thrive in a world that frightened most folks.

"Nepi," she spoke, pulling me from my thoughts.

Wii'si was touching the water and smiling when I looked at her.

I nodded and smiled. "Water is nepi?" I asked, moving closer, sitting by the river, and placing my hand in.

"Water, nepi," she agreed, smiling broadly.

"Go?" I asked, hoping my request wouldn't anger her.

I did want to learn but I wanted to be free more. And as badly as I wanted to believe Wilma and I would have a say in our future, I couldn't.

Wii'si had been kind and proven her opinion mattered to the people. But I wasn't convinced she wielded the power in the village. And time was of the essence. So after I spoke, I prayed the woman would understand my predicament and not be angry with me.

She wrinkled her face and quickly looked around.

Her nonverbal actions worried me. It also forced me to understand that if Wilma and I were going to get away, it had to be as soon as night came.

"No," she answered. "Bad."

I wasn't happy with her response and was once again thrown into near panic when she spoke the word 'bad.'

Before I could mask my emotions, I pulled my legs up to my chest, wrapped my hands around them and began rocking. It was a habit I didn't think I would ever break. The movement had stopped me from falling into hysterics numerous times in the past. So, again, I found myself silently praying for strength.

Some part of me wanted to know what she meant by the word. Bad could mean numerous things but I was afraid. Did they plan on killing us? If so, why hadn't they done it already? But those questions were too weighty and wordy to pose to Wii'si.

After blinking away the tears that polled in my lower eyelid, I bit the inside of my cheek and took a deep breath.

"Sorry," I stated, doing my best to keep my bottom lip from quivering.

Wii'si moved to sit beside me. Once she was close, she held her arms open but didn't lean into me. The woman didn't grab me and force me into an embrace like she had with Wilma. She merely offered comfort and even though I was again internally fighting with the notion that I should invite death instead of fight it, I was touched by her manners.

Her offer was difficult to deny because I was sure being comforted by someone would have helped me in some way.

When I shook my head, I smiled sadly.

The woman seemed to understand and not be hurt or angered by my denial.

I was quietly battling all the emotions that were threatening to take hold. All the while doing my best to believe that if the people did kill me, it would be less painful than some of the beatings I had taken. It was enlightening when I realized that was what scared me the most. I didn't care if my life ended. It really wasn't much of a life anyway. I was slightly saddened to accept that I would never see Moses again but I was sure he would go on living a relatively pleasant life. I was most frightened at the thought of the pain that would usher me into the afterlife. It might have been selfish, maybe even a sin, but I thought I deserved a peaceful death.

"Come," Wii'si said.

Instead of attempting to respond to my apology, the woman stood, gathered the water containers, and was standing in front of me with the habitual smile on her face and her hand offered out.

My hand shook as I placed it into hers and when I realized, I looked away.

She sighed and as soon as I was steady on my feet, she broke our contact.

I may have been experiencing a delayed sense of shock because it felt as if I were walking in a dream. The edges of my sightline were slightly blurry and I even seemed to be moving slower than normal. My legs felt heavy and my thoughts jumbled.

The last effect might have been a blessing but I didn't have time to reflect on that.

I felt Wii'si touch my arm and slowly looked at her.

She was concerned, but still maintained a cheery exterior.

"Sleep," she explained as she wrapped her arm around mine and began guiding me back to her home.

Sleep wasn't a bad suggestion but I doubted if my mind would slow enough for me to attain any peace. I didn't share my opinion with the woman. I didn't tense up when she took my arm and led me toward her home either.

My vision wasn't clearing. In fact, it appeared to be growing fuzzier by the moment. But I was sure I would make it to the home before I was blind.

As we walked, I was finding it more challenging to take a deep breath and the shallow ones I was able to take in rapid succession were doing little good. All I kept telling myself was, 'We are close. You can do this'.

The man guarding Wii'si's house was standing in the doorway looking inside.

I didn't question his actions because I could hear the wailing from a distance.

Wii'si picked up her pace and dragged me beside her.

I was worried about Wilma but still couldn't seem to pull myself from my funk.

Once we were inside, Wii'si let go of my arm and quickly moved to comfort Wilma.

"Where did you go?" Wilma asked between hiccups.

I sat on the robe and attempted to take a deep breath. I knew if I couldn't breathe, I couldn't talk, so I began trying to calm myself before answering her.

Wilma pushed Wii'si from her and looked at me. Her expression was one I had never seen on her face before. She was mad and hateful.

"You are the reason this is happening," she yelled as she pointed at me.

I recoiled instinctively when I heard her statement.

Wii'si grabbed Wilma's outstretched hand and forcibly pushed it down to Wilma's side.

The woman had no idea what was being said but there was no missing the intent. Wilma clearly blamed me.

I hadn't thought about the whys of our predicament and when forced to, I couldn't argue with her. I didn't think I had done anything to ask for our situation but I may very well have been cursed and poor Wilma and everyone else was just paying the price of being in my company.

I had been told as much all my life. It was my fault I got beaten. It was my fault when the congregation was stingy with the offering. It was my fault my father wasn't a better man. So, it really wasn't much of a stretch to think Wilma might be right.

But before I could agree with her, Wilma continued sharing her thoughts with me.

"Tobias was right. You are trouble and it follows you. You know he was planning on leaving you in the wilderness, don't you?"

I was shocked because I didn't know, but my shock quickly turned to an almost overwhelming melancholy. If my dead husband had simply left me to fend for myself, I might have been able to build a new life. But I still wasn't sure I was to blame.

Moses hadn't attacked our group. The men who killed Adam, Tobias, and Howard were complete strangers. So even I couldn't connect the dots. No matter how easily I could have accepted the blame.

I stayed silent and watched as Wilma opened her mouth to berate me further.

Wii'si gently placed her hand over Wilma's mouth and made a noise meant to both quiet and comfort the woman.

"I did nothing to cause this. I am sorry we are in the position we are in. But if there is any chance of getting out of this alive, you are going to have to trust me," I explained, forcing myself to smile and sound as if she hadn't shattered me with her words.

I was speaking more than I wanted to in front of Wii'si. But it was a risk I was suddenly willing to take. If for no other reason but to stop Wilma's outburst. The real possibility that we were only hours from death was enough for me to believe if she continued to make noise, it would hasten that inevitability. And strange as it was, I found I would rather die running than cowering at the hands of a Native.

Wii'si still had her hand covering Wilma's mouth but from the look on Wilma's face, she did not agree with my statement.

I was tired and the fog was beginning to reach the point where I could no longer fight it but I still wanted Wilma to hear me. It was a new desire but I was holding to it. I had been soft-spoken, if spoken at all, my whole life and telling Wilma how I felt held no consequence that concerned me. I would help her if she wished but she would keep me from escaping. The only reason I felt comfortable sharing my thoughts was she couldn't tell the others anything. I was sure Wii'si didn't know enough words to understand a hysterical woman.

So, with a burgeoning backbone, I laid my hands on the fur robe and took a deep breath before blinking several times to clear my vision as much as possible.

Before I could continue, Wii'si gave Wilma a warning look and lowered her hand. The woman held it at the ready until she was satisfied the yelling had ceased.

She smiled and turned her attention to me. "Sleep."

I nodded and gritted my teeth when she stood and walked back to tend the fire.

"You are scared and I am too. If you don't come with me, they will kill you. Now I am going to get some sleep. Wake me when it is dark," I instructed the woman.

I was having trouble focusing but thought that Wilma appeared to be considering my statement.

"I don't trust you and honestly can't decide whether death at their hands wouldn't be preferable to trying to escape with you. But I will wake you up," she informed me with a wicked look in her eyes.

"Just wake me, please," I murmured as I nestled into the soft fur.

I heard her response and knew she could ruin my escape. All she would have to do was cry out. But what I couldn't understand was why the woman turned on me so quickly. She was the one who was in the wrong for most of our relationship.

We hadn't had much interaction. The most we had spoken was on the trip. But she had never seemed so hateful as at that moment. I was exhausted but sleep did not come. My mind was full of too many questions. While my body was worn to the bone, my increasingly foggy brain was still attempting to solve life-changing challenges.

"Maybe I want to stay here," she stated, sounding as if she was sitting up and moving around.

I rolled to my side and tried to focus on her form. "I don't think that is a possibility," I mumbled more than spoke.

I heard her make a noise that was meant to ensure me I had no idea what I was talking about.

She was right, I didn't. But I was sure a white woman in an Indian village was something that was not done.

I was too worn out to continue to talk to her. My brain was still firing on all cylinders but I couldn't keep my eyes open or gather the energy to speak.

I was torn between running without Wilma and staying and taking whatever came my way. In the midst of my inner turmoil, I learned one interesting thing. The more I continued to accept that death was a strong possibility, the more I understood that I didn't want to die. So as I fell into a fitful slumber, I knew what I was going to do. When I woke up, I was going to gag Wilma and make my way from the village. The plan was not a good one but I was determined to not easily accept death.

A warm, welcoming, dull peace began to envelop my body and I took a much-needed deep breath.

My stillness was short-lived. As soon as I was in worry-free, almost sleep, I heard yelling and people moving about in excitement.

I couldn't force my eyes open but I did hear Wilma begin to whimper again.

"Stay," I heard Wii'si warn before she left us alone.

I may have been given the perfect opportunity to run but my body was just too exhausted.

"I will go with you," Wilma informed me in hushed tones.

It sounded as if she were rethinking her hateful attitude and very much like she was moving closer to me.

After attempting to wake from my daze, I knew it was useless. But I did manage to allow the frightened woman to hold me without flinching.

## Chapter Twenty-Five

Lone Crow woke to a dull ache at the back of his head. It was not a pain he was unfamiliar with but it had been a long time since someone he trusted intentionally inflicted pain upon him. The Warrior understood the reasons well enough and knew the anger and anxiety he was experiencing needed to be kept in check.

Before opening his eyes, his hands instinctively moved to touch his wound. When his hand felt the cool, sticky, wetness, he knew Pathkiller meant to keep him in the village. And he understood the lengths the man was prepared to go to ensure his people were protected.

It was not a trait Lone Crow could argue with. But he was still battling anger and resentment when he slowly opened his eyes to take in his surroundings.

The first thing he saw was Otter. The old man was sitting close to Lone Crow and was displaying both sadness and regret.

"This is for the best," Otter stated.

Lone Crow didn't speak. There was nothing to say. The Warrior had been selfish and impetuous. Accepting the truth did not change his desperate need to find Faith but it did force his silence.

"Would you like help sitting up?" Otter asked.

Lone Crow knew his father was trying to help but did not enjoy the strange new awkwardness they were experiencing.

The Warrior understood he was acting like a child but he also knew there was nothing he could do to change that. And rehashing those facts with his father was not something he wanted to do.

"I will be fine," Lone Crow replied, doing everything in his power to keep his simmering anger hidden.

Otter shook his head and rubbed his wrinkled forehead.

"Would you like some water?" the old man continued to drive the unwanted conversation.

Lone Crow appreciated his father's efforts but he was still in no mood to pretend that all would be well.

"I would like to be able to come and go as I always have," he answered as evenly as possible.

Otter sighed deeply and stood but didn't comment on Lone Crow's statement.

"If you were thinking as you normally do, then all would be well. But you are not, so you cannot leave. I am sorry, Son. I do not relish your pain and sadness. But the Aniyunwiya are what is important. One man's happiness is not too high of a price to continue to keep the settlers happy."

Again, Otter was speaking the truth. Lone Crow's thoughts still didn't shift. Faith was all that mattered.

"I do not know what I will do if she has been killed or touched for that matter."

Lone Crow had not had time to consider Faith could be raped. When the possibility dawned on him, he attempted to stand.

His vision went dark and he wobbled on his feet as the throbbing in the back of his head intensified.

"Sit. Pathkiller hit you pretty hard," Otter demanded as he moved to Lone Crow and physically pushed the man to a seated position. "What is done is done. But we will know any time now. I know this is difficult. But just allow yourself time to recover from the wound."

Lone Crow's spirit was strong but his body was failing him and that fact angered him further.

"Here, drink," Otter offered as he dangled the water bladder in front of Lone Crow.

The Warrior grabbed the vessel and laid it on the ground before reaching to again check his wound.

"I will wash it," Otter offered.

The old man was doing his best to shift the anger in the room to the usual peaceful banter but Lone Crow couldn't seem to attain any other emotions but anger and fear.

"Do what you want," Lone Crow stated, lowering his head in a defeated manner.

"If I did what I wanted, I would be following you as you follow your heart but we cannot always do as we wish. There is a greater good. If I failed to instill that in you, then I am truly sorry."

Again Lone Crow knew he was in the wrong. He did not enjoy knowing his father and Pathkiller were disappointed in him. But instead of admitting his feelings to his father, he remained silent while the man wetted a rag and gently cleaned his wound.

It was painful but Lone Crow embraced the discomfort.

"It will heal nicely," the old man decided as he returned to sitting in front of his son. "I am not going anywhere and I plan to continue to speak until the rider returns so you can remain silent, or we can try to discuss what your next move should be."

Lone Crow smirked after hearing his father's statement.

"Speak your mind. It is only us here and I intend on helping you if you decide on a plan that makes sense and brings no possible retribution from the townspeople," Otter prodded.

"I know I have been acting strangely," Lone Crow admitted, still looking to the ground. "I have never felt this strong of a need before. Father, they could be forcing her to endure terrible things. I cannot sit here and allow it to happen."

Otter sighed again before reaching for Lone Crow's chin.

After raising it, he looked at his son. "You will. I know all the horrible things that are running through your mind. And all of them are possibilities. But not probabilities," the old man began explaining calmly, still holding Lone Crow's head. "I can only surmise the men who caused the deaths were young and stupid. If the men Pathkiller sent to dispose of the scene are able to accomplish the task before it is discovered by anyone else, there is a chance all of this will blow over."

When Otter stopped to take a breath, Lone Crow fought the desire to speak his opinion on the matter. He wanted to point out that Otter was making a good case for the deaths of the women but he waited for his father to finish his thought and let go of him.

"The men did not kill the women too. So maybe they are discussing the best way to return them. And perhaps they are gone. I do not believe they would be mistreated for the fun of it. I am sure the Shawnee village is in more of a state of panic than we are."

"Will Pathkiller trade for them?" Lone Crow allowed himself to hope when he voiced the question.

The Warrior watched as Otter thought about the query. After a few moments of torturous silence, the old man wiped his forehead. "I do not know what Pathkiller will do," he admitted trepidatiously.

It was not the answer Lone Crow was looking for but it was an honest reply.

"Is he still in the village?" Lone Crow continued his interrogation as he once again attempted to stand.

Otter stood quickly and steadied his son. "I believe he is. But going and looking for him is not a good idea," he replied, not hiding his disappointment with the question.

Lone Crow rubbed the back of his head and considered his limited options. He had only one that wouldn't irreparably harm his relationship with his family and village. He had to do as he was told.

As his brain slowly began clearing, he looked from the exit to his father. "If they harm her in any way," the Warrior began in an even manner. "I will kill every last one of them."

His statement was not meant as a threat. It was a promise. But accepting his place wasn't a simple task. While he began slowly pacing the length of his home, he repeatedly told himself all would be well and his father had been right about everything.

The anger he was tortured with slowly began turning into a feeling of complete helplessness. It was an emotion he hadn't endured since he was a child and he did not enjoy it. So he quickly began reasoning that he hadn't been in Faith's life for years and she'd somehow managed to survive. The proven knowledge was not as helpful as it should have been. And that reaction caused more questions. Why did he feel so strongly about her? Why had he so quickly decided to change the woman's life? Faith hadn't asked him to. He knew she was frightened but she hadn't given him any real sign that she wanted to be with him. Only that she wasn't happy and wanted to be free of her husband. Was it because he realized he loved her, or was it because he carried guilt for leaving her the first time? Were the feelings he was experiencing love at all? The Warrior had never wanted to be with a woman as much as he did Faith. But he had to admit he did feel a deep sense of responsibility for her also. And no matter how hard he tried to reason all his feelings away, he couldn't. She had returned to his life and he again failed to protect her. That was what bothered him the most, next to the thought she could be mistreated. If the Great Creator was testing him, the Warrior was again failing.

"And if the worst happens, I am sure all the warriors in the village will happily accompany you," Otter declared, breaking Lone Crow's concentration.

The statement was heartfelt and Lone Crow appreciated it. But he didn't speak to it.

Instead, he began asking all the questions he wanted answers to.

"Does Faith want me? If we manage to help her and the other woman and the plan goes well, Faith will be free of any man. She could very easily return to the town and live a fulfilling life," he began as he stopped pacing and reached down for the water vessel.

Otter looked shocked by the direction their conversation had taken.

"Did she not tell you to leave her?" he asked, standing and moving toward the fire to stoke the flames.

"She did," Lone Crow answered before taking a seat across from his father. "But I believe she was doing so to keep me safe. She did tell me as much. We have had this conversation before," Lone Crow informed his father as he watched the old man through the smoke.

Otter smiled and nodded his head. "We have," he admitted. "But your answers are different this time. She said she loves you. There are many types of love."

Again, Lone Crow did not enjoy the direction the conversation was headed. He knew Faith felt something for him but was it the same as he felt for her? Was it selfish to ask her to stay since her life had changed so much? Would she accept his offer because of the shared trauma they experienced or because she wanted a life with him? Was it wrong to offer her anything but a safe return? Was the right thing to just allow her to go? Wasn't her happiness more important than anything? The unanswered questions were not going to answer themselves. And no matter how Lone Crow tried to embrace his old self and sit patiently, he couldn't. He had to go to her and he could only pray Otter didn't attempt to stop him.

"Lone Crow, you must be patient," Otter warned, seeming to read his son's thoughts.

Lone Crow stopped thinking about standing and shook his head before looking to the ceiling and stifling a scream.

"I have never been more tormented in my life," the Warrior shared almost in a whisper.

It was the raw truth. Everything had been black and white until he saw Faith again.

"What is the right thing to do? You have loved, tell me what to do," Lone Crow urged, employing a tone that bordered on begging.

It was not one of his proudest moments but he needed guidance and hoped he would be able to follow his father's.

Otter smiled and pulled his pipe from a beaded bag he wore around his waist.

Lone Crow knew his father's movement meant he was preparing to tell the Warrior a story. Lone Crow gritted his teeth and forced himself to sit still and open-minded while Otter finished filling the pipe.

"Everyone is different," the old man began before lighting the dried leaves and inhaling deeply. Only after exhaling the smoke did he continue. "I believe you love the woman called Bird. But you live very different lives."

Lone Crow reached around the flames, took the pipe his father offered, and bit his cheek harder in an attempt to remain silent and patient.

"If you decide to offer her a life with you, there will be many challenges. You cannot stay here. A white woman in the village is not something we are willing to allow. Our mission as of now is to peacefully coexist with the white men. If she were the only survivor, that might have been an option. She was not. If the other woman says anything that could arouse suspicion, there will be bloodshed. I know this is not what you wanted to hear," Otter admitted, clearly experiencing no joy in his opinions. "If you really love her, my advice is to see her safely back to the town."

Again Lone Crow knew the answers his father provided were correct and allowed himself the time to grapple with the knowledge. He wanted her. More than any woman he'd ever encountered. In truth, he wanted to hold her in his arms and show her what it felt like to be loved. But if that did happen, would it make it more difficult to allow her to leave? He was sure of that but he still wasn't convinced it wasn't something he would attempt. And when he realized that, he knew he was being selfish and a feeling of shame overtook him. All he should have been concerned with was Bird's future and he had no part of that. So he settled on doing everything in his power to do as he was told.

If and when he saw Faith again, he would offer to accompany the two women back to town and explain that an accident at the river crossing had caused the deaths of the men. It was a good, sound plan and he was determined that was what he was going to do. The thought hadn't fully rooted when he remembered that he didn't know if Pathkiller would attempt to trade for the women. The Warrior was still battling with the changes he needed to make when he took a draw from the pipe.

"Do you think you can do that?" Otter asked as he reached for the pipe once again.

The tone his father was using was the same as he did every time the two had a difficult conversation. There was understanding but also sureness.

"I will do my best. But I meant what I said," Lone Crow stated as he stood up. "If they have hurt her in any way, I will kill all the men of the village."

Otter looked up at his son and smiled. "And I meant it when I said the whole village will aid you in that task. I understand none of this has been easy for you and for that, I am sorry. But all will work out as it should," the old man assured. "Where do you think you are going?" he asked when Lone Crow took a step toward the doorway.

Lone Crow turned and sighed before rubbing the bridge of his nose. "I would be grateful if you would accompany me to Pathkiller so I can ask if a trade is something he is considering," the Warrior explained.

He knew he was pushing his boundaries but even after accepting he would do what was best for Faith, he still found sitting and waiting for a rider to return was simply something he couldn't do.

Otter stood and walked to his son before patting Lone Crow on the back and smiling a proud grin. "I will gladly accompany you. But maybe it would be best if I inquire about the plan."

Lone Crow nodded his head and followed his father out.

196 Elizabeth Anne Porter

It hadn't dawned on the Warrior to ask how long he had been asleep so he was shocked to see the sun had again retired for the day and the moon was the only source of light. When he realized he had slept most of the day away, he turned to his father.

Otter was again smiling a knowing grin. "I told you when you woke, it would not be long before we heard from the rider," he assured his son as they began walking toward the council house.

For the briefest of moments, Lone Crow felt hope. Maybe things would work out. Maybe he could be the man he wanted to be.

It was the first time since being reintroduced to Faith that he thought there was a plan in place that could actually work. It wasn't exactly how he wanted things to happen and it would take the rest of his life to get over Faith. Everything and everyone was telling him to do the right thing by the woman.

Otter stopped near the doorway and peeked his head inside before looking back at Lone Crow and ushering him inside.

Pathkiller was sitting alone in the large house. It was an occurrence that didn't happen often and Lone Crow took it as a good sign.

"Have you come to your senses?" Pathkiller asked Lone Crow when the Warrior took a seat beside the Leader.

Lone Crow understood the validity of the Chief's question but it was still difficult to speak. The Warrior was relieved when Otter spoke for him.

"It has been a difficult journey but my son will do what is right, for our people and the woman."

Pathkiller looked skeptical but nodded his head. "The rider has not returned if that is why you are here," he informed the pair.

"We have come to discuss the option of trading for the women. Have you come to any decision on that option?" Otter continued.

Pathkiller opened his mouth to answer but was interrupted by an excited man's voice emanating from outside.

The Chief stood and motioned for both Otter and Lone Crow to stay seated as he walked outside.

The Warrior who sounded so excited seconds earlier lowered his voice and the two men spoke in hushed tones.

Lone Crow tensed to stand but Otter laid his hand on the Warrior's leg. "Stay. We will know something soon."

Pathkiller returned to the fire and sat down. The look on his face was not in any way helpful to Lone Crow.

"What did he say?" he asked, doing his best to remain calm.

"He said the Shawnee would gladly trade for the women but one has run away."

It was all Lone Crow needed to hear and he was on his feet readying to ride out and look for Faith.

The Warrior half expected one or both of the men to attempt to stop him but was relieved and gladdened when he realized they were beside him and planned on helping him locate Faith.

## Chapter Twenty-Six

Wilma did not wake me. She was still lying beside me, sound asleep, when I was gently awakened from my fitful slumber.

I slowly opened my eyes and saw Wii'si was kneeling next to me, smiling.

When I attempted to sit up, she shook her head and placed her finger to her mouth, showing me she wanted silence.

I was confused and still fog-brained but I nestled back into the robe and waited for whatever was to come.

She shook her head and pointed to Wilma.

I had no idea what she was trying to convey but tried to look confused and questioning.

"Stay up," she whispered as she moved to cover Wilma and then walked back outside.

I was left battling anxiety and genuine fear but I didn't move. I remained tensed and tried not to allow my mind to begin to add to my stress.

My throat was dry and my palms were sweating when I heard her return.

She again knelt beside me and placed her hand on my shoulder. "Go?" she asked quietly as she pointed to the doorway.

If she hadn't looked frightened, I would have been overjoyed with her suggestion. But I quickly found I couldn't move. Her concern was overpowering.

I blinked and tried to swallow.

Wii'si smiled weakly and gently pulled at my arm while continuing to point to the outside.

Tears began pooling in my lower eyelids and my lip started quivering.

She was offering me a chance to get away and I was pretty sure that was what I still wanted but suddenly, I needed to understand her motives.

I shook my head and wiped my eyes. "Why?" I asked hoarsely.

Wii'si continued to look nervously at the entrance. "Bad, stay." She whispered, pointing to a leather bag that was sitting against the wall near the door. "Go. Run," she continued as she began pulling me to a sitting position.

I gestured toward Wilma's sleeping form. "Wilma?"

Wii'si shook her head. "No. You." She replied, miming a large stomach as she continued to look at Wilma.

I was doing my best to take in all the new activity and the change in Wii'si's personality but was pretty sure the woman was assuring me Wilma would be fine because she was with child.

The knowledge still didn't make me feel good about considering Wii'si's offer.

"Run," Wii'si urged in a more persuasive tone as she pulled me up and ushered me to the packed bag.

"Why?" I asked again, still fearful that I might be making a mistake by doing as the woman demanded.

"Bad men," she whispered as she grabbed my upper arm and slowly pulled me from the dwelling into the darkness.

As soon as we were both outside, she placed her arm against my body and pushed me close to the wall of the home.

The air was crisp and goosebumps broke out all over my body before my teeth began chattering.

Wii'si paid no attention to my discomfort but she was watching our surroundings closely.

Without any warning she yanked me into a run and we didn't stop until we were at a large clump of fir trees.

I was out of breath and still not convinced I was doing the right thing when Wii'si grabbed me by the arms and turned me to her. "Run," she urged, pointing in the direction she thought I should take.

I nodded my head and wrapped my arms around myself in an effort to find some comfort.

Wii'si took a small robe from around her shoulders and gave it to me before securing the bag across my body. "Go."

I wanted to run away but my legs felt heavy. It was my chance to be free and yet I couldn't find the courage to take the first step.

Wii'si had been nothing but kind and caring but her demeanor changed quickly when she realized I was still fighting her plan. Her smile disappeared and she furrowed her brow before pushing me several times. Every backward step I took concealed me more.

A final shove caused me to stumble a few steps further into the forest.

I wanted to argue with her but knew if I didn't keep my footing, I would run into a tree. Once steady, I turned and saw that she was gone and the night was quiet.

I was still confused and unsure but tried to move all the worries to the back of my mind and stood tall. After taking a shaky, deep breath, I pulled the robe tight against my body, adjusted my bag, and began running in the direction Wii'si pointed. I ran until I couldn't catch my breath. Once I stopped, I leaned over and placed my hands on my knees until I could once again breathe easily.

The darkness of the night was a perfect cover. The moon was obscured by clouds and the wind blew with a strange fierceness. I knew both were signs of impending rain and also understood I needed to get out of the weather and take a minute to allow the events that just happened to sink in.

All I could see were thick trees. There would be no dwellings, no premade shelter from the weather for me. Finding refuge from the storm was left entirely up to my own prowess.

I was terrified but forced all the negative responses floating in my brain to silence and began looking for a large tree that offered many leaves and branches that I could use as cover. I had no plans of staying put long but had to sit for a minute and digest everything.

I walked for another few minutes and found a tree I thought would be adequate. My brain was in a fog but I was sure that was better than what was to come once I settled.

As soon as I sat down, I pulled the bag from my side and began looking through the contents. Wii'si had packed everything I would need for the next few days and even a beautiful pair of beaded moccasins. The first thing I did was remove the water container and take a long drink, then I rested my head against the rough bark of the tree and slowly began to think on what had just transpired.

I ran away and left Wilma alone with Natives. She was more than likely experiencing a new level of fear and I felt horrible about that. Although I did not believe anyone was going to hurt her, I had no idea what they planned to do with her. Wii'si had been worried about me. And while I appreciated that, I still didn't feel comfortable or pleased with myself. But going back would do nothing. It would only result in me being treated roughly and watched constantly. After a few minutes of berating myself, I decided the only thing I could do was try to stay alive and find my way back to a civilized town. Once I made it there, I would tell my story. Of course, I would make sure the military men knew my captures had been kind and were not Cherokee and then leave the rescuing to them.

The plan did have some drawbacks. The most troubling one was the three dead bodies left with the wagons. I felt sadness but not the kind of overwhelming melancholy I thought was warranted. And yet I couldn't seem to force myself to cry over the deaths. I wasn't sure what that said about me but didn't have the time to do much more soul searching than I already was. I was hopeful that I would be able to come up with a story that would satisfy the military men and not endanger the Natives more. Most of my life, I'd believed the military was doing an excellent job of protecting the towns but I wasn't sure they cared enough to not attack the first village they encountered. And that village, to the best of my knowledge, was Moses'.

What I honestly wanted more than anything was to run to his village and explain what happened, ask them to help free Wilma, and then beg them to allow me to stay there.

Going back to town was not something that excited me like the thought of spending time with Moses. I knew his name was Lone Crow and I thought the name fit him well. But I didn't imagine I would ever think of him as anyone other than Moses. I wanted a chance to just get to know the man he grew up to be. But my foolish desires were squashed almost as quickly as they were formed.

Staying in a Cherokee village just wasn't an option. And running to them would more than likely prove to do nothing more than cause them more trouble. No. I needed to take a few bites of the dried meat, stand back up, and travel in the shadows as long as I could. Going back to town was the smart thing. Even if it wasn't what I really wanted.

As I slowly walked the tree-laden path, I forced myself to accept that doing what was right was my only choice. I may not get to know Moses but wasn't sure his life wouldn't be better for not knowing me. I loved him with every fiber of my being, probably always had. So it was challenging to dismiss the thoughts of the impossible.

It didn't matter that the scenes that were playing in my mind were painful to endure, I still allowed it.

Moses and I would never sit and talk about the 'nothings and everythings' like we used to. I would never feel his arms around me again. If I managed to make it back to my town, there would be no man in my life. I would embrace being a spinster and continue to miss the one man I truly wanted. As sad as it seemed, I knew I wanted what was best for Moses.

The pale light from the sun trying to break the horizon was cascading through the leaves of the trees in breathtaking beauty. The walking had taken its toll and I was exhausted. As soon as the morning sun peeked over the horizon, I started looking for another place to hide. There was no way I could know how far I'd walked or even if I had been moving in the right direction. But I hoped the fact that I hadn't heard horses or men looking for me was a good sign that Wii'si really had my best interest in her heart.

Still, I worried about Wilma and knew I would until I could find some help. My concerns and anxieties didn't lessen when I sat in the center of two large fallen trees and covered myself with the robe. For the briefest of moments, I allowed myself to feel pride in the seclusion I'd found. I was well hidden and even had room to sit up and take a drink without being cramped.

My satisfaction lasted only until I heard the sounds of horses and men whispering.

## Chapter Twenty-Seven

As soon as Pathkiller spoke the words, 'one has run away,' Lone Crow was on his feet.

The Warrior knew the runner was Faith and all the promises and accepting he had done over the last few minutes were forgotten. He had to find Faith and he wasn't going to listen to any arguments or allow himself to be blindsided by the Leader again.

When he saw the two men mount their ponies and wait for him to leave, he was both humbled and touched. It didn't matter to the men that Lone Crow had been argumentative and unthoughtful. All that mattered was things had changed.

"Thank you for coming," he spoke to the two men as soon as he was sure he wouldn't allow his emotions to bleed through.

"Are you sure we are looking for the right woman?" Pathkiller asked as he rode beside Lone Crow.

There was no anger or judgment in the Leaders voice, only curiosity.

Lone Crow was positive Faith was the runner. The action was her only chance at freedom. And she may have been held back and afraid for her whole life but she was braver than she knew.

"Yes," he replied as soon as there was a gap in the trees. "I will not stop looking until I locate her. I cannot allow the Shawnee to find her first."

"If they were looking for her, they would have found her quickly," Otter said, joining in the conversation.

Lone Crow felt his stomach knot and his heart rate quicken.

"Squirrel told me they were thankful she had gone and they are willing to trade for the irritating one," Pathkiller informed the others. "If you hadn't moved so quickly, I would have explained the rest."

Lone Crow calmed considerably when Pathkiller spoke. It was good to know Faith wasn't being chased. That fact freed up more of his brain. Enough for him to stop his horse and think about which way she would have headed.

The Shawnee village was another few miles away if traveling at a quick rate, but Faith was on foot. He also knew the direction of the town well enough. If Faith were walking in the right direction, it would take her the better part of a week to reach the homes at the outskirts of the nearest town.

The forest was thick and dense. Faith had never been far from her home and Lone Crow was sure she was frightened.

"We can split up," Otter offered, stopping his pony in front of Lone Crow.

The Warrior again experienced a feeling of doom. He, and the men riding with him, were proficient trackers but the area they were scouting was vast and Lone Crow knew the odds of finding Faith were slim.

"Lone Crow, let us try to track her. There is only one direction from which she could have left the Shawnee village," Pathkiller suggested as he stopped his pony beside the Warrior and looked from Lone Crow to Otter. "All other routes are watched. We should travel there and hope we can pick up signs of her."

The Chief's idea was a good one. Maybe even the only one that made any sense but Lone Crow didn't want to suffer the loss of time by backtracking.

"I know you are anxious, Son," Otter spoke as he turned his pony around. "If we do not return to the beginning, we are wandering blindly. Bird was not hurt or she wouldn't have been able to slip away. We will find her," he continued as he slowly began moving toward the Shawnee encampment.

Pathkiller continued to ride beside Lone Crow.

"Will we face any opposition when we near their camp? Were the men able to hide the evidence of the attack?" Lone Crow asked, slowly beginning to think like a warrior once again.

He was not averse to taking a few Shawnee lives but he wanted to be ready if there was a chance he would.

"It is done. If the women agree to the story of how they came to be alone, all should be well. And I do not believe we will have any trouble from the Shawnee. From what Squirrel told me, they are in a state of near panic. Besides, they are waiting for us to return some of their herd for the other woman. You do know locating the woman will not be easy. She has to be scared and if she isn't used to the elements ..."

"We will find her before anything else can happen to her," Lone Crow interrupted, keeping his tone even.

The Warrior understood Pathkiller's motives. The man was simply warning Lone Crow of the possible outcomes. It was meant to allow Lone Crow to slowly accept the facts but the Warrior was not going to allow that to happen. Faith had to be alive. He just would not believe the Great Creator or the white man's God could be that vengeful. Faith was a good, pure woman and she deserved a chance.

Pathkiller smiled and quickened his pony's gait leaving Lone Crow at the back, alone with his thoughts.

As Lone Crow rode, he assured himself nothing else had changed. He still couldn't be with Faith. And he needed to remember as much when he did locate her. As soon as both women were back at his village, he would accompany them back to town. It was the right thing to do. He was aware that the trip might end in his death. It was an acceptable outcome. As long as Faith was well, he would die without regret. But sharing that knowledge was not something he planned on doing. Everything inside him longed to spend the remainder of his years with the woman. Still, he knew the feelings he battled at present would only intensify with each passing moment he was in Faith's company. The Warrior had never faced such a challenge but knew whatever pain he was forced to endure would be worth it. Lone Crow quieted all his concerns and fears and began doing what was second nature to him. He started watching for signs of Faith.

"Look," Otter spoke, pulling Lone Crow's attention from the ground.

The old man was allowing his pony to circle around a spot when he spoke.

Lone Crow moved his ride closer and looked at where his father was pointing.

There were several footprints near the edge of the Shawnee camp.

Lone Crow dismounted and knelt beside the marks before laying his hand in one. The foot had a small heel so it was surely Faith's. Around those was another set of footprints, also a woman's. Those appeared to return to the village while Faith's footprints pointed away.

It was a good sign and Lone Crow welcomed the feeling that accompanied it.

"Who was the woman who helped her?" Pathkiller asked in hushed tones, sounding more like he was wondering out loud.

Lone Crow was thinking the same thing. "And why?" he asked, jumping back on his pony and steering him in the direction Faith clearly took.

Pathkiller followed closely behind. "Maybe they thought we were a bigger threat than allowing her to fend for herself?" the Leader answered, sounding as confused as Lone Crow felt.

"I am going to try to speak to the members of the village," Otter stated, causing both Lone Crow and Pathkiller to turn at the waist and look at the old man. "It will keep the men busy and we are at peace for the moment," Otter continued. "Once the woman is secure, I will return to our village."

Lone Crow was curious as to why his father changed his plans but could see by the look on the old man's face that there would be nothing he could say that would change his mind.

The Warrior nodded his head and continued to look at his father. "You can explain this when we see each other again."

"Try to learn who the women were staying with," Pathkiller added before looking away.

"Why would he chose to go to the village?" Lone Crow asked as he again focused his attention on the broken, twisted limbs laid out in front of him.

He was feeling more confident that he would locate Faith with each step.

"He is old and unwell," Pathkiller shared. "He is probably tired. I believe he is attempting to help you as much as he can and then he will welcome death gladly."

Pathkiller's answer was not what Lone Crow expected. He hadn't noticed his father was in ill health. And the two had spent more time together in the last few days than in the previous couple of years.

"He is unwell?" he asked, doing nothing more than stalling for time to digest the news.

"Yes."

The answer was short but it was an answer that saddened the Warrior. He hadn't considered his father wouldn't be around to help guide him for many years to come. He also knew the man well enough to know his father would do all that was in his power to help Lone Crow. But Otter was an old Warrior who would much rather find death in battle. The Warrior was still uncertain if Otter would be able to help him with Faith but knew there was a better chance Otter would die in battle. So peace with the Shawnee needed to be short-lived. Lone Crow said a quick prayer asking that the Great Creator watch over his father and allow the old man to die on his own terms.

"Look, here," Pathkiller said, pointing to a large tree.

There was evidence that Faith had been there recently and that knowledge excited the Warrior. So much so, that he had to temper himself before replying to the Leader's statement.

Lone Crow cleared his throat and slid from his pony's back.

Faith had been there and it looked as if she at least had a robe for warmth. He quickly found himself questioning her escape again. The more he learned, the more he was convinced she was aided.

Lone Crow knelt by the base of the tree and touched the bark where Faith leaned against it. He knew there was no other reason for doing it other than just knowing she was close.

Pathkiller stayed atop his horse and cleared his throat to garner the Warrior's attention.

Standing, he saw a piece of leather stuck in a grove of dead tree limbs. It was just another sign Faith had help.

"Did they expect her to die?" he asked, as he got back on his pony.

"I do not know what they were thinking," Pathkiller admitted as he patiently waited for Lone Crow to again take the lead. "But the sun is up now so it should be even easier to find her. I am sure she will tell you everything."

After experiencing a full range of emotions in the last few hours, Lone Crow gratefully accepted the latest. Relief and Hope. They were interesting and he found himself again concerned that his resolve would crumble when he did locate Faith. The woman had a way of making him lose his reason.

"Maybe you should be the one to find her," Lone Crow offered, feeling like a coward for suggesting it.

Pathkiller smiled widely and stifled a laugh when he heard Lone Crow's request. "I am sorry," he spoke once he cleared his throat. "I wish there were a way. And I know you feel weak when it comes to this woman. You plan to avoid her until I find someone to take them back to a town?" he asked, raising his eyebrow and looking truly interested in hearing the plan Lone Crow had accepted.

The Chief wasn't asking anything unusual and Lone Crow would have been glad to share his thoughts if everything hadn't once again changed. If he weren't sure he could remain stoic when he located her, then how was he supposed to accompany the two women? Being standoffish was not the ideal action and he knew Faith would be confused and hurt. He did not relish that and prayed for strength before explaining his plan, excluding his fear of not being able to behave if the two were left alone for long. That was one thing he wasn't going to share with anyone.

Lone Crow explained as they continued to move slowly through the underbrush.

"I do know doing what is right is not always easy," Pathkiller spoke as soon as Lone Crow finished. "And that you are stronger than you believe. All this will work as it should."

Lone Crow was glad the Leader thought so because he could never accept that sentiment.

Why had he and Faith been subjected to beating after beating? In what world were those things supposed to happen. But he didn't argue because he understood Pathkiller was trying only to lift his spirits. And the Leader was right as far as that was concerned. He shouldn't be concerned with himself. He should have been overjoyed that any minute they would find Faith and she would at least be comfortable and warm when she laid her head down for the night. And maybe, most importantly, she would not be frightened.

The trail continued to be simple to follow for almost another hour and then all signs of Faith vanished.

"She is lucky she found a safe place to hide. If the tracks hadn't been so easy to follow, we might have missed her," Pathkiller whispered as they neared the two downed trees.

"If she is not sleeping, she has to hear us," Lone Crow cautioned as he watched Pathkiller slide from his mount and move toward the robe covering.

Pathkiller stopped moving and turned to Lone Crow before pointing.

Lone Crow had no idea what his next move was going to be. He wanted nothing more than to be the man everyone else saw when they looked at him. But he wasn't that person. Deep down, he was scared and unsure. Over the years, he had learned to think about things from every angle, and usually, he could find a way of ensuring his success. The Warrior just couldn't do that when it involved Faith.

While Lone Crow was overthinking his next move, he saw the robe ripple. He jumped from his pony and pushed Pathkiller out of the way.

Pathkiller was not angered by Lone Crow's actions. The Leader looked slightly impressed as he quickly made his way back to his horse.

"I will see the two of you back at the village. I will have a place for the women to stay and we will plan the next move when you return," the Chief informed him barely above a whisper.

Lone Crow heard what the man said but kept his eyes glued to the covering. It had stopped moving except in the center and from the looks of its motion, Faith was rocking herself.

## Chapter Twenty-Eight

I was terrified when I heard the men's hushed conversation and tried to make myself invisible.

They didn't seem to be angry. It sounded more like the two were just out on a ride, enjoying the beauty of the day. But I still couldn't stop shaking and rocking in an attempt to soothe myself.

The whispers made it difficult for me to hear much but for the briefest of moments, I thought one of the voices sounded like he was speaking Cherokee. Because my life wasn't one where impossible things happened, I found myself silently crying for even allowing myself to think I might be correct. No. I was wrong and needed to do everything in my power to stop moving altogether and hold my breath until I could be sure the two were gone. If they were Shawnee, the punishment for running would be severe.

Once I forced my movements to stop, I tried to listen for signs of them passing by without realizing I was there.

I held my eyes tightly shut, bit the side of my cheek, and remained still. When I noticed the robe I was using as a covering being gently pushed down, I held my breath and prayed I would survive the next few minutes. And again, I was struck at my desire to survive. All I wanted was a chance at a life that wasn't full of fear and pain. I might have even been beginning to believe I deserved that much. But nothing was quelling my anxiety at that moment. So, I steeled myself for the unknown.

"Tsisqua? It is me. I am going to uncover you."

My heart leaped and my stomach flipped when I heard Moses preparing me. And then I did something without thinking. I quickly moved the robe aside and leapt up. Wrapping my arms around the man I loved. He was all I needed. I needed to feel his strong, protective arms. I needed to tell him how sorry I was for everything. I just needed him and that wasn't any reason to be ashamed. He was the only man who ever cared about me. The only person who ever told me I was a good person. The only one who hadn't tried to control me. And as impossible as it was, he was the only man I wanted to share my life with. Moses was there with me. He had found me and I was afraid I wouldn't be able to hold my tongue when he held me and lifted me from my hiding spot.

Nothing was said for minutes. Moses simply held me and rocked me in his arms. It was the first time since he left me all those years earlier that I could remember feeling safe and loved. So, it was difficult to allow the man to put any space between us.

"You are safe now," he spoke as he gently pulled from our embrace and looked down at me.

I tried to stop shaking but couldn't. In fact, my body was trembling uncontrollably.

Moses smiled and pulled me back into a hug. "Did they hurt you?" he asked in a choked voice.

I still couldn't form words but did shake my head and cling harder to him.

I felt his hand moving through my hair and down my back.

"Who helped you escape?" he continued his gentle interrogation.

"A woman called Wii'si," I answered into his chest, still fighting my chattering teeth.

Moses continued to run his hand down my back and I was overcome with a new feeling. Maybe for the first time in my life, I wanted a man to kiss me; that man. But more than that - I wanted him to make love to me. But I knew if that happened, I would never be able to get on with my new life. As sad as it was,

I knew we needed to remain friends and nothing more. My brain and body were not in agreement. I was shocked when I found myself pushing harder into him and allowing my hand to run down his sculptured chest. My breath was labored but the fear-induced trembling had gone. It had been replaced by excitement and happy anxiety. A strange warm feeling played havoc on my belly. Before Moses again placed some space between the two of us, I was sure a strange, moan-like noise left my lips.

I felt I should have been embarrassed by my actions but couldn't summon the strength. Wanting the man wasn't wrong or anything to be ashamed of. But it was something that wasn't going to happen.

My eyes were closed tightly when I felt Moses place his hand under my chin and gently raise my face so that he could look at me.

When he softly ran his finger down my cheek, it was difficult not to reach for him again. Tears were slipping from my closed eyes but they weren't tears of pain or fear. They were tears of relief and love.

"I will not allow anything bad to happen to you," he vowed, letting his hand linger on my shoulder.

While I was still very much attempting to keep my sudden wantonness in check, I had managed to completely forget about Wilma. When I realized what I had done, I pulled my hands from him and clasped them at my chest. If I was going to use my brain, I needed the small amount of space between us.

Moses didn't stop me from moving away but he did reach to cup his hands over mine. "What is the matter?" he asked, looking and sounding just as affected by our closeness as I was.

"Wilma," I stammered, doing my best to place the woman's safety at the front of my mind.

Moses smiled and squeezed my hands tighter. "She is fine. At least, I believe she is. My father is at the village and we are trading horses for her," he explained, keeping a hopeful tone.

"What now?" I asked, hoping he would suggest we run away together and never look back.

I knew it was wrong and dangerous to have those thoughts. Still, it was what my heart (and body) wanted. I did my best to quash them as soon as they popped up.

"I am sure you are hungry and tired," he replied, not really answering my question. "Come, we will talk more while we ride. Our village is half a day's ride."

While he was speaking, he broke our contact and reached for the bag Wii'si packed me. "This woman was nice to you?" he asked as he placed the long leather strap over his shoulder before picking up the robe.

"She was," I answered, suddenly feeling as if Moses was waiting on me.

The feeling made me uncomfortable. Nobody had ever offered to make my life easier. And he was doing it without a thought. The feeling manifested itself in the form of another tear.

Lone Crow held his hand out for me to take and we walked to his waiting pony.

My answer seemed to confuse Moses and I did want to know why but was busy preparing myself for what was to come; my body's reaction to him lifting me atop the horse.

I managed to keep my noises to a barely audible level and was surprised when Moses made a similar sort of sound as he mounted the pony behind me.

His hands went around my waist when he grabbed some of the pony's mane and when the muscles in his legs tensed, my body again began trembling.

"I have got you," he spoke into my hair as the horse began to carry us toward the village.

My trembling body exposed my desire. Gone was the fear. I felt protected and safe. I was trembling because it was difficult not to throw myself at the man.

I leaned back into his muscular body and sighed deeply. "I know you do. And I am so incredibly grateful you found me."

I heard him clear his throat and felt him relax against me.

"Are you cold?" he asked as he grabbed for a heavier robe from the back of his pony and wrapped the two of us in it.

"No, but don't move," I boldly spoke before I could stop myself.

"I think I am just shaking because I may still be in shock," I admitted, hoping to convince both of us that my reaction wasn't solely because of our contact.

We rode in silent bliss for a while before he broke the calm with words of a plan I knew would eventually come.

"The other woman should be at the village when we return. Part of the plan is to convince the both of you to explain the wagons were swept away by the river," Moses began speaking as we slowly rode.

His voice was having an incredibly calming effect on me and I was finding it challenging to keep my eyes open. But when he mentioned Wilma would have to lie, it woke me up a little.

"I don't know if we can get her to lie. She is a strange woman," I mumbled, not able to hide my sereneness.

I knew I should have been worried more about the part Wilma needed to play to bring our adventure to a peaceful conclusion. Yet I couldn't force myself to feel overly concerned. I knew where I was sitting and who had me in their arms. The pure bliss I was experiencing was not going to last but I was determined to enjoy every minute I could. Wilma was something I would worry about only when forced. She was apparently unharmed and I was sure she was still frightened, but I wouldn't allow her to root in my thoughts. I couldn't recall a time when I felt safer and more loved. I wasn't willing to let go of those feelings until I was obliged to do so. Whether the actions would cause more pain later on or not, I simply didn't want what I was feeling to end.

"I believe we will be able to convince her," Moses stated as he gently laid his chin on the top of my head.

His declaration was enough for me to feel I could change the subject and not appear selfish or uncaring.

"I am sorry I told you to leave me," I began because I couldn't stop myself. I didn't want to sleep. I wanted to talk to Moses as much as possible while we had the time.

And the statement was probably one of the most honest things I had ever uttered. I hadn't told him to leave because I wanted to live with Adam. I told him to go to protect him. And even if some part of me knew continuing to speak would only intensify our feelings, I couldn't help myself.

"I know," he said after reaching into another pack and offering me water. "I am sorry I left. If I had been there, you would not have been taken."

Moses was attempting to keep his tone even but I knew he felt responsible. There was no reason for him to feel that way but the realization did cause me to wonder if responsibility and regret were the reasons for his actions. The thought made my stomach ache, and all the butterflies flitting around in my stomach to quiet. I began trying to convince myself it would be best if the man didn't love me like I loved him. All I should have wanted was for him to be happy and not feel the guilt he seemed to still be burdened with.

"Since the first time I laid eyes on you, you have done everything in your power to help me. What my life turned into was not your fault at all," I spoke slowly and chose my words carefully. I was on the verge of crying once again and did not want Moses to be aware of that fact. So after swallowing several times, I continued my thought. "I am just going to choose to be blissfully happy for a few minutes. And when I have to, I will accept the next step in my life."

I cringed when I finished my statement because I realized how in love I sounded and did not want to pressure Moses into feeling things he didn't.

It was a position I had never been in before. I had never loved anyone except the man riding behind me and never would feel those emotions for another. But sharing any time with him was a blessing so I silently promised I would stop allowing my true feelings to bleed through.

"Tsisqua, hearing you are at peace makes my heart happy," he said as he kissed the top of my head.

218 Elizabeth Anne Porter

Tears again threatened to fall but I took a deep breath and continued to mold myself into him.

"But things would have been different if I would have taken you with me the first time, maybe even the second time," he continued, sounding as if he were growing displeased with himself.

I was not going to listen to anyone, even Moses, talk bad about him. In my eyes, he was perfect and had done everything right. It had taken me years to let go of my anger but as I sat cocooned in his arms, I allowed myself to understand what he had done was the only option he had.

I shook my head against his chest. "No. I was angry with you but you were and are the only peace I have ever experienced. So I will be thankful for that. Please don't think you ever did anything wrong."

"I will make sure the rest of your life is a good one," he promised.

There was a determination in his tone and everything he said made it more difficult to continue looking ahead and not turn to embrace him face to face. I was sure my mind and body couldn't fall into a deeper state of satisfaction. It was the happiest event I had ever experienced and it was intensifying with each moment.

"Sleep now," he suggested as he patted me on the leg. "You have been through much and we won't reach my home for a time yet. Do not worry, you are safe."

His recommendation was all I needed to give into sleep. But before I allowed everything to darken, I again quietly informed the man just how much he meant to me.

## Chapter Twenty-Nine

Lone Crow couldn't have guessed how Faith was going to react when he uncovered her hiding place but he had not expected her to jump into his arms.

It was an action he enjoyed. Holding Faith silenced his mind and filled his heart with love. So he gladly held the woman as long as she needed.

He was aware they were carrying on a conversation but he had no idea what was being said. All he was doing was repeating that she would be safe and reminding himself they were just close friends. That was all they would ever be. And yet he was still silently attempting to think of a way they could be together. It was maddening because that outcome was no longer an option. The Shawnee had seen to that.

Once they were riding, he told her he would keep her safe and apologized again for leaving her.

Faith had been acting strangely but Lone Crow attributed her need for comfort to shock. Until her voice began displaying a huskier tone. The more she molded herself into him, the more difficult it was to discount the idea that Faith might be willing to put aside the comforts of living in the white town and join him in his village.

He needed to think and stop allowing his imagination to run away with him. What good would it do if she did love him enough to stay? Before suggesting she sleep, he decided once again that distance was needed as soon as it was possible.

But even after coming to that conclusion, he found himself keeping the same amount of pressure on his thighs to hold her tightly, his free hand still resting on her leg. And, instead of backing away, he kept his chin gently resting on the top of her head, the scent of her hair intoxicating his brain.

When Faith informed the Warrior that she was at peace and wanted to enjoy the feeling as long as she could, his immediate reaction was to reply with the same sentiments. But he hadn't. He couldn't. Her statement was a weighty one that both excited and hurt him. He knew being excited was pointless and quickly dismissed the emotion but the pain was something he knew he was going to carry for some time. He didn't enjoy being in pain. When he was, he was usually mean. And that was the last thing he wanted to be to Faith. It wasn't her fault they were different.

But while she slept in his arms, he did allow himself to dream of a world where they could be together.

From the moment he and Faith reconnected, he wanted to be with her but wondered if he would still feel the need to be alone. While she was safe in his arms, he realized the fear had been unfounded and the reason for the shift was apparent. He had managed to overcome most of the trauma of his childhood and when he confronted the white men for the first time as an adult, he felt as if he had healed even more. And yet, he sought solitude even after that. The draw to go off on his own and be alone was still present. There was still something that wasn't right. He knew the missing piece to his full recovery was Faith. Her presence soothed his tormented soul. The discovery led him to question if he did the same for her. And if that were the case, he simply wouldn't allow himself to continue to send her away for the third time. If she needed him a fraction as much as he needed her, Lone Crow was going to make it happen. Another jolt of excitement coursed through his body and instead of tamping it down, he embraced it. There had to be a way and he would find it.

The Warrior knew he couldn't share his change of heart with Faith but he was not going to shy away from her. Once sure of her feelings, he would ask her to give up the only life she ever knew, give it up and learn to live as a Cherokee for him. Shock could explain some of her actions and he hadn't forgotten that fact. He had to be certain of her mindset, convinced that she wanted him and his life. He knew that it would take some time.

Pathkiller was not a man to be put off so Lone Crow didn't believe the Leader would allow the white women to linger in the village. More than likely, the Chief would want them moving away as soon as the they had been fed and rested.

Taking the time to learn about Bird's true feelings would not be simple. They would not easily be afforded the luxury of being alone. Pathkiller would certainly want both of them on their way as soon as possible. Lone Crow didn't know the other woman but he was concerned she was going to be trouble. He hadn't shared his opinion with Faith. In fact, he told her the opposite of his true belief. The woman had suffered and Lone Crow knew how strangely people reacted to trying events. He still hoped he would be able to convince Wilma that telling the truth would cause a war. But he knew that would mean little. The Shawnee had killed three white men and the townsfolk would demand justice if they learned of the men's true fate. As severely as Lone Crow wanted to object to that way of thinking, he couldn't. He would want revenge too. Before he forced the dark truths to the back of his mind, he decided to talk to Faith alone before attempting to sway Wilma. Maybe if he promised the murderers would pay, he could convince Wilma. It was a stretch to believe that would make any difference but he wanted to think on happier things.

At the rate they were traveling, it would be midday when they arrived at the camp, so Lone Crow slowed his pony and hoped that their later arrival would ensure the women would stay the night. Again he knew he was wishing for events that could cause trouble for his people. It was strange to be so conflicted in his mind and so comfortable in his body.

For the remainder of the ride, he played many scenarios in his mind. Each ended in failure. But he was stubborn and had managed to come up with one conceivable argument for

Pathkiller. If the townsfolk were concerned with the missionaries, they would still have to send the sheriff. When the lawmen found no sign of an attack, they might continue to the village. If they did, they would have no reason to think his people had anything to do with it. The visit would be only to ask if the missionaries had been there. Lone Crow knew as well as anyone that counting on the white men to act a certain way was never the wisest thing to do. But it made sense in his mind so he was going to at least voice his thoughts when he saw the Chief.

The Warrior was pulled from his jumbled but hopeful thought when Faith began murmuring and shaking her head against him.

"I ... love you," she mumbled, sounding as if she were on the verge of breaking down.

Lone Crow fought the desire to wake her. It was clear she was in some distress but he needed to hear whatever she was going to say next.

"It's, always, been ..."

The Warrior took a deep breath and pulled her tighter to him. "Tsisqua, wake up," he urged gently. "I am here."

Faith took a prolonged intake of breath and then slapped her hands over her mouth before saying something that came out as a muffle and nothing more.

The Warrior smiled but stayed silent because he didn't want to add to her unease. Faith may not have called his name but he was sure she was speaking about him. The realization made it challenging to be silent about his plan. Typically, Lone Crow was a patient, pragmatic man. He couldn't seem to stay that way when it came to anything to do with Faith.

After a few minutes of wiping her eyes and sniffing, Faith sat up straighter. "Are we close?" she asked, still sounding half asleep.

He was relieved when he heard her question. It was something they could talk about that wouldn't cause anyone to feel awkward. The Warrior was unhappy with the present state the two seemed to be experiencing. It was the first time he felt as if he couldn't say whatever popped in his mind and he hoped his feeling was only because they were both too worried to share their thoughts.

"We are," he answered, lifting his head from its resting place and reaching back for one of his packs. "Are you hungry?" he asked, waiting for her reply to search its contents.

"I am but I am more thirsty than anything," she admitted, leaning closer to the pony's neck and looking around.

Lone Crow felt the coldness when she moved from him and fought the desire to pull her back. Instead, he grabbed the water container and two long, thick strips of dried deer meat.

Faith placed her hands on Lone Crow's pony and stretched to take in her surroundings better before sitting back down and returning to a snuggled-in position against the Warrior.

Without turning, she took the offered water and proceeded to quench her thirst before wiping her mouth with the back of her sleeve.

"Thank you," she said before taking a deep breath. "It smells so good here."

Lone Crow was used to the smell of wildflowers and herbs that naturally blanketed the ground. But he remembered how wonderful it smelled when he ran away. The scent banished the odors of the town and gave him his first hope that he was actually free.

Lone Crow quickly learned he enjoyed it when Faith was happy. "Here is some meat."

She turned her body slightly and smiled at him as she took the meat from his hand. "I want to just be happy," she admitted, sounding sad instead of pleased.

His emotion went from enjoyment to trepidation as soon as he heard the sadness in Faith's voice. He was determined not to take another step until he understood why Faith felt the way she did.

"What is the matter?" Lone Crow asked, prompting his pony to a stop.

She shook her head and forced a smile before turning back around.

"We will not move until you answer me," the Warrior stated as he reached for her shoulder.

Instead of pulling away from his touch, she rested her head on his hand. "I am just worried about Wilma," she admitted, allowing her voice to denote the guilt she was experiencing.

"We will do what has to be done," Lone Crow replied, doing his best to sound confident in his statement.

It was a problem he had been worrying about and still had no idea how to guarantee the woman's cooperation. But he did not want to talk about the predicament with Faith. Not yet, anyway. He still wanted to speak to Pathkiller and his father.

Talking to his father would be difficult since the Warrior had been made aware of Otter's declining health. Why hadn't Otter been the one to inform him? The Warrior was of the mind that his father still had no idea that Lone Crow knew about his illness. Lone Crow knew it would be difficult not to allow the knowledge to shade their conversation. The Warrior wanted more time in the day. He had many things to do and little time to do it.

"I have never been allowed to act as I wanted," Faith began explaining after chewing a piece of meat and returning herself to a relaxed position. "But I promise you, I will not allow Wilma to blame you or your people for anything."

He had heard and experienced all of Faith's moods when they were younger and he was pleased to know somewhere deep inside, she still had spirit. Lone Crow believed her vow but knew there was little Faith could do to follow through. If Wilma proved uncooperative and they did make it back to civilization in one piece, she would tell her tale to the first person who would listen. Lone Crow would most probably be shot on sight and the men with guns and large weapons would wreak havoc on his village. A lot was depending on the woman and Lone Crow didn't believe there was much hope. But he wasn't going to share his feelings with Faith. He wanted her to be happy instead of worried.

"Look," he said, pointing in the direction of the horse herd grazing at the outskirts of his village.

Faith leaned forward and looked before again resting against him. "I know this may be forward but I would very much like it if you would sleep with me tonight," she said lazily before sitting straight up and turning to Lone Crow, displaying a look of horror and profound embarrassment. "I didn't mean it like that," she corrected, fanning herself with her outstretched hand. "I meant, would you sleep near me tonight."

Lone Crow was momentarily at a loss for words. He very much wanted to lay with Faith and her embarrassment caused his body to shutter.

He leaned closer to her and gently removed the hand that quickly moved from fanning herself to covering her mouth before speaking softly into her ear. "I will stay as close as you wish."

The deepness of his voice surprised him and caused Faith to shiver. She cleared her throat and cautiously placed her hand atop the one Lone Crow still had resting on her thigh. "You just make me feel safe," she whispered.

Lone Crow clenched his teeth together and looked to the sky in an attempt to calm himself. He was finding it increasingly difficult not to turn her around and hold her in his arms.

"You make me feel whole," he admitted before he could stop himself.

He was stating the truth but found he wasn't looking forward to her reply so he was grateful when he saw the outline of his father walking toward the pair.

"I like that man," Faith informed the Warrior when the old man came into view and waved.

"That is my father. He is called Otter and he likes you too," Lone Crow said before pulling the robe from the two and sliding from the ride.

Before reaching for Faith, he focused on his approaching father. The man appeared to be in no distress and that gave Lone Crow some hope that so far the strategy had gone as planned.

"Hillo," Otter said, waving at Faith.

Lone Crow held his arms up for Faith to fall into and saw the woman was smiling. It warmed his heart that she liked his father.

When Faith's feet landed on the ground, she and Lone Crow were face to face.

Time seemed to stop and it was just the two of them. Faith looked up at him with an unmistakable look of love and desire. Her eyelashes still held the remnants of tears and before Lone Crow could talk himself out of it, he gently took her face in his hands and used his thumbs to wipe the wetness away.

He felt Faith swoon but was still unprepared for her arms to find their way around his neck.

Lone Crow knew kissing the woman was not the smart thing to do but couldn't help himself. He felt himself being gently pulled into her.

Faith's hooded eyes closed and he leaned down and placed his lips against hers.

"Lone Crow, everyone is watching," Otter stated excitedly as he moved to block the pair from view.

Lone Crow gently pulled away and watched as Faith's eyes widened and a red flush crossed her cheeks. She was beautiful and it was difficult to pull away.

She placed her hands over his and smiled sweetly as she attempted to slow her breathing.

"Come," Otter continued to invade their space as he grabbed both by the arms and began pulling them apart. "The other woman is loud and very frightened," he continued as he practically dragged the pair into the center of the village.

"What is he saying?" Faith asked as she looked around Otter to Lone Crow.

The woman didn't sound afraid. She didn't look frightened. She still had a very becoming glow about her that he planned on coaxing out as soon as they were alone again. It was going to happen whether it was right or wrong. They would be together at least one time. He would show her how a man loved a woman.

## Chapter Thirty

When I fell asleep, I was gifted with the sweetest dreams and felt free to speak my thoughts. Until I realized I might actually be speaking out loud.

When I heard Moses tell me I was safe, I was embarrassed to my core. But he didn't say anything more before offering me food and drink. Again I was touched by the simplest of things. He was thinking about my needs first and it was difficult not to cry.

I was still concerned with how Wilma was going to react. But those thoughts clearly weren't occupying much of my mind. Moses was making me so calm and happy I couldn't concentrate on her for long. I was also keenly aware that I was being wanton by pushing myself so firmly to Moses. But I didn't care. My emotions were still pretty much all over the place and I couldn't seem to stop tears from forming in my eyes. After taking a moment to get a grip on myself, I continued speaking simply because I wanted to keep talking to the man. I hadn't expected to ask him to share my bed but that is how my question sounded. When I realized exactly what I'd said, I was mortified.

While quickly explaining the true intent of the statement, I noticed a look on Moses' handsome face. It was fleeting but I knew the look. Not because I'd seen Moses employ it before but it was a look of enthusiasm. The thought of lying in bed beside me excited him. The realization took my breath away for a moment and then I told him how safe I felt when he was around. Was that the smartest thing to do? Again, no. But for some reason, I didn't care to be smart any longer. I wanted happiness, even if it was fleeting. Accepting that my change in attitude could have been brought on by the events of the last few days didn't stop me from wanting any happiness I could find.

When he told me that I made him feel whole, my bones turn to mush. The things my body was doing were foreign to me but they were another thing I quite liked.

There was a second of forced silence before Moses pointed to the man I had spoken with before we left the Cherokee village.

He had been kind to me and I was pleased to see him again. Learning he was Moses' father made me like him even more.

I slid off the pony and into Moses' arms with a smile on my face. But as soon as I was standing face to face with him, the smile disappeared and my breathing changed.

No man had ever looked at me like that. I had been kissed many times but never had I desired to feel the warmth of someone's lips against mine.

I stood on my tiptoes and reached to place my arms around his neck.

When his lips met mine, I was sure my heart stopped and would have gladly stayed entwined with the man if Otter hadn't been so excited in his tone.

Strange as it was, the old man's manner caused another smile to brighten my face.

I did manage to ask why Otter was dragging the two of us toward a house.

Moses smiled back at me and informed me that Wilma was being loud and was afraid.

"Then we should do what we can," I replied, still not ready to let go of my blissfulness and fully acknowledge just what the answer meant.

Otter was gentle in his handling of me but I noticed he was a little rougher when it came to Moses. But the man I loved stayed calm and waited for his father to place us inside a dark home.

Once we were inside, I heard Wilma whimpering in the corner. As soon as my eyes adjusted to the darkness, I pulled away from the old man's grip and ran to her side.

She was lying on a robe in a fetal position with her eyes clenched shut, switching from crying to praying as she rocked herself. I noticed she was neither tied up nor gagged and was pleased to see the people choose to treat her with dignity.

"It's going to be alright," I soothed as I ran my hand down her back.

When she heard my voice, her eyes opened widely and she reached to hold me. "I thought you were dead," she confessed as she rocked me. "I can't understand anything anyone is saying," she continued. "What are they going to do with us? Is this any better than where we were before? I am so happy to see you. Are you well? How did you get here?"

It was impossible to forget all the horrible things she said to me before I left her. I was shocked she wasn't once again telling me that all her misfortunes were entirely my fault. And I did understand where some of her queries were coming from. But I couldn't hold a grudge against her. It was an ugly thing to do and I knew if I were in her position, I would be frightened too. So instead of pointing out her rudeness of late, I continued to pat her on the back as she held me tightly in her arms.

Wilma sniffed loudly and broke our embrace before looking at the other two people in the home. Her gaze focused again on my eyes with a mixture of question and fright. The adrenaline her body was experiencing was obvious.

I shook my head and smiled at her. "They are friends," I began explaining.

Wilma looked unconvinced but she settled a little. I was worried that she would scream without warning so I continued to explain the situation as best as I could.

"This is where we came to before. These are good people," I said, pointing to Moses and his father.

The two men were deep in conversation until I pointed at them and then they both looked our way.

Moses smiled and Otter waved before they returned to their conversation.

"When can we go home?" she asked, moving away slightly before sitting up and making herself comfortable. The look on her face was rapidly changing. "The savages who killed our men have to die."

I was disappointed that her dissipating fear brought out her anger. I understood her feelings and knew I should be taking my husband's death harder than I was. Still, I was not going to allow her to cause a problem for Moses or his people.

I choked back all the arguments I had for her and smiled before taking a deep breath. "I am sure they will. But we must make sure the Army doesn't take out their anger on the wrong people," I explained with as much patience as I could garner.

Wilma was shaking her head and looking like she was in the throes of remembering the scene.

"Are you thirsty? Hungry maybe? What do you need?" I asked, easily falling into an accommodating mode and pulling away to get her some water.

Wilma scanned the dwelling once more and nodded. "I am. They are going to let us go, aren't they?" she asked, reaching to stop me from standing.

I smiled and gently moved her hand from my arm to her lap before getting up. "They will," I assured her. "Just relax and I'll get you some water and food."

Wilma still looked unsure but seemed to be gathering herself. The tears were gone and she was speaking normally so I had hope that whatever shock she was suffering from would ease and I would be able to convince her to lie about the deaths of the men.

"Thank you," she whispered.

Moses and Otter were still deep in conversation when I approached the two.

As soon as I stood next to Moses, he reached to place his arm around me. The action caught me off guard but I easily moved into to him.

As soon as our bodies were pressed together, I heard a gasp escape Wilma's lips. An action that made me feel so very safe and loved clearly repulsed the woman. And I found the knowledge angered me.

I was readying to pull away from Moses and tell Wilma about herself when I felt his hold tighten.

When I turned to him, I saw he was smiling sadly and Otter was looking unsurprised by Wilma's actions.

"What is wrong with her?" I asked in a low whisper before continuing to wriggle free of Moses' grasp.

"She is reacting perfectly normal to the thought of a Native and a white woman sharing love," Moses answered, clearly attempting to keep his disdain as bay.

"Well," I stated, embracing the anger. "I will remind her that hate is not Christian-like."

"I will bring her food and water and be at your side as soon as my father has gone in search of Pathkiller," Moses informed me, still looking at me in a way that made it challenging to keep my knees from buckling.

After taking a brief second to assure I would remain standing, I turned my attention back to Wilma. Strange as it was, my anger had lessened by the time I was once again standing in front of her.

"That man saved us," I pointed out before sitting beside her. "He is the only reason we will be able to return home. And he is also seeing to your needs as we speak," I ended when I saw him follow his father out of the home.

"He is a savage," she informed me, sounding as if maybe I hadn't heard that word used to describe the people we invaded.

I had listened to the same sentiment for years and had never believed that talk. I'd always believed there were good Natives and bad Natives, just like any other peoples. And because of my relationship with Moses, I would never be convinced otherwise.

But I did understand where the woman's beliefs came from. So I bit the inside of my cheek and began attempting to placate her.

"He is no savage," I assured her as Moses entered the dwelling and slowly walked toward us. "He has done nothing but help you. What happened is terrible and the men who murdered our men will pay," I promised easily enough, even if I knew I had no right to speak on their punishment.

"I can see that. They didn't even tie me up. But I want the men who did this to suffer," she said, sounding stronger with every word.

Moses smiled politely and laid the bag beside me before walking to the fire and stirring the embers.

I was waiting on Moses to speak to her statement while he stood and pulled a clay pot from the place it hung on the wall.

"How do you know him?" Wilma asked, breaking the considerable attention I was paying to the man.

I looked at her and wondered if telling the truth would shift her thinking. There really wasn't much to our story but suddenly, I felt overprotective of it.

While I was considering a story to tell Wilma, Moses spoke.

"Faith and I grew up together," he stated, watching both of us closely.

"You are the man who killed her father?!" Wilma asked louder than necessary.

Moses looked disappointed by Wilma's reaction and before I could stop myself, I grabbed her arm and forced her to look at me. I wanted to be sure she heard what I had to say.

"My father beat Moses and me. Almost every day. He shot my father in self-defense and if your parents had said something or questioned why the two of us were always walking around bruised and bloody, it wouldn't have come to that. And stop looking at me like that. I did not escape when my father was gone. I went from one abuser to another. You know that. You were sleeping with one of them. And still, no one spoke out. My life has been one misery after another and this man, well, he is the only person who ever took care of me or wanted to protect me. He is no savage, nor are the others in this village. You will be respectful and you will do as you are told."

I was pleased with my declaration and could tell Moses was proud of me. When I looked at Wilma, she was shaking her head and looking concerned about her situation once again.

It was mean of me but I preferred when her mind was occupied. When she wasn't concerned with something else, she was a mean, hateful person.

"I couldn't help you," she argued weakly while she reached for the water vessel I offered. "I understand why you are not mourning Tobias but he did have a good side," she continued after taking a drink and holding the gourd next to her body protectively. "And Howard was a good man. I want vengeance and nothing you can say will change that."

I was well aware that my mourning was less than Wilma's but hearing her say that Tobias had a good side made it difficult not to slap her. In my opinion, Tobias was an animal. And as hard as I tried to hide my anger, I knew I hadn't. Wilma looked both sorry for speaking and embarrassed.

"But I will make sure the military knows who committed the murders. I promise you that. And if that man ..." she said, pointing at Moses.

"His name is Mose…his name is Lone Crow," I interrupted simply because I couldn't abide Wilma not calling Moses by his name. And again, I was surprised to learn how protective I was of the name I called him. I was quickly learning; I wanted to keep everything about Moses to myself.

Wilma nodded and continued. "If Lone Crow can speak our language, then I am sure he can explain everything to the Army."

I was naïve when it came to ruling powers but was still reasonably sure nobody was going to take Moses' word for anything.

"You will feel better after you eat," Moses said, walking to us and searching his bag. "Here. This will hold you over until I retrieve more food from my home."

I watched as Wilma reached for the piece of dried meat Moses offered her. Her hands were shaking but she was attempting to hide her fear.

Moses smiled and didn't seem to be near as angered by the situation as I.

"Can I do anything?" I offered when he bent over.

"No. I will take care of everything," he answered as soon as Wilma was busy eating. "Do you still want me to bring my robes back?"

The roughness of his voice was enough to make my mind blank. But I quickly recovered and looked at Wilma before answering him.

Wilma was busy concentrating on the meat so I smiled and reached to touch the side of his face. "I do."

I knew it was a brazen statement but the anger and irritation I was experiencing were gone and all I could think about was Moses. A small voice in the back of my mind warned me to remember how vital Wilma was to my future happiness. But the voice was quieted quickly. I had been cheated out of a normal, content life and was going to enjoy true happiness - even if it was fleeting.

## Chapter Thirty-One

Lone Crow understood the gravity of the situation as his father spoke. It was essential to keep the white woman calm and he was the only one who could do it. But he still couldn't think of anything except the soft eagerness of Faith's lips.

Her inquiry conveyed that she, too, was still being affected by their contact.

As soon as Lone Crow explained Wilma's situation to Faith, she seemed to take charge.

The change in Faith was surprising. And although he did question the cause, he hadn't really considered she could still be acting out because of the shock of the last day. He needed to be sure she felt the same way for the same reasons. The last thing he wanted was to add to her pain.

As soon as they were inside the dwelling, Faith ran to the crying woman who laid in the corner.

"We must calm that woman," Otter stated quickly.

"Bird will do what she can. She is the best chance we have. The woman has been taught to distrust us. I understand how vital she is to our plan," Lone Crow said, finding it difficult to stay focused on the problem at hand.

Otter smirked at his son. "This is important. Stop looking like a love-struck youth."

Lone Crow shook his head, stopped trying to hear what the women were saying, and concentrated on the critical conversation at hand.

"I understand what is at stake," he assured his father. "While I see to feeding them, will you locate Pathkiller?"

Otter looked confused but stayed silent.

"I know we need to begin our journey to town as soon as possible," Lone Crow continued, finding himself choosing his words carefully.

His logic was valid but he knew his reasons for wanting more time with Faith were selfish. And he wanted to be able to walk the line between what was right for his people and what was right for himself.

"The longer they stay, the more danger we are in," Otter interjected when Lone Crow took a breath. "The scene is cleared. If anyone comes looking, they will not know there was an attack ..."

"If they find two white women and no white men when they are visiting, we will not be able to explain it away. No, son. I understand what you are proposing but I do not agree."

Lone Crow never enjoyed being told 'no.' "If you do not agree, I understand," he stated, tamping down his growing irritation. "But I will at least speak to Pathkiller."

Lone Crow overheard Bird speaking about him and turned to glance at the two women. Otter smiled and waved before immediately continuing to talk.

"We must think of the people."

Lone Crow understood his father's opinion and knew arguing would do no good. Even if he didn't agree with Otter, he kept his thoughts to himself and listened while his father continued.

It was unlike Otter to be so stubborn and Lone Crow was reminded of his father's illness. Was his personality changing, or was he acting totally out of character? Arguing his point or pushing his opinions on Otter would do nothing more than strain their relationship. And the Warrior did not want that. So, until he could figure out why they were suddenly at odds, he decided to change the subject.

"I will feed them and we will meet at the council house. I have no plan to cause trouble, but I will be heard," he informed Otter in non-threatening tones.

While the Warrior was talking, Faith had returned to the men. Instead of fighting the urge to swallow the woman into his arms, he pulled her into his side. As soon as he heard the gasp emanate from Wilma, he felt Bird pull away. Her anger induced feelings of pride and sadness. As she pulled away, he informed her of his plans to gather food and yet he didn't follow Otter out. He stayed and offered the water from his bag and the little dried meat he had remaining. Wilma questioned their relationship after displaying her disgust. When Bird remained quiet, he felt the need to speak the truth. He was prepared to be called a murder, so when Wilma said as much, he was not as shocked as Bird.

While Bird continued to inform Wilma of her past, he busied himself with stoking the embers and marveling at just how strong the woman he loved was. He watched her begin to come into her own with a sense of profound pride and love.

But he wasn't blind to the fact that Bird was doing little to sway Wilma. She was chipping away at Wilma's resolve but Lone Crow could see Wilma was still distrustful and frightened.

He stayed silent as he approached his pack and heard Wilma suggest that he could explain everything to the military. Lone Crow clenched his jaw and didn't voice his opinion on the proposal. The Warrior understood Wilma knew little of the workings of the military and was sure if Bird thought about it long enough, she would realize his death would be a certainty. He didn't want anything more to concern the woman he loved. When she looked like she was once again going to explain the problem, the Warrior handed the dried meat to Wilma, telling her she would feel better once she ate.

The distraught woman took the offering from Lone Crow and promptly began to chew. He was caught off guard when Bird asked if there was anything she could do. If Wilma hadn't been there, he would have answered differently but because they were not alone, he told her no. But he couldn't resist asking if she still wanted him to sleep in the dwelling.

When she said she did, he was hesitant to leave her. Only after telling himself they would have time to talk later did he stand and leave the home.

Lone Crow wasted no time gathering the needed supplies before approaching the council house. After setting his bag at the entrance, he announced himself and waited to be called inside.

He had not given much more thought as to what he was going to say because his mind was full of Bird. The excitement and adrenaline running through him were new and he found it to be enjoyable. Before he walked inside, he cleared his throat and tried to settle his mind. Lone Crow was walking into the most important meeting of his life and was the least prepared he had ever been.

When he walked inside, the murmurs died down and all looked toward him. Their actions made him uncomfortable and he wasn't sure how to react.

"Sit, Lone Crow," Pathkiller suggested, patting the vacant ground beside him.

Lone Crow did as he was told and took a deep breath, hoping the next few minutes would not be a waste of time or end in hard feelings.

"Otter tells us you think we should allow the women to stay the night," he said, pointing at the old man as he spoke.

Lone Crow was shocked to hear his father had spoken to the council of his proposal even after telling him it was a bad idea.

Lone Crow nodded and waited to hear the rest.

"While we do not want to appear to be cold or uncaring about the welfare of the women, I do believe the quicker they are out of the village, the better."

The decision was not what Lone Crow wanted to hear.

"This whole plan is dependent on the woman called Wilma," the Warrior began explaining, keeping his voice friendly even though he was disappointed and hurt. "If she does not agree to lie, we will see bloodshed. Time is what is needed. Time to gain her trust."

It was a weak argument at best, but it was the truth. Pathkiller looked pained before shaking his head. "I will not put the future of my people in the hands of a frightened white woman."

It was evident the Leader was taking no joy in his statement and even though reality had begun to creep into Lone Crow's foggy, overcrowded brain, he was still taken aback when the meaning of the Chief's statement sunk in.

"If you are suggesting we kill the women …" Lone Crow began, fighting to remain respectful.

"No one savors taking a life," Otter interrupted from across the fire. "But we cannot take the chance."

Lone Crow was having trouble believing his father agreed with the idea of killing the women. It was unlike the man and something Lone Crow simply would not allow.

"There has to be a way to fix this," he argued, knowing full well the men were right.

In the simplest of terms, the base of all the impending doom was the pair of women. But he was not going to allow anyone to hurt Bird and he was still not willing to give up on Wilma. He also knew he couldn't take on the whole village.

"You and your father will leave before the sunrise and when the time is right, a decision will be made," Pathkiller declared, watching Lone Crow closely.

When Lone Crow heard the beginning of the declaration, he experienced mixed emotions. He was pleased his father would be with him and confused that Pathkiller would choose the man. Lone Crow didn't think Otter would kill a woman if he weren't forced to. And the Warrior was planning on fixing everything as soon as possible. But he was still puzzled at the choice.

"I need to go feed the women and then we will leave," Lone Crow said, standing and walking to the exit.

He knew if he didn't leave, he would say things he wouldn't be able to take back. And he also knew the Chief and members of the village hadn't arrived at their decision easily. The plan was the only way the people could be sure no one knew of the attack.

"Lone Crow," Pathkiller called to him before he walked out.

The Warrior took a deep breath, turned, and looked at the Chief.

"I know this is not easy but I believe the other woman will be helpful in keeping the scared one in line. It is the only way I see the two surviving."

Lone Crow clenched his hands into fists and took a moment to collect himself.

Everything Pathkiller said hurt him more. He had no intention of letting Bird go unless she wanted to leave. He was still trying to think of a way they could be together, still holding to the plan he had before the Shawnee interrupted. It was extremely difficult to walk away without saying another word but, he did. Once outside, he began walking in circles while attempting to understand just how much everything had changed in such a short amount of time.

Before he'd walked into the meeting, his biggest worry was getting Bird alone. Wilma had been a problem but he had managed to not accept the true weight of her importance because he was too occupied with Bird.

While he walked and desperately attempted to think of another way, he found it difficult to draw a deep breath and realized his heart was racing. The Warrior hadn't experienced those symptoms since he was a child but he knew what had brought them on. He felt helpless.

While he was in the throes of convincing himself there was still a chance everything would work out, he was pulled from his thoughts by Otter.

The old man was standing beside him, holding Lone Crow's arm in an attempt to stop the Warrior from continuing to walk in circles.

"There was a time when you had faith in me," he said, not hiding his disappointment in his son.

Lone Crow stopped and swallowed the desire to walk away. He had been angry many times in his life but he had not been helpless since he was a boy and he was not sure his father could or would say anything that might give him hope.

"Listen to me," Otter demanded.

Lone Crow bit his tongue and gave his father his undivided attention.

"Pathkiller is coming as well."

Lone Crow wasn't sure how to take the latest development.

"Is that news supposed to change anything?" he asked, allowing a small amount of the despair he was experiencing to seep through.

"We will speak more as we ride. Do not give up hope yet."

While Lone Crow appreciated his father's attempt to help, he didn't find much comfort in it.

The woman who held his happiness in her words was a woman he wished he'd never met. Wilma held all the power and the Warrior was beginning to dislike the woman. But as his thoughts grew darker, he still did not allow himself to wish harm to the woman. She was a definite thorn in his side and her actions could cause his death but she was still a woman and a bringer of life. She had done nothing wrong and had witnessed a terrible attack before being swept away by the killers. She had been through more in a few days than some people would experience throughout their entire lives. So the task of changing the way the woman viewed the world was daunting.

"Are you listening to me?" Otter asked when Lone Crow remained silent and staring off in the distance.

"I am. When are we leaving?" he answered with no emotion in his tone.

He realized how badly he wanted to be on his own and understood a little more about himself.

Otter read his son's thoughts quickly enough. "No, we need to face this head-on. There is no time for seeking solitude. If this does not go as planned, I imagine we will see little of each other. And for that, I am sorry," the old man professed, sounding as if he meant every word to the core of his being. "I will pack the animals while you see to the women. I know they are in need of sleep so we will not travel far. The main concern is that we are not in the village."

Lone Crow let out a sigh and turned in the direction of Bird and the troublesome woman.

The plans of their night spent lying in each other's arms were no longer a possibility. But he would be with the woman. That was non-negotiable.

While he slowly walked toward the women, he attempted to clear his mind and appear as if nothing soul-crushing had happened. His hope was that his being confident and strong would lessen any stress felt by Bird. It would be easiest for her and the other woman if they thought he approved of the plan.

He had never lied to Bird before and he knew it was not going to be easy.

Lone Crow stopped at the entrance and listened to what was happening inside.

The sounds coming from the home were hushed voices but Lone Crow heard enough to know Bird loved him and she knew she would have to return to her people. He was proud of her strength and prayed he would be as strong as her when the time came.

He would have continued to eavesdrop if Wilma hadn't decided she wanted to leave. The Warrior was sure the woman was the only one who wanted the ordeal to be over. That knowledge made it difficult to walk inside and pretend that all was well.

## Chapter Thirty-Two

As soon as Moses left, my mind took over and began planning our evening. Wilma certainly hadn't agreed to behave but I was so desperate to believe everything would work out that I didn't want to allow my mind to linger on what if's. Being with child was always a tiring and uncomfortable time for me so I hoped she was feeling the drain too. All I wanted to do was aid her in sleeping and in the morning, urge her to see the reasoning in doing as our hosts asked.

"They are gonna let us go, right?" Wilma asked for the third or fourth time after she finished the strip of meat.

I rolled my eyes and pulled myself from my imagination and back to reality. The truth was, I wasn't sure. Moses hadn't talked to me about what was going to come next. I was pretty sure escorting us to the nearest settlement was the smartest thing to do. It made sense but even as I tried to bury the probable outcome, I realized being in the company of Natives might not end well. And I honestly wanted only to stay with Moses. There were many things I wanted to talk to the man about but hoped when he returned, he would run to my side and carry me to his robe. So, it was disappointing when I realized there was no putting off all the other life-changing things that were going to happen.

"I believe they will. But what are you going to do when you get home?" I asked before I could stop myself.

I was suddenly employing a new tactic and had no idea where I was headed.

When I saw the look on her face, I knew instantly that I needed to return to being comforting and play on her sympathy. "I will tell my story to anyone who wants to listen," she answered.

I wasn't sure she knew exactly what she was saying. "If you tell everyone what happened, there will be a war. Is that what you want?" I asked, doing my best to control my rising panic.

"I told you before, I will inform the military that the men who committed the murders were not from your friend's village," she repeated, sounding as if she actually believed in what she was saying.

"Wilma, can we take some time before we easily condemn these nice people to untold horrors?" I asked, clenching my teeth together and standing up.

"You will be an outcast if I tell anyone about your friend," she stated as she moved from a sitting position to lying on her side.

Her tone was full of judgment and superiority.

Since I was finally free to embrace my emotions, I held to my anger when I began pacing. I would have preferred it if we could have been friendly with one another. I had even been cordial when she was openly having an affair with my husband. So, I was finding it impossible to hold my tongue when she threatened me.

"I will be an outcast?!" I asked, stamping my foot to exhibit my aggravation. "What about you? I am not doing anything wrong. You, on the other hand, were sleeping with a married man; a married man you were afraid would hit you if you tried to leave. And you say he had a good side? Wilma, this would be so much easier if we could come to an agreement."

I meant what I said. I wanted everyone to get along. But for the first time in my life, I knew I would continue to be ugly if that was what Wilma really wanted. At that point, I wasn't sure she knew what she wanted. But my patience was wearing thin and I found it incredibly freeing to not worry or censor myself before I spoke.

246 Elizabeth Anne Porter

"What I did was wrong. But you are in love with Lone Crow. If him being an Indian isn't enough, he killed your blood," she continued to spew forth and became so self-righteous she again sat up.

I balled my firsts several times and rubbed my temples before taking numerous deep breaths and calmly sitting beside her once again. She was an infuriating woman and I had no idea what Tobias saw in her.

"He saved me. Plain and simple. And yes, I do love him," I said, growing more confident with every word. "I am just now realizing that I have always loved him. But there is no way we can be together. Because of the way our people look on them. It is sad, Wilma. Lone Crow is a loving and giving man. Someone who would never raise his hand to me in anger. The only man who made me feel safe and protected. So, why should the color of his skin, or the way he lives, have anything to do with it?"

Wilma looked as if she were thinking about my impassioned statement so I continued.

"Will this deceit be easier for you if you understand just how badly leaving Lone Crow again will hurt me? Because I know that's the only way this ends," I continued.

Wilma was looking at me with her mouth hanging open slightly and I was quickly learning the more I spoke, the more I understood about myself. So I kept talking.

"You, at least, have a chance at living a normal life. I am sorry Howard is gone. He was a good man. Adam was a fine man too. But you are with child and widowed. There are plenty of people who will help you. I have always been kept in the shadows. Oh, the townsfolk know me but they very often look right through me. And since I cannot possibly be with the man I love, I will wither away. But at least these people who have done nothing more than shown us kindness will be safe. And since I have control over so very little in my life, I will make sure that happens."

"The men who killed our men are savages. They attacked us unprovoked and they will not get away with it," she countered, making it clear she cared little about my pain.

Her reasoning was something I could not argue with. I was well aware our treatment could have been much worse in the hands of the Shawnee but I was sure the people had laws and punishments.

"I will speak to M … Lone Crow when he returns and I am sure he will tell you the men will be punished," I offered after giving it some thought.

"Then I will think about telling a different story if he can promise that," she decided after taking a deep breath.

I was overjoyed with her conclusion because I desperately wanted to believe everything would work out. I quickly found myself returning to the daydream of my time alone with Moses.

"Well, unless what they want me to say is ridiculous," she added before standing and walking to the fire.

I hadn't been able to drift off when she spoke again and wasn't thrilled with her sudden amendment.

"I am sure the story will be one that makes sense," I assured her.

Wilma warmed her hands near the flames and began walking. It was apparent the woman was stiff from riding and being tossed about. I felt for her and what she was going through but couldn't place myself in her shoes.

"Did Lone Crow say he was going to cook something?" she asked, smoothly moving on from a topic that my future depended on, to her hunger.

"He did and I am sure he will be back any minute," I assured her, hoping I was right.

"After we eat, I want to go home," she declared as she returned to the fur and sat down.

I was on the verge of telling her that she wasn't the one who made the decisions about our travel, when Moses walked back in.

My heartbeat quickened and the butterflies in my stomach awoke.

"Then we will eat and begin our travels," he agreed as he walked toward the fire and began placing corn, wild onion, and meat into a cooking vessel.

Wilma seemed pleased with the news but I was devastated.

"What is this story you want me to tell?" she asked, looking at Moses.

I was interested in his answer but was still battling disappointment and was concerned as to why he did not look as happy as he had when he left.

"We would like it if you tell the townspeople that your wagons were taken by the river and you were the only survivors," he began, focusing his attention on the wonderful-smelling food he was preparing.

His voice was flat and it only served to concern me more.

"I can't even consider that until I know the murderers are punished," she replied confidently as she reached for the water vessel that sat beside her.

Her sudden sense of being in control was unwarranted but her nerves had calmed and she was having a normal conversation with Lone Crow so I held on to hope that something would still go as planned. I was sure the intimate night with Moses that I was looking forward to was not going to happen.

I watched as Moses clenched his jaw when he heard Wilma's demand. "They will be punished," he replied before looking directly at her. "Would you like a finger or some sign that I speak the truth?"

I was taken aback by his anger and Wilma almost swallowed her tongue.

"Of course not," she answered quickly. "I just think our men deserve justice."

After she spoke, she began picking on a loose thread at the hem of her dress.

I was glad for her silence but for the briefest of seconds, I considered staying beside her instead of moving next to Moses. As soon as I was able to convince myself the bold move would have no bearing on Wilma's final decision, I stood and walked to Moses' side.

He smiled and reached to hold my hand.

"What happened?" I asked as I caressed his hand in mine.

"We must move out before the sun arrives," he answered, shifting his attention between me and the food.

I knew there was more to it but also realized we would have time to talk when we traveled. All I needed to do was have a little patience.

"Can we ride together?" I asked, hoping we would still be able to be alone.

The smile that crossed his face made me go weak at the knees.

Before answering my question, he looked around to see if Wilma was still occupied and then leaned over and kissed me.

It was innocent and I knew that was for the best but I still wanted to wrap my arms around him and cuddle.

"We will be together every moment we can," he answered against my lips.

My body was being bombarded by new sensations so I was shaky on my feet. Moses appeared to enjoy my reaction to him.

"The quicker you eat, the quicker we can leave," he said, looking around me.

I sighed and stood beside him while he filled three bowls with food.

We ate in silence but Moses kept his leg pressed against mine. Wilma ate quickly and then fought with an episode of hiccups.

"I need to be alone," she informed the two of us when Lone Crow reached for the empty containers.

He nodded his understanding and offered out his hand to help her up. After hesitating for longer than I was comfortable with, she took his hand and stood.

"You can step away on the way to the corral," Moses said as he placed the dirty utensils in a thin sheet of leather before placing it outside the door.

As soon as I realized he was packing his belongings, I began rolling the fur and held it in my arms while I waited.

Wilma looked around and when she began slowly walking toward the exit, I followed.

It looked dark outside but I could still hear people moving about. I silently wondered if the people ever really settled. They had homes and grew crops and appeared to have a town much like the one I grew up in. And yet it seemed as if they never rested. When the sun went down in my town, people were in their homes and an almost eerie silence overtook the place. The town was one of the few that didn't allow a pub to be open late and I was sure that had something to do with it. But I slowly grew to understand that the quiet I was used to did not give me the peaceful feeling the Cherokee village did.

"My father and the Chief will be waiting," Moses explained as he gestured for us to exit the dwelling.

The village wasn't so dark that I couldn't see but I was not as surefooted as Moses.

After seeing me stumble for the third time, Moses slowed his pace and offered his arms to both Wilma and me. I gladly accepted the offer and waited until Wilma finally saw the sense of it and did the same.

"Where are we going?" she asked, sounding a little winded.

"We are taking you back to your people," Moses answered unenthusiastically.

"Thank God," she said, smiling.

I was nowhere near as enthused with the idea and still had a feeling Moses wasn't telling me everything. I smiled and continued to keep my thoughts to myself.

Moses stopped near a tall growth of grass and pointed. "I will be here."

Wilma removed her arm from Moses' and began walking away quickly.

I needed a moment alone myself but wasn't going to move until Moses answered the question I suddenly had to ask. "Everything is going to be alright, isn't it?"

As soon as I asked, I realized that maybe I didn't want an honest answer.

Moses smiled and pulled me into a quick kiss before guiding me to take the same path Wilma had taken.

He hadn't answered me but he had made my mind go momentarily blank.

When we rejoined Moses, he was standing by a man I assumed was the Chief.

Wilma stopped walking and pulled me back when she saw the man.

"Who is that and why is he coming too?" she whispered, keeping a tight grip on my arm.

"I don't know but I'm sure Lone Crow will explain everything," I replied, smiling at her and pulling free. "Now, shall we?" I asked, holding my arm out for her to take the lead. "Like you said, the quicker we leave, the quicker we get back."

Wilma seemed swayed by my statement, even if I wasn't sure I was telling the truth. The only reason I wanted to get moving was to give me time to speak to the man I loved.

252 Elizabeth Anne Porter

# Chapter Thirty-Four

Lone Crow fought the almost overwhelming desire to walk inside and sweep Bird up in his arms. Instead, he forced himself to begin to cook the meal while doing his best to act as nothing had changed and the very lives of the two women still were in the balance.

He was surprised when Wilma began speaking to him directly. But because he was desperate for any sign that the woman could be swayed, he was pleased. And just as soon as he thought there was hope, the woman demanded the Shawnee Warriors be punished.

Instead of attempting to explain that the Shawnee were different than the white man in many ways, he allowed his anger and lack of control take over.

He knew his offer of a body part would force Wilma to think but hadn't considered Bird would be affected by his proposal.

His question did quiet the woman and her silence allowed Bird to walk to him.

When he took her hand, his mind slowed and his anger faded.

The question Bird asked was one he did not want to answer simply because he hadn't fully accepted the reality of it.

His answer was the purest form that was still true.

The Warrior was doing his best to appear as if he had everything in control even as his future plans were crumbling before him. But when Bird asked if they could ride together, he found doing so was all that occupied his mind.

While they ate, Lone Crow tried to reconcile his future and accept that he would take the happiness Bird brought him for however long it lasted.

Soon the food had been consumed and he began packing and clearing the house. But his mind was still on finding a way to be alone with Bird when they rested.

The Warrior stopped and offered Wilma a place to be alone when Bird asked if everything was going to be alright. The last thing he wanted to do was worry her. When it was all said and done, the women would both survive. He wasn't sure how he was going to accomplish that feat but he was sure it would happen. Instead of answering Bird's question, he kissed her, promised her he would be waiting for her return, and watched as she followed Wilma behind a tall patch of grass.

As soon as he was alone, he saw Pathkiller walking his way. The Warrior still respected the man but at the time, he didn't like him much.

"Where are the women?" he asked as he reached to pat Lone Crow on the back.

It was difficult for the Warrior to stay still.

"They are seeking some privacy," Lone Crow answered in a clipped tone.

Pathkiller looked hurt and confused by Lone Crow's attitude.

"Does your mood mean that the woman cannot be trusted?" he asked, appearing genuinely curious.

"My mood means that I am concerned and because I am, I will tell you now that no one will harm Bird. I cannot allow that." Lone Crow answered, hoping he was still able to keep the right amount of reverence in his statement.

Pathkiller watched Lone Crow closely and raised his eyebrow after hearing the Warrior's proclamation.

"That is not the outcome I wish for but you need to know just how far I am willing to go to ensure the safety of our people.

Now, the women are returning. I will meet you at the ponies,"
Pathkiller stated as he smiled cordially at the women and walked
away.

Lone Crow was still angry and conflicted but he knew he
needed to keep his emotions to himself so he turned to the
women and smiled warmly.

Wilma appeared to be as calm as he had ever seen her but
he knew Bird had concerns and questions for him.

"How long will it take us to see civilization again?"
Wilma asked as she began following the path.

Lone Crow offered his arm to Bird and began following
Wilma.

She leaned into him and sighed. Her action stopped him
from replying to Wilma.

"We will have time to be together, won't we?" she asked
dreamily.

Lone Crow knew he couldn't promise it would happen
but he again wasn't ready to share his concerns about the
obstacles they faced.

"We will. And as soon as we get on the pony, we can
begin to get to know one another."

"I missed you. And I am sorry that because of me, you
have to deal with Wilma."

Lone Crow thought he heard Bird's voice catch and did
not want her crying so he stopped walking and gently lifted her
chin up. "None of this is your fault," he stated ardently. "You
must believe that. And we will make the best of the situation."

Bird's eyes widened and a blush crossed her cheeks. "I
know it may be wicked to say but I am glad we got to see each
other again. I know the circumstances are not ideal but I am
thankful for you."

Lone Crow watched as Bird's bottom lip began to quiver
slightly and could not stop himself from leaning down and
kissing her.

The Warrior meant for it to be a quick peck but when Bird
reached for him, he pulled her closer and kissed her deeply.

"Faith," Wilma called, sounding irritated.

The woman was aggravating to Lone Crow but he felt Bird smile against him and his anger disappeared.

"We should be going," Bird said, sounding disappointed in her statement.

Lone Crow smiled and slowly moved away from their embrace. "I know we should," he agreed. "But I do enjoy kissing you."

The Warrior noticed his voice had deepened and enjoyed watching Bird swoon.

"Lone Crow."

The impatient voice belonged to the Chief and when Lone Crow looked up, he could see everyone on a horse and waiting for them.

Lone Crow was certain the Leader was expecting an apology but the Warrior just couldn't muster one up. And it didn't help that Bird was giggling. It was a sound he hadn't heard in years and he did not feel the slightest bit bad about taking the time to be happy.

Otter was the only one waiting who seemed to be enjoying the ease Lone Crow and Bird were sharing.

"Here are your horses," the old man said, pointing at two waiting ponies.

Lone Crow saw Bird's disappointment when Otter spoke.

"We will be riding together," he informed everyone as he reached for Bird and helped her get on the horse before sliding into place behind her.

Lone Crow was sure the other members of their party had feelings about his decision but did not bother to look at any of them until they were headed out of the village.

Otter's pony was pulling a travois that was packed with everything the group would need for at least a week without stopping to hunt. Lone Crow was hopeful that if their party crossed paths with others, it would appear that they were simply trying to return two lost women. But he would not allow the thought to continue. He wanted to talk only to Bird. So he slowed his ride and waited for Otter to ride beside him.

His father looked at him with a knowing grin on his face but Lone Crow could see there was more going on in his father's mind than the man was sharing. But because of his need for intimacy with Bird, he chose not to question the man.

"We will travel until the sun is up and then begin looking for a place to camp. The waterhole is not a good idea but we will try to stop close enough to travel there," the old man informed Lone Crow.

"We will follow behind," the Warrior told his father, shocked at how uncomfortable the conversation was.

Lone Crow decided that when the task at hand was seen to an end, he would take the time to speak to his father and let him know how much the man meant to him. It was a talk that Lone Crow knew he couldn't put off for long, when in truth, it was a conversation he wished he could put off for years to come.

"What are you saying?" Bird asked, using an extremely calm tone.

Lone Crow was pleased that he had been able to keep at bay any thought of the trip not ending well. But still, he felt the sting of his conscience. It was not like him to keep anything from Bird or tell half-truths. And even after understanding what he was doing, he couldn't seem to force himself to tell her any more than she already knew.

"I was just telling my father that we will be following behind," he answered, patting her on the leg before resting his hand on her thigh.

The Warrior heard Bird's sharp intake of breath and felt as she arched her back against him.

"How long will it take until we reach a town or a ranch?" she asked.

Wilma had asked the same question earlier but Bird's query failed to embody the excitement Wilma's had.

"I do not know," he answered truthfully as he rested his chin on the top of her head. "But I hope it's not for a few days at least."

"What happens if Wilma does not cooperate?" she asked quietly.

Lone Crow knew she deserved an answer but he still wasn't ready to share the details with her, at least not yet.

"I am sure she will," he answered, hoping his tone conveyed the confidence he lacked.

Bird seemed to either believe his statement, or at the very least, want to believe it because she quickly changed the subject.

"She is with child. And the baby could very easily be Tobias'," she informed him effortlessly.

"She is with child?" he asked, wanting to be sure he hadn't misheard her statement.

The news was delivered in such a blasé manner, he didn't know whether to apologize for Bird's further humiliation or hold her tighter in an attempt to make her feel safer. He wished he had more time to continue to ask the woman about her feelings but the news she had just told him was too important not to garner his full attention. If Wilma were carrying a child, then there was no way Pathkiller would have the heart to kill her. It also brought up a whole new set of problems.

"She says she is. Why?" Bird asked as she laid her hand atop his.

"It is news that needs to be shared with Pathkiller," Lone Crow answered.

Bird sighed deeply and sat up straight. "Why isn't it as easy to talk to you as it was when we were young?" she asked, turning to look at the Warrior.

Tears were pooling in her eyes and she looked confused and hurt by her own question.

Her emotions tore at his heart.

"I am sorry. When we were young, everything was easier. It was us against the world," he answered as he steered his pony to a quicker pace. "Now it seems that everyone is against us and even we are swayed by the talk."

Lone Crow knew he had said too much when Bird collapsed against him and he felt her shoulders begin to shake. He knew she was crying and wanted nothing more than to be able to stop and comfort her. But the news he was carrying was just too important to be put off.

The Warrior moved his hand and wrapped it around her waist. "All is not lost, Tsisqua," he soothed. "We will have time."

"I hope so because, damnit, I deserve to be happy," she agreed, before sniffing and once again laying her head against his chest.

They passed Otter and were greeted with a smile. The Chief was a few paces in front of his father and Wilma was riding beside Pathkiller. She did not appear to be experiencing any uncomfortableness and seemed to be entranced by the man.

"You don't look happy," Wilma spoke as soon as she realized Lone Crow and Bird were close by.

Bird sniffed and turned to look at the woman. "I told you I would end up broken before this was all over."

Bird's statement surprised both Wilma and Lone Crow.

"You must have faith in me," he said, holding her tighter before kissing her on the top of the head. "We will stop soon and I promise we will be alone and everything will be easier. Our world has gotten bigger but when we shut that world out, we will be able to enjoy each other," he vowed before shifting his attention to Pathkiller.

The Chief was waiting to hear why Lone Crow rode to catch up with him. His expression was one of concern and fatigue. "Does this woman know that she is speaking a language I do not understand?" he asked, looking from Lone Crow to Wilma.

"I am sure she does. Why do you ask?" Lone Crow knew his news was important but he suddenly needed to understand why the Chief was looking so haggard.

"She has not stopped speaking since we left the village. Please explain to her that there is no need. I do not understand."

At any other time in Lone Crow's adult life, he would have found the Chief's predicament funny. But he didn't.

"I will do my best," he replied. "But I have news that will change everything."

Pathkiller instantly looked more aware when he heard Lone Crow's statement.

"What is that?" he asked.

"Wilma is with child," the Warrior informed the Leader.

Lone Crow got no joy from delivering the news. He knew it changed everything and he had no idea how to fix things but it wasn't his decision.

Pathkiller rolled his eyes and looked to the heavens. "We will smoke while the women sleep," he decided after giving his answer some thought.

It was not what Lone Crow wanted to hear.

"I wish I could understand you," Bird spoke barely above a whisper. Lone Crow heard her declaration and felt a mixture of pride and the ever-present sadness.

"I will teach you a few words," he informed her before returning his attention to the slow-moving Chief. "I would like to spend time with Bird. If I am not needed…"

"But you are needed," Pathkiller interrupted, using his authoritative voice. "There will be time for you to spend with the woman later."

Lone Crow hid his reaction to the news and nodded politely at Pathkiller before stopping his pony, allowing the others to move away.

"What happened now?" Bird asked as she turned at the waist to face him.

"Our reunion has been delayed again," he answered honestly, not hiding his disappointment.

Bird looked disappointed but slowly smiled before she leaned in to kiss him.

"No one will stop this from happening. Not Wilma, or your dad, or the Chief. I will not allow it," she spoke with determination.

Lone Crow smiled and remembered the gift the Chief had given him. After reaching into his medicine bag, he caressed the soft leather and beautiful beading before reaching around Bird and showing it to her. The Warrior was pleased when a squeal left Bird's lips as she took it from him.

"This is beautiful," she gushed, holding the small bag against her heart. "No one has ever given me a gift as beautiful before. Thank you so much. I will keep this with me always. It will be the one thing I have to remember you," she said, sounding as if she were once again on the verge of giving into tears.

The gift was meant to make her happy, and it had. But as soon as she began to think of the future, her mood darkened. Lone Crow wanted to do everything in his power to keep her from thinking about the next day. Today was all that mattered.

"It dims to your beauty," he argued lightly. "But I am glad you like it. Now, while we ride, tell me about your life. And know this. I do not wish to hear about your marriage," he added quickly before continuing to coax the woman into a normal easy conversation. "What did you want to do when you were finally free from Father Silas?"

"My life is depressing. Tell me about you. How did you end up with these people? Are they your family? Just talk to me. And please don't stop holding me."

Lone Crow let go of his horse's mane and wrapped both arms around her. "The first thing I did when I thought I was safe and free of any man hunting me down was prayed that we would see each other again and if not, that you would live a full, happy life."

Bird moved away slightly and placed the leather bag around her neck before again pressing it to her heart. A sound of contentment left her lips when she heard the Warrior's answer. "Keep talking. Just hearing your voice makes me happy. But before you continue, please tell me things will work out alright."

Lone Crow heard the need in her voice and almost immediately decided to tell her what she wanted to hear, whether it was the truth or not.

## Chapter Thirty-Four

Our reunion might have been delayed once again and I was convinced Moses was keeping things from me but I was still happier than I had ever been. It was maddening that we couldn't just have a conversation like we had when we were young. But Moses was right when he said our world was bigger. So, I held on to hope that once we were alone, it would be more natural.

Wilma was a constant concern because even if the plan was a sound one, I still wasn't sure the fate of Moses' people was in good hands.

There were many things I should have been worrying about but as long as I was being cocooned by Moses, I couldn't feel anything other than joy and comfort. In fact, I wouldn't allow my brain to think of what could happen after Moses and I were alone. I had spoken to Wilma about the only future I saw for myself. A future without Moses. As bleak as it sounded, it was the future for me. Of course, as I rode with my head resting on his muscular chest and cradling the beautiful bag in my hand, I did fantasize about life with Moses. I desperately wanted the world to be one where we could walk into town together and start a family. But the idea was just as preposterous as me staying with him. And just as deadly for the man I loved.

"You are supposed to be telling me about your family," I reminded as I brazenly moved his resting hand a little further up my thigh.

I was a grown woman and absolutely not a virgin but the reaction my body had to Moses' hand was extraordinarily pleasurable and something I had never experienced before.

When I heard a soft moan escape his lips, a warmth spread from my lower belly to my toes.

"Otter found me and took me to the village. The people have treated me well and allowed me to hold onto ways and behaviors which are strange to them. I was so frightened for the first few years, I wouldn't allow anyone to touch me," Moses continued, sounding as if he were far away.

I placed my hand atop his and gently squeezed it. "I am glad you found some peace," I said because it was the truth.

It warmed my heart to know he had years to be free and loved without fear. And it reinforced my desire to feel and act the same way for the time we had.

"I always hoped the same for you," he replied, sounding saddened.

"No," I stated as I patted his hand and sat up a little straighter before turning and looking at him. "We will not speak of anything that makes us sad. We will speak of only good things."

I was determined but even as I spoke my thoughts, I began to understand that Moses and I didn't have many good times in our youth. There were occasions when we would giggle about some of the hats women wore to church or something funny we saw on the way to church but most of the time we were together, one of us was comforting the other. The discovery caused a pain in my heart. Did I remember more than there was to our relationship? Was I asking for an easy conversation when we had never actually had one before? Did he love me, or was he only overcome with guilt? Was I making a fool of myself?

"I remember one happy time we shared," Moses spoke before leaning down and kissing me. "The first time we did that."

His eyes were hooded and he was breathing in a slightly labored manner.

Moses' reaction to kissing me was enough to banish any of the questions I'd been fretting over a second earlier. And once again, I was sure that he was all I needed. He would fix everything. And the memories we made would keep me going until I died.

Since I was momentarily struck speechless, he smiled and kissed me again.

"We have much to talk about," he promised as he slowly pulled away from me. "But this is not the place."

I went from excited to disappointed in the time it took for him to end his thought.

"I know there is more going on than you've told me and I understand you are concerned about Wilma. And please do not tell me why that is," I added when it looked like Moses was readying to interrupt me.

When I placed my finger against his lips to silence the interruption, he smiled and kissed it, all the while looking into my soul.

"All right," I stammered as I slowly turned back around. "Who were the men who attacked our wagons and why did they do that?" I asked, knowing if I didn't turn around and change the subject, I would end up being disappointed when we stopped for the day and we couldn't continue kissing.

Moses cleared his throat before answering. "They are Shawnee and I can only imagine they attacked you because we had taken most of their horses and you were an easy target. Of course, they must not have been thinking clearly. And before you ask, they will be punished," he answered in a breathy tone.

I tried to pay attention to his answer but it was challenging to think straight. And since I very much wanted him to continue to talk, I again changed the course of the conversation.

"Did you ever marry?" I asked before I could stop myself.

It was a loaded question, at best, and I had no idea where it came from. Moses didn't seem to want to discuss Tobias and the knot that formed in the pit of my belly was a good sign I really didn't want to hear if Moses had found love with someone else.

But I had asked and the question hung in the air for a few seconds.

Before Moses answered, he pulled me back into his chest and inched his resting hand a little bit further up my thigh.

"I have known women," he stated flatly. "But even as I laid with them, my thoughts were with you. I may have been blessed with the family who found me but I couldn't stay with them for long. I would run and seek solitude whenever I remembered Father Silas. And strangely enough, those thoughts were brought on by the most mundane things. But I wouldn't allow myself to believe you were anything other than happy with many children. The truth is, I am still broken. I hadn't seen another white man until your wagons came into the village. Seeing the men helped me to heal some and then I saw you. I had no idea how your life was. I couldn't know you weren't madly in love with your man. But when I saw you again, I knew it was always you. You were a girl when you captured my heart and it has always been with you."

Moses' declaration was the most beautiful thing I had ever heard and it was impossible to not cry.

My tears were not from sadness alone. I was touched to my core by the things he was saying but devastated because there was no future. Still, I had the present and I had decided to make the most of it. So, I wiped my eyes and nestled deeper into him.

"I have never spoken so openly about my feelings," he offered when I continued my silence. "That is a start."

"It is," I agreed quickly. "You know, I thought I had been able to put you out of my mind and then Tobias brought you up. I still didn't consider there was a chance we would travel to the village you lived in. After he talked about you, I couldn't drive the memories away. I think I still blamed you a little but that was wrong of me. I know now if you had taken me, they would have hunted us down and killed you. But, here we are, together again and I have no husband in the way."

I stopped talking because I could hear how I sounded. Tobias had beat me for years, threatened to kill me on several occasions, and I had fantasies about killing him myself. I did understand that I should be sad that he was dead, and feel guilt over wanting another man so quickly. I just couldn't force myself to feel those emotions. But I wasn't sure I didn't sound cold-hearted. And I didn't believe that was the case. Tobias was a man whom I didn't love. At first, before he showed me his real self, I tried to make myself believe it would be a loving marriage. I had read enough books to understand; sometimes, it takes some time to get to know a person. My childish dreams did not last long.

But I felt love for Moses, a deep, profound love; even if the voice in the back of my mind still wanted to know if he felt the same. I worried for him and was willing to be strong and not cause a scene when we parted forever.

"Tsisqua," he said, pulling me from the increasingly stressful thoughts. "You are perfect in my eyes and always will be."

I smiled and laid my hand on his knee. I was well aware of how selfish I was being in wanting the man all to myself but I still did.

"When are we going to stop?" I asked, not bothering to hide my eagerness.

I heard Moses sigh before rubbing his chin on the top of my head. "Not soon enough. I will set up a shelter for you and Wilma while the others finish the camp. Pathkiller has informed me that we will talk while the two of you are resting. The meeting will not last long and after we have scouted the area I plan on coming to you and we will take a long walk. How does that sound?"

"It sounds like heaven. I am sleepy, though," I admitted. "So I will nap while you are busy."

Our reunion had been put off several times but the mere thought that we had another chance was enough for me to feel almost giddy with excitement.

"If we stop close to the water hole, we could go there," he offered, sounding slightly apprehensive.

I understood his concern. It was a beautiful spot but it was the spot I lost my husband. Again I was faced with accepting my true emotions and tried to not feel guilt.

"I think that would be a nice place," I agreed, still attempting to talk myself into being accepting of my feelings and not sorry.

"I saw you bathing before you came to the village," He admitted before removing his hand from my waist and gently turning me to face him. "And you were looking away but I knew there was something about you. I felt I knew you but told myself it was just too much to ask."

As soon as he finished speaking, I leaned in and kissed him. It was not a very comfortable position and I was readying myself to turn when I heard Otter call Moses' name.

He smiled and directed his attention to his father.

I watched as the two carried on a conversation. Otter seemed to be a happy man but his eyes were expressive and even if he hadn't wanted me to see it, I knew he was troubled.

Moses didn't raise his voice or sound as if he was arguing. I had no idea what was being said but I did enjoy the way the language sounded. It was similar to the other language I'd heard but the Cherokee was almost lyrical and strong at the same time.

While I was waiting for the two to finish, I remembered Moses promised to teach me a few words. I knew it was pointless and I would never hear the language again but I very much wanted to learn to say I love you.

Otter nodded and smiled at me before turning his pony and moving away.

"We will stop soon. Father says he thinks Wilma is taken with Pathkiller," Moses informed me with humor in his tone.

At first, the thought terrified me, next, I didn't think it was possible, and I finally settled on finding it just as amusing as Moses.

"If that would help her to understand why lying is the only thing we can do, then I am all for it. But please believe I am not above telling her about herself," I informed him after I settled back against Moses' chest.

"I do understand your desire to do just that but we need to be gentle with her. I wish everything didn't depend on her."

I was sure Moses thought he was being covert but suddenly I understood, or at least had a good idea, what was at stake. And I didn't like it one little bit. Not for a second did I believe Moses would allow Wilma or me to be hurt but I was still shaken to the core when the reality sunk in.

"They are planning on killing us, aren't they?" I asked before I could stop myself.

Moses stopped the pony and turned me to look at him.

Before he could answer, I spoke. "I know you won't allow it but they are considering that, aren't they? What are you going to do?" I continued to interrogate him while the panic settled in.

"I will not let that happen. And Wilma is with child so that changes everything. That is why Pathkiller wishes to speak to us. You have to believe I will not let anything bad happen to you. As long as I am near, you will be safe."

I believed him but accepting just how close to death I had been for the last few days was still difficult to digest.

"What can you do other than trust she will not tell the truth someday?" I asked because I really wanted to know the answer.

# Chapter Thirty-Five

The ride was enjoyable and something he never dared to wish for. Even in his dreams, he hadn't seen any way that they would be together again.

Lone Crow was not the type of man to exhibit affection but found he enjoyed doing so. And Bird appeared to be just as eager. But he did understand her questioning why their attempts at conversation were strained. He had spoken the truth when he said they had more going on in their lives but he wasn't convinced that was the real reason.

He loved Bird and would do what was best for her but he wondered if he weren't holding back in some way. The Warrior was aware of just how bad it was going to hurt to tell her goodbye. It would be the last time, there was no other way. Lone Crow would hope and pray she was well and he would enter into a new phase of his life where he would be more careless. The Warrior had escaped death many times over the years and he wondered if he hadn't done so because he still had a task to accomplish. Seeing Bird safely back to her people was that task and once it was complete, he would be fighting against time. But he had no plans of dying without taking many of his enemies with him. There was no depressive state lingering in the back of his mind. A small part of him valiantly fought to believe there still was a way he and Bird could live happily ever after but as difficult as it was to shut those wishes down, he did. There were truths and rules that came along with the invaders and it was what it was. One Warrior couldn't change that and if he tried, would it be the right thing to do by Bird?

Lone Crow did find it effortless to express how much she meant to him and needed her to believe he would not allow anything bad to happen. But he made sure to add 'as long as he was near.' He hadn't thought explaining that statement further would be a good idea. Bird seemed to calm and accept his words. Telling her the truth of the matter would cause her distress. The truth was, he would die trying to protect her and Wilma but if Pathkiller killed him, well, that would be the end of his protection. It was a hard truth but it was the truth.

Her excitement and willingness to spend time alone with him made it almost impossible to think about anything else but he tried to keep their conversation and contact to a level that was safe. Making love to her was all he could think about. And then Bird asked the question that snapped him out of his daydream. It was also a query he would have rather not answered.

He had already assured her that he wouldn't allow her to be hurt and she had already surmised that her and Wilma's lives were in the balance. Wilma being with child did change things but he wasn't sure how much. It was still vital that the woman keep the secret of what really transpired. Trusting her was still a long shot and placed a lot of responsibility squarely in Bird's hands. If the plan was to work to perfection, Bird would have to stay close to Wilma for the rest of her life. The obligation everyone assumed Bird would gladly accept, came with its own set of drawbacks. He had questions but knew no one had any answers. And that knowledge was maddening. But he did not want to burden Bird with the truths of the situation until he had to. It may very well have been selfish on his part but he wanted her happy and carefree for as long as she could be.

"So, you don't want to tell me?" Bird asked, employing a docile, unbothered tone.

"I would rather talk about things that are not difficult," he admitted. "And believe that this is all part of a bigger plan. One where things work as they are supposed to."

Bird giggled and Lone Crow's heart stopped. The sound was so pure and clean; it washed him in joy.

"You are beautiful," he said into her hair. "Do you not believe we were meant to come together again?"

The Warrior attempted to keep his tone light but the question was vital to him and he found he needed to hear her answer.

"I want to believe this wasn't just a wonderful coincidence," she admitted. "But I am glad it did happen. I guess I am having problems with accepting this was all part of a master plan if the ending is so tragic."

Lone Crow was taken aback by her raw honestly and once again gently turned her and kissed her deeply.

He wanted to tell her just how hard saying goodbye was going to be. He knew he couldn't put off telling her all the information he was keeping from her but, he just couldn't. Nor could he argue with her assessment of their situation.

"There is always hope," he found himself assuring her without having any proof of his statement.

The Warrior wanted to believe his declaration as badly as he wanted her to.

Bird sighed deeply. "Moses," she began as she sat forward and turned to him. "My plan is to forget our situation and all the unknowns it entails and to enjoy you. I do know it may be wrong but that is what I plan to do. We will be blissfully happy and intentionally ignorant for the remainder of the trip. Does that sound like a good idea to you?" she asked as she inched closer to Lone Crow. When she finished speaking, they were lip to lip.

Lone Crow looked to the heavens for help and quickly took her face in his hands and slowly opened her mouth with his before nipping gently at her bottom lip.

Bird surprised him when she moaned and pressed herself closer to him.

"Lone Crow, every time I seek to tell you anything, you are entangled with the woman," Otter stated, causing the Warrior to quickly finish their kiss before turning and looking at his father.

Otter was not wrong but Lone Crow was not about to apologize for his actions so he was relieved when he saw his father was still smiling. The old man still had a concerned look in his eyes but he seemed less stressed than when they left the village.

Bird smiled shyly and the Warrior noticed her face reddened as she righted herself and looked forward.

"Because I love this woman," he answered truthfully.

Otter shook his head and waited until Lone Crow's pony caught up to his.

"Pathkiller and the woman have stopped and they are waiting on us," he informed his son. "Our Leader does not seem to be in a patient mood, so we should hurry."

Otter's voice was serious but there was a spark of humor in the old man's eyes.

Lone Crow was enjoying the easiness he was experiencing with his father but did feel as if he was leaving Bird out of the conversation. So, he took a moment to tell her what had been said.

"Earlier, Wilma was telling me well, practically threatening me, by telling me I would be an outcast if anyone found out about our relationship and now, she is acting as if your Chief is fascinating. I don't know whether to laugh or cry," she said, shaking her head and resting back against Lone Crow's chest.

Lone Crow had to tamp the irritation that rose as soon as he heard Wilma had threatened Bird. And after telling himself that chastising the woman would do no good and could cause irreparable harm did he relay what Bird told him to his father.

Otter smirked and shook his head. "The woman is strange but she is the result of her environment. We, well, you and your Bird, will have to make her see that we are not all the same. It will not be an easy job but if we are not successful, then everything changes."

Lone Crow was still desperately trying to maintain his block on all the things that could go wrong so he was not pleased when he realized Otter was right.

He had already prepared Bird for the eventuality but had somehow left himself out of the situation. He realized he had an important part to play and he accepted it begrudgingly. Spending time with Wilma was not something he was looking forward to but he placated himself by remembering Bird would be beside him. They may not be totally alone but they would be together. As soon as he accepted that, he nodded his head in a respectful but dismissive manner and turned his attention back to Bird.

"We will be spending time with Wilma. I believe it is our best hope in convincing her to do ask we ask," he informed her gently.

"As long as we are together it won't be so bad," she replied softly.

Lone Crow could hear the heaviness in her voice and knew she was growing tired.

"We will stop here," he said, pointing to a wooded area where Pathkiller was working and Wilma was sitting atop her horse watching the man intently.

Bird moved her head slowly from side to side before speaking. "She is looking at him like I look at you," she appraised, sleepily.

Bird's opinion only served to excite the Warrior more. But he did his best to stay in the moment and not in his head.

"I know you are tired," Lone Crow stated as he slowed his pony to a stop. "But I need to get down so I can build your shelter," he continued as he quickly turned her and planted a kiss before sliding from his pony's back.

Once on the ground, he held his hands out for her to fall into.

"Allow me," Otter offered, moving Lone Crow out of the way. "If you help her down, we will all have to watch the two of you embrace once again. While it is beautiful to see two young people in love, we have a job to do."

Lone Crow couldn't be angry with his father. He was right and there was no malice in the old man's tone, only a touch of sadness.

Bird stayed atop the horse and looked at Lone Crow in question. "What happened?" she asked as she turned her attention to Otter, who was still standing with his arms outstretched.

"Hillo," he said smiling broadly, while he wiggled his fingers.

"He says if he helps you down, we will set up camp quicker," Lone Crow explained.

She smiled warmly at Otter and effortlessly slid into his arms.

The fact that the woman he loved and his father shared a relaxed relationship warmed his heart.

The calmness of the situation was broken when Pathkiller spoke.

"This would go a lot faster if I had some help," he stated, stopping what he was doing to address the others.

The Chief's tone was one of near exhaustion and Lone Crow wondered if the man's condition was all because of a white woman, one who was still watching the Chief with much interest.

"Come," Otter urged, shepherding both Bird and Lone Crow closer to the center of the grove of trees.

"I will talk to Wilma while you are busy," Bird said, looking across the old man and smiling at Lone Crow.

"And I will work as fast as possible," Lone Crow promised, before once again reminding himself that Pathkiller's predicament was not as funny as he thought.

## Chapter Thirty-Six

I was practically floating when I stood on my own. Otter smiled and backed away. Moses stood still until his father grabbed him and pulled him in the direction of the Chief. When my true feelings began flowing from my mouth, I was afraid I would say something to frighten Moses. But he didn't shy away. He spoke the same words to me. And I was not about to allow the little voice in the back of my head to even speak. I was well aware of the time constraints on our relationship but I had never been so ready to accept the fallout.

Still, I was a little shocked to witness Wilma's change in attitude. At least I hoped her attitude had changed because she was looking at Pathkiller in a way I'd never seen her look at Howard or Tobias. And, I very badly wanted to ask her why it was acceptable for her to act like that but it wasn't for me. But because I did not want to do anything to upset the chances of the plan working out, I bit my tongue and smiled as I walked to her.

She was oblivious to my nearness so when I called her name, she was startled and looked at me as if I were interrupting her. Her reaction only made it so I had to bite my tongue harder.

"How was the ride?" I asked, with all the forced curiosity I could muster.

"I am tired and hungry again," she answered, giving me only half of her attention. "But I can see some truth in what you were saying earlier," she admitted quickly.

I smiled and reached to help her down from the pony. "I am glad to hear that," I stated because I knew she wanted a reaction and it was all I could think to say.

276 Elizabeth Anne Porter

I was overjoyed at the sudden turn of events. But I had suffered too many disappointments in my life to believe she had magically changed her fundamental thinking. So, I was leery but was not going to share my concerns with her.

She slid into my arms and thankfully, we did not end up on the ground.

"You really do love that man, don't you?" she asked, again effortlessly turning her attention from me to the three men who were quickly setting up a beautiful camp.

Instead of answering, I reached for her arm and gently pulled her toward the nearest clear spot.

She followed but not without dragging her feet.

"I do wish I could tell the Leader thank you," she mused as I pointed to the ground and waited for her to sit down. "No. I think I need to stretch my feet. I am not used to riding this much," she continued as she began walking back to the working men.

I reached for her arm to slow her movement. "They are busy and we will have time later," I informed her.

It was difficult to not follow her and gawk at the men. But I knew it was best if I continued to work on Wilma while she was pliable.

The woman had endured much over the last few days. I was sure she was still suffering from the lingering effects of shock but I also knew her pining over the Leader of Moses' band was not going to end well. So, I was going to have to walk on eggshells. But that was something I had done for the whole of my life.

"You said you were hungry again," I reminded her as we began to walk the perimeter of the small camp. "I am sure we will eat as soon as possible. And the reason we didn't travel far is because they know we need to rest. I am pleased you are changing your views."

Wilma didn't seem to hear anything I said so I stopped talking but continued to walk beside her.

"How will we know for sure that the murderers will pay?" she asked, sounding deep in thought as she carefully walked over a fallen limb blocking her path.

After I tripped, I thought about what answer she wanted to hear.

"M ...Lone Crow," I corrected myself before continuing to share my name for the man. "Lone Crow asked you if you maybe wanted a body part," I reminded her before I slapped my hands over my mouth.

She stopped and turned to me with a horrified look on her face before her expression turned a little dark.

"I am trying to be as helpful in this situation as I can. I do not need a sign because, quite frankly, how would I know if the body part belonged to the murderers. But I want assurance."

My attempts at being sweet and helpful were being pushed to their limits but I smiled at her and nodded my head to show her I understood her desire.

I wasn't as concerned with the Shawnee's punishment and knew Wilma had every right to be angry and hurt but it frustrated me that she hadn't taken Moses at his word; because I had. The man had never lied to me so I couldn't imagine he would do so when the situation was so dire. Keeping things from me for my own protection, which I was sure he was doing, was different than lying to me.

After taking several cleansing breaths, I looked at the men.

They had finished setting up a comfortable, covered place for Wilma and me to rest in and the fire pit was ready to be lit. Several furs were laid out and Otter was leaving the lean-to with a smile on his face.

Pathkiller was busy starting the fire and Moses was walking toward us with a solid look of satisfaction.

I could tell it was forced but hoped it was because he knew he was going to have to speak to Wilma and not because we were facing yet another delay to our time alone.

"Wilma, Tsisqua," he greeted before holding his hand out to me.

I moved closer without pause and held his hand tightly.

"The shelter is ready and we have food and water. If you would like, go inside and sleep. Or you can stay here and eat with us. The choice is yours."

Wilma looked around us and at the Chief before answering. "I am tired," she admitted. "But I might enjoy eating with other people."

Moses smiled and gestured for Wilma to walk ahead and pulled me into a hug as soon as she was on her way.

"Are you sure you want this?" he whispered in my ear, with a desperation in his voice that made my knees buckle.

"I am. I honestly don't believe I have ever been so ready or looking forward to anything as much as I am looking forward to being with you," I answered, cringing when I realized how tongue-tied I was.

He made a noise that was a cross between a low growl and a moan before nipping at my earlobe. I was slightly disappointed when he righted himself and we began taking the few steps to join the others.

Nothing was being said but everyone gathered was watching us. It did make me a little uncomfortable so I moved a little further behind Moses.

"They are jealous," Moses assured, before turning and kissing me.

I heard both Pathkiller and Otter speaking to Moses so I wasn't shocked when the Warrior slowly pulled away from me.

"I will go back to the tent if you don't mind. I want to be rested when you come for me," I explained, still breathing in a labored manner.

"And while you are resting, I will be trying to think of something other than you," he informed me in a deep voice.

I smiled and was sure I blushed before I nodded my goodbyes to everyone except Wilma. I walked to where she was sitting and looked down at her before leaving.

"Lone Crow may be able to help you speak to Pathkiller," I informed her, hoping I was not making the situation even more perilous.

For reasons I couldn't explain, I felt that if Wilma got to know the people, she would see they were not so different than we were.

Wilma smiled and blushed before eagerly taking a strip of dried meat from Otter's outstretched hand.

"I will join you shortly," she assured me after turning her attention back to the men.

I knew when I was being dismissed so I turned to look at Moses one more time before leaving.

He was watching me with hunger in his eyes and I found it quite arousing but I forced myself to behave like a lady and walk to my new shelter.

There wasn't much to the dwelling. Thick branches were laid strategically and covered with a few thin strips of leather. It was surprisingly roomy inside. The men had laid out robes and the whole of the floor was covered with them. There was no fire pit inside but when the opening was uncovered, a beam of light permeated the space. It looked inviting and I was looking forward to resting. Sleep would have been wonderful but I doubted if I could calm myself down enough to achieve it.

After debating where to sleep, I decided to stay near the entrance but not so close that Wilma might trip over me.

I hadn't bothered to close the flap so a cool breeze was blowing through the lean-to. Everything was conducive to sleep so I took several deep breaths, rolled to my side, and clenched my eyes shut. After tossing and turning several times, I settled on my back and looked up at the intertwined limbs.

I was suddenly afraid I would disappoint Moses in some way. It was a terrifying thought so I quickly pushed it from my mind and concentrated on the conversation taking place around the fire.

They were speaking in a normal tone but I had to really listen to make out what was being said.

I didn't feel as if I were eavesdropping and hoped the sound of Moses' voice might help me to attain some sleep.

"So, I have your Leader's word that they will be punished for their crimes?" I heard Wilma ask.

The woman was nothing if not persistent.

After Moses spoke to the others in Cherokee, he answered Wilma.

"We can promise that," Moses assured. "And in doing so, we do hope you will tell the townspeople the wagons were swept away by a strong current."

"Will they believe that?" she asked quickly. "Does that happen?"

"It does. Quite often. The water is dangerous."

It sounded to me like Moses was growing a little impatient with Wilma and I didn't blame him.

I heard more Cherokee before Moses spoke again.

"Pathkiller says he understands your concerns but hopes you understand why we need you to misinform your people. Most of the settlers care little about which of us did what. It is easier to take out their anger and aggression on the first band they come into contact with. We have been in our home for many years and do our best to live in peace with you. But the truth in this instance would do nothing more than cause a war. A war we do not want. It will be difficult to keep a secret and we do not ask lightly."

When Moses stopped to take a breath, Wilma interrupted.

"I really am terrible with secrets," she stated shyly.

In my opinion, she was not speaking the truth. She had kept her affair with Tobias secret enough. And I wondered if she were not attempting to appear coy with the men. It was an extremely interesting turn for her and the longer she did it, the more I wondered if she weren't still in shock. Her attitude had changed in the span of a few hours and although I did find some humor in her actions, I was more offended by them than anything. And the more I thought about her, the more worked up I got.

How dare her? She had threatened me with my relationship with Moses and was blatantly flirting with Pathkiller. My emotions quickly went from indignance to concern when I wondered if the strain might have been too much for her and something in her brain had broken. While I continued to hear what I could, I decided we were going to have a heart to heart talk.

"I know this is really none of my business," I heard Wilma preface. "But why do you choose to love someone you cannot have?" she asked, employing a tone that sounded as if she were genuinely interested in the answer.

My answer to that question was easy enough. I wanted to be happy for as long as I could but I waited anxiously to hear Moses' reply.

Moses didn't answer her right away. I heard him talking to the other men first.

"You know nothing of our relationship," he began in a gentle tone. "I have loved Bird since we met. I will love her until my last heartbeat. Life is not always easy and rarely is it filled with joy. So, where I would much rather spend the rest of my life trying to make her happy, I will be content with a few short days."

I believe I actually melted when I heard his declaration. And found it difficult not to get up and run to the man.

"You would want to keep her with you?" Wilma asked, employing a tone of disbelief.

The woman had missed all the beautiful things Moses had said and homed in on the one soft spot.

"If there was a chance and she would agree, I would ride into the wilderness with her. But that is not possible. So, I would very much like to get this meeting over," he informed her.

"Oh," she replied, sounding embarrassed when she understood the meaning behind Moses' words; she had overstayed her welcome.

"My father will escort you if you would like," Moses offered.

"Oh, no. I can walk. Would you please tell your Chief I said thank you for taking care of me?" she asked, sounding like she was just outside the opening.

"If you like, I will teach you the word tomorrow and you can tell him yourself," Moses offered.

"Thank you," she stated, sounding like she meant it.

I was torn. I did need to talk to her to ensure her sanity was intact but I also needed to rest because I did not want to miss a moment with Moses. So while I lay there and waited for her to enter, I held tightly to the beaded bag Moses gifted me before slipping it inside my dress. It was one more thing I wanted to keep to myself.

"I will do as you ask, Faith. And I think it would be best if we try to be friends. We will share this secret until we are old and gray," she informed me while she began moving the robes and making herself comfortable.

I wanted to believe her. I really did. But in my experience Wilma was mercurial.

"I am glad you feel better," I said, purposely sounding half-asleep. "We will talk more when we wake up."

Once she was settled, I again tried to listen to the voices but only heard a low, beautiful chant. It was not long before I drifted off to sleep.

## Chapter Thirty-Eight

As soon as Bird was inside the structure, Lone Crow's mind returned to the task at hand.

Wilma's prolonged presence was delaying the meeting but he knew there was prudence in talking to the woman. And Wilma seemed to be smitten with Pathkiller, so there were signs that the woman was beginning to understand the wisdom in doing as they asked. An event that made Lone Crow happy because he did not want to fight his father or his Leader. And as uncharacteristic as it was, he didn't want to listen to the men while they smoked a pipe and discussed what Wilma's pregnancy changed. He wanted to go get Bird and walk to the waterhole.

After again explaining the situation and answering questions from Wilma that he considered a little too personal, she reluctantly rose to leave.

When the Warrior offered to teach the woman a few words of his language, he smiled. Not because he was attempting to be helpful but because he knew it would add to Pathkiller's dismay.

Once Wilma left, the Warrior returned to a seated position between his father and Pathkiller and did his best not to appear as anxious as he felt.

"That woman seems taken with you," Otter stated, looking like if he didn't speak his mind, he might explode.

Lone Crow stifled a smile and looked toward the Leader to gauge his reaction to the declaration.

284 Elizabeth Anne Porter

Pathkiller did not appear to enjoy the tone in Otter's voice any more than he liked the smile Lone Crow found impossible to hide.

"I think she will ride with you tomorrow," he decided as he pointed to Otter in a slightly threatening manner.

Again it was difficult for Lone Crow to not find humor in Pathkiller's situation. And if he hadn't desired the time alone with Bird, he would have continued to engage in the conversation.

"So this meeting is over?" he asked hopefully.

When he saw Pathkiller reach for his bag and pull his pipe out, the Warrior knew he was not going to be able to leave.

"I understand your need to be with your woman," Pathkiller prefaced as he began filling the bowl of the pipe while watching Lone Crow closely. "But it is an act of futility."

Lone Crow did not like the direction the conversation was going and definitely had an issue with the Chief's last statement. But before he could ensure his response would be calm and emotionless, Otter spoke.

"He will not listen to honesty," the old man said in a light-hearted way.

"We rarely do when the heart is so deeply involved," Pathkiller agreed as he raised the pipe to his lips.

Lone Crow was growing more unhappy with his situation with each passing second.

He was not one to enjoy being told what to do and he absolutely did not enjoy being talked about like he wasn't there.

"I do understand just how much you are giving up for the people," Pathkiller stated thoughtfully. "And I do wish these events would have gone differently. There is still a very good possibility that one, if not all of us will be fired on. Until the women are back in the white man's hands, none of us are guaranteed to survive. And as badly as I would like to put distance between the woman called Wilma and myself, I will not. It will be my duty to bear the uncomfortable weight. Since we have no need to rest, I will scout the area. Otter," Pathkiller said, turning to the old man. "I think there is game nearby. Why don't you do some hunting and keep alert."

Otter nodded his head and slowly stood up. "How long are we going to allow the women to sleep?" he asked as he began walking toward his pony.

"We cannot afford to stay here for long but I believe we will stay until the midday," Pathkiller answered, looking at Lone Crow. "If you choose to be with your woman, be alert. And do not allow your guard to completely drop."

Lone Crow wanted to quickly assure Pathkiller that he never completely relaxed but he couldn't. All he could do was hope nobody showed up unexpectedly.

The Chief's warning did not roll off the Warrior's back like it should have. It did plant a seed he wasn't sure he could stop from growing.

Explaining why the three men were in the company of two white women was tricky enough. If a white man found Bird and him in a compromising position, it would absolutely end in death. And that realization had him rethinking the waterhole as a place to take Bird.

It was yet another obstacle that presented itself but Lone Crow was tired of being put off.

"Son," he heard Otter call his name and snapped out of his racing mind.

Lone Crow sighed and looked up at his father.

"It does not matter where the two of you spend time. And there are plenty of places that are well hidden close by. Now, we will speak soon. Enjoy yourself. And remember there is always hope," he said as he urged his pony forward.

Lone Crow decided to take his father's advice and locate a private, hidden place before waking Bird.

While he was making his way to his pony to unpack extra robes, he heard Pathkiller.

"Do not let your weapon out of your reach," he warned before turning his horse and leaving the small camp.

286 Elizabeth Anne Porter

Pathkiller's caution should have bothered the Warrior more. The Chief seemed to have more on his mind than a troublesome white woman and at any other time, the Warrior would have been desperate to know what was bothering the man.

But he only nodded and placed his quiver and bow across his back before beginning his search.

There were several suitable sights close by but Lone Crow wanted Bird to know that no one could hear them. He wanted nothing to occupy her mind, except him.

As soon as he felt he found the best available spot, he cleared some limbs and placed several robes on the ground. Once that was done to his satisfaction, he gently laid a thin but sturdy sheet of leather over the opening. It was not extraordinarily roomy but it would work.

Lone Crow realized he was nervous when he began walking back to Bird's shelter. It was the first time he was worried about being enough for a woman. All he wanted to do was show Bird what love truly felt like and he found himself standing in front of the opening of Bird's shelter, unable to move.

Only after reminding himself Bird was happy merely being in his company could he reach for the covering.

It didn't take long before his eyes adjusted to the darkness. When they did, he saw Wilma was still awake.

The knowledge instantly angered him but he forced a smile and waited for the woman to ask why he was there.

"I know I can be difficult," she began speaking, just above a whisper.

Lone Crow grumbled quietly and waited for her to finish.

"But a lot has happened to me in the last few days. I lost my husband and my lover. And to be completely honest, I have no idea whose child I am carrying. And yes, I do know how that makes me sound. Like I should be ashamed of myself. Well, I am. Anyway, I have been laying here praying and I realize what I have to do."

Lone Crow felt his muscles tense when Wilma stopped talking to lift her head and lean on her elbows before continuing with her rather long-winded statement.

"I am the one who is in the wrong. I have sinned and was punished. I wanted to blame you, or Faith, or anyone really, but I can't. And I believe you when you say the men will be punished. So what I am trying to say is I will keep Faith's secret and your secret and the real ending of our men a secret. But Faith will have to keep mine."

Lone Crow didn't reply but he did raise his eyebrow and look from Wilma to the still sleeping Bird.

"I don't think I am asking for much. I want both of us to keep our reputations intact," she continued when Lone Crow remained mute.

The Warrior knew he couldn't speak for Bird, even if he was sure she would have no problem doing as Wilma wished. But he felt a huge weight lift when he realized the woman had decided to do as she was asked. It was a strange calming feeling that he did not want to lose right away.

"I understand what you are asking but that is for Bird to decide. Thank you," he said, thinking there was not much else to discuss.

Wilma smiled. "You are taking her somewhere to be alone, aren't you?" she asked with a giddy tone in her voice.

Lone Crow sighed and rubbed the bridge of his nose. He was aware just what Wilma had agreed to and knew he hadn't been appreciative enough but every minute he spent talking to Wilma was less time he had for Bird.

"That is what I planned," he replied as he moved closer to Bird and knelt beside her sleeping form.

"Well, don't let me stop you. I will hold you to teaching me to thank your Chief, though," she said quickly.

Lone Crow took a deep breath and turned to ensure Wilma was lying back down. She was and had conveniently turned her back to him.

His hand trembled when he reached to touch Bird's shoulder.

"Tsisqua," he whispered as he gently shook her.

She smiled when she heard his voice and stretched in an arousing way before opening her eyes and looking up at him.

"Hi," she said shyly.

The Warrior watched as a blush crossed her cheeks. She was the most beautiful woman he had ever seen.

"Hello," he replied, feeling slightly awkward himself.

Bird slowly sat up and looked around him to check on Wilma. "Is she asleep?" she asked quietly as she stretched another time.

"She is not," Lone Crow answered. "But she has an offer for you," he added, mentally chastising himself as soon as the words left his mouth.

He did not want to delay their time together any longer and yet it always happened.

Bird looked curious about the news but smiled and reached for Lone Crow instead of asking him for more information.

As soon as her arms reached for his neck, he moved and scooped her into his lap.

"I don't think I want to hear about Wilma right now," she informed him breathlessly. "But I would prefer it if we could be a little more alone."

Lone Crow saw a look in her eyes he had never seen before. It was one of hunger and it was all he needed to stand with her still in his arms and quickly walk from the small space.

Bird remained quiet except for the sounds of laughter that he could feel when she buried her head into his chest.

He efficiently carried her to the spot he had prepared and tried in vain to remind himself he didn't need to be anything except himself and Bird would be happy.

She didn't move her face until he stopped walking.

"It is beautiful," she quickly decided, sounding as if she genuinely meant it.

Lone Crow knew it was nothing special and had wished he'd had the time to make a spot truly magical for her. Still, he appreciated her opinion.

"*You* are beautiful," he commented, as he gently lowered her feet to the ground.

"Is this really happening? Are we really going to be alone?" she asked as she shifted the weight on her feet and wrung her hands.

Lone Crow was relieved to see Bird was battling with nerves as well. "I think so," he answered as he reached for the thin covering and pulled a few sticks out of the way to help Bird climb inside easier.

As soon as she was situated, he climbed in and replaced the covering. The sound of rolling thunder in the distance was not worrisome enough to garner more than quick interest.

There was no room to sit up so he wriggled in beside Bird and leaned over to look at her.

She was having trouble catching her breath and the Warrior could see the heartbeat in her chest.

He carefully leaned down and kissed her.

"Are you sure this is what you want?" he asked, before slowly unbuttoning the row of buttons on her thin dress.

Before Bird answered, he felt her back arch to his touch and a moan escape her lips. "I want this. I want you. I want us. I want forever," she replied in a ragged voice.

## Chapter Thirty-Eight

Moses made me feel loved, beautiful, and safe. I knew that loving the man was an experience I would never forget.

Everywhere he touched me, my body burned and the gentleness he employed made me melt.

He drove me to heights I never imagined attainable and while he was worshiping me, he never stopped repeating how much I meant to him.

It felt as if I were floating above my body and when he told me he loved me, I lost myself for a moment.

The man woke feelings in me I didn't believe I possessed. And I very much wanted to stay lying in his arms for the rest of my life. I wanted my forever.

\*\*\*

"Are you alright?" he asked, as he reluctantly began to button the front of my dress.

I was more than alright. I was better than I had ever been. But I was having trouble forming words.

My silence seemed to worry Moses. "Speak to me, Tsisqua," he urged as he placed his elbow on the ground and looked down at me.

I reached to cup his handsome face in mine and smiled. Before I could answer the man, I began crying.

He quickly rolled me into him and held me tightly.

"Did I hurt you?" he asked, concern thick in his voice.

"No," I blubbered quietly as I held to him. "You made me feel loved and I don't want to let you go."

Moses kissed the top of my head and began running his hand through my hair. "I love you, Tsisqua. And I know how hard it will be to say goodbye but I am glad we got this time."

I kissed his chest, held back a new barrage of tears, and slowly pulled away from him. It was the first time a man had told me he loved me and it was both heartbreaking and euphoric at the same time.

"I love you too," I declared before reaching for him and kissing him deeply.

I didn't want to think about the future. All I wanted was to make love to Moses again.

"I wish I could give you forever," he said before rolling me on my back and looking down on me and the buttons he had closed.

"I will be happy with now," I replied as I helped him with the rest of the clasps.

\*\*\*

Making love the second time was even more enjoyable than the first.

I laid in the crook of his arm and lazily ran my finger down his chest, doing everything in my power not to cry again.

The tears were not because of the profound sadness I would experience soon. I was crying because there was no other way to express all the beautiful emotions that were awakening inside me. But explaining why I was being weepy was not what I wanted to do. I just wanted Moses to keep holding me.

"Can we do this again when we camp again?" I asked as soon as I was sure I had my emotions mostly under control.

He chucked and held me closer to him. "I plan to love you at every given opportunity," he said, before yawning.

I knew he was sleepy and I needed to sleep too so I cozied up against him. The opportunity to sleep with him was something I hadn't thought possible. But I was sure I would sleep better than I ever had.

Before I closed my eyes, I told him I loved him again.

"I will love you forever," he answered sleepily.

I don't know how long we slept but it wasn't long enough and I wasn't happy about the way we were awoken.

Moses woke with a start and I woke quickly too.

I could hear Otter calling Moses' name and knew the man would not come after us if it wasn't unavoidable.

Moses replied and sounded disappointed and concerned by the interruption before smiling at me and quickly helping me button my dress.

"We will have time again later," he promised as he sat up and slowly began moving the roofing.

Moses climbed out and began speaking with his father. I sat up, rearranged my dress, ensured my bag was concealed, and attempted to flatten my hair.

"There is a wagon nearby," Moses informed me as he held his hand out.

Disappointment slammed through me and I had to steady myself when I heard his news.

"Do not be sad yet," he suggested as he helped me from our special place. "I do not know how close they are or who they are but we will find out. Come," he urged as he held my hand and we began walking the short distance back to the camp.

It was difficult not to fall into tears again. But I valiantly attempted to remind myself that I should be thankful I had been able to make love to Moses. What was taking place was inevitable and I was sure I would never be prepared for saying goodbye, no matter how much time we had. It didn't work as well as I had hoped. No matter how hard I tried, I couldn't see the bright side.

As soon as we were close enough to see the rest of our traveling party sitting around a small fire, Moses stopped and turned to me.

He let go of my hand and held my face. "I love you. Just keep telling yourself that. And we will be together again."

His voice was deeper than usual and I believed every word he spoke.

Instead of replying, I leaned in and kissed him. We would have continued to enjoy our contact if Pathkiller hadn't spoken.

Moses smiled against my lips and sighed before letting go of me and turning his attention to the others.

"I love you," I whispered as I reached for his hand and took a deep, cleansing breath.

If I was supposed to feel embarrassed or ashamed by our rendezvous, I didn't. And as surprising as it was, I looked Wilma, Otter, and Pathkiller in the eyes before sitting between Moses and Wilma.

Moses smiled and patted me on the leg before speaking to Pathkiller and Otter.

"Do you know what is going on?" Wilma asked, looking as if she were woken up too.

"I think there is a wagon near," I answered, doing my best to embrace my happiness and not give in to worry.

Wilma looked relieved by my answer and wiped her eyes before yawning and stretching.

"Well that is good news," she decided. "Did you and Lone Crow have a nice time? You are glowing," she shared as she warmed her hands near the fire. "I remember when love was that good."

I didn't feel like our relationship was close enough to speak of such intimate and private things so I nodded and turned to see if I couldn't read the conversation the men were having.

"We could offer to cook something," she said, after standing to stretch her legs.

Moses didn't seem angry. At best, he was not enthusiastic about what was being discussed. But I knew he would tell me what was happening as soon as he could and Wilma's suggestion was not a terrible one.

I noticed when Wilma stood, the conversation paused briefly but when I joined her, it continued to flow.

I took that as a sign that the men trusted me and I was touched to know that fact.

But before I could step away, I felt Moses gently reach for my ankle.

I smiled and looked down at him.

He looked up at me and waited for Pathkiller to finish his thought before smiling.

"You do not need to cook," he stated, looking at me in a way that made my stomach flutter. "I will feed you when we are finished."

I was amazed to learn Moses had been participating in a talk with the men and yet heard what Wilma and I were saying.

I blushed and looked at Wilma. "We should probably sit back down and wait," I suggested, gesturing to the ground.

"I need to be alone for a moment," she argued gently as she wiggled uncomfortably while explaining her situation to me.

"We will be back in a few minutes," I informed Moses as I leaned down and spoke in his ear.

He nodded and watched as we walked behind the nearest tree.

I was desperate to know how long Moses and I had before we were forced to part forever but knew once I found out, my happiness level would drop. No matter how many times I told myself I would always remember everything about Moses, I was devastated. Leaving the man would be the hardest thing I had ever done. And I wasn't sure I was strong enough.

"You look so different than you did when I first met you," Wilma informed me once we were hidden from the others.

I wasn't sure how I supposed to take her observation so I stayed silent.

"Did you ever love Tobias?" she continued interrogating me.

The question was easy enough to answer. "No. I have never loved anyone other than Moses."

It was difficult but I managed to answer without allowing my voice to catch.

"Well, I am sorry for that. I have loved men but never to the extent of the love you share with Lone Crow. I have to admit, I am envious."

I hoped the woman was finished speaking about Moses' and my relationship. It was another thing I wanted to keep for myself.

"You should not be jealous. We have no future," I reminded the woman and looked to the heavens.

"I am not expected to be part of their meeting, am I?" she asked as we began walking to rejoin the men.

"I don't know. Why?" I asked quickly.

"If I cannot eat, then I would like to return to the shelter and pray. It's funny how sometimes language isn't needed to understand some things," she mused as she looked longingly at the dwelling.

I had no idea what she was talking about but she did sound as if she were willing to go along with the plan and I was pleased to know that. And, since I didn't see where the harm would be if I kept an eye on the shelter to ensure she didn't slip away, I answered.

"Go ahead. I will wake you when the food is ready," I decided, watching her slip back inside and close the flap.

She was a hard woman to figure out but I wanted to believe what we were asking from her was something she could do. Because if she did tell the truth, I was sure I would die trying to protect Moses.

## Chapter Thirty-Nine

Lone Crow wanted to hold onto his happiness but found it difficult when he heard a wagon was close. He hid his disappointment and did his best to lift Bird's spirits. Before talking to the men, he made her a promise he was not going to break. He vowed they would have more time together and he was going to keep that pledge. No matter what obstacles were thrown his way.

Loving Bird was spiritual. She was everything he ever wanted. The woman made him whole.

As soon as they sat down, Pathkiller began speaking.

"A wagon is a day's ride from here," he stated as he handed Lone Crow the lit pipe.

It was not what the Warrior wanted to hear but he had been forewarned so he nodded his head and took a pull from the pipe before speaking. "Do you plan on staying here, or are we going to meet them?" he asked as he handed the pipe back and clung tighter to Bird's leg.

Pathkiller handed the pipe to Otter and looked like he was unsure of his answer.

"I think it would be better to be riding," Otter stated, joining the conversation.

"This plan could so easily go the wrong way," Pathkiller admitted, in a thoughtful tone.

The Leader was not acting like himself and that concerned Lone Crow even further.

"We have at least a day. How many people are there? Did they look like they were well armed?" Lone Crow asked, snapping out of his melancholy and embracing the Warrior within.

They were not going into battle per se, but it was always smart to know as much as possible about any threat encountered.

"It was a lone wagon and two well-dressed men were on the bench. I have no idea if they are looking for our missionaries or if they are just looking for land to build a house. But it is the perfect opportunity to hand the women off."

Lone Crow did not hear the certainty the Chief usually employed when he discussed matters.

"I do not claim to know much about white men but I would be concerned with whom we are handing the women off to," the Warrior stated. "Not all men are good or kind-hearted." He added when both of the men looked at him in question.

"There was one of their crosses pained on the side of the wagon," Pathkiller assured Lone Crow.

Both Father Silas and Tobias had hidden behind the cross but were still abusive men. So religion was no guarantee the men were good.

Lone Crow had been listening to two conversations at once and when he realized Bird was going to find food to prepare, he stopped and told her he would cook.

He wanted to do everything in his power to take care of her.

The two women went to seek privacy and he returned his attention to the critically important conversation.

"It might be best to allow the women to begin walking. The less we are seen, the better," Pathkiller said, looking from Lone Crow to Otter.

The Chief's latest idea was a terrible one. And one that did not assure Wilma would keep her word. The only thing keeping the woman in line was Bird.

No. Lone Crow wanted to escort the women and explain the accident. He needed to hear that giving up the only woman he would ever love was not done in vain. He needed to hear Wilma tell the story of the tragic accident with his own ears.

"No," he stated, after some thought. "In the morning, we will ride toward where you saw the wagon. Once we are close, I will fly a white flag and allow the women to ride ahead of me. You and Otter can stay back but be ready to fire if need be. Once Wilma has explained the situation, I will return to you and the continued conversation with rest with Bird."

Lone Crow had attended numerous meetings in his life but he had never spoken with such authority before. He was sure it was the best idea, even if it would break him.

Pathkiller looked like he was considering Lone Crow's suggestion when Otter stood and took a seat next to his son.

"I know this is difficult. I wish there were another way. But if there is not, then we tried our best," he said, patting Lone Crow on the back.

The Warrior looked up and saw Bird talking to Wilma before the woman returned to the dwelling.

"Father, I would do anything for Bird. But this will be shattering. Now get up, old man. She is returning to my side," he said, doing his best to lighten the heavy mood.

Bird smiled and sat between Lone Crow and his father before smiling at both the men.

"Are you well?" he asked after he leaned into her and kissed her neck.

"How can I not be?" she asked, giggling. "I am sitting by the man I love."

"Our word for love is gvgeyu'i. It means so much more than love. It means I will protect you and care for you until my last breath," he explained, looking into her eyes.

Bird seemed to be struck mute and then sighed dreamily and repeated the word.

"Gvgeyu'i."

Lone Crow would have continued staring into Bird's eyes if he hadn't heard Pathkiller clear his throat and stand.

"Things would be different if this all didn't depend on the woman's word," he stated as he began to walk away.

Lone Crow was captivated by Bird but the Chief's comment was something he could not allow to go unquestioned. Before turning to Pathkiller, he smiled and kissed Bird. "I need to speak to him a little more. But I will return quickly," he assured her before standing and following the Leader.

"What did you mean by that?" he asked as he reached to stop the man from walking.

"I do not enjoy seeing you so happy when there is no way to stop the crippling pain that will follow," Pathkiller said, dodging Lone Crow's question easily.

"Is there a way? Can you see a way for the two of us to leave like we discussed earlier?" the Warrior asked, feeling a mixture of emotions at the mere thought that the Chief might still be entertaining other options.

"There is no way," Pathkiller assured Lone Crow, sadly.

"Humor me," Lone Crow argued. "I understand it is impossible, but I would very much like to hear your solution."

"If the other woman was not involved, I am sure you could travel further from white civilizations and join with another band. But the Wilma woman makes that an impossibility," he ended looking unhappy.

Lone Crow wondered if Pathkiller shouldn't have kept his idea to himself. Because it was another heartbreak he was forced to accept. If not for Wilma, there might have been a way.

"I should not have brought up a plan that is impossible. Lone Crow, I am not trying to make this more difficult. I wish there were some way. But short of the woman's death, there is none."

It was the brutal truth and Lone Crow knew his Chief was not suggesting they kill the woman. But the truth was still not easy to swallow. And although he wasn't proud of himself, he considered taking Bird and riding away. If the good of his people hadn't been at risk, it would have been an easy decision.

"I know you are doing what you think is best," Lone Crow stated as he turned back toward the fire. "And I know I need to hold on to my happiness while I can. Food will be ready soon."

"I will go back to the lookout and see how far the wagon has traveled," Pathkiller informed him as he began walking toward his horse.

Lone Crow walked back to Bird and Otter while swallowing the latest pain and holding to the joy Bird brought to him simply by being in her company.

Otter was cooking a rabbit on the fire and Bird was watching the man closely.

"What happened?" she asked, holding to her cheery disposition. "How far are the wagons? And how long do we have?"

Lone Crow patted his father on the back before walking to Bird.

He didn't want to answer her questions. He wanted her to be happy for as long as she could.

## Chapter Forty

As soon as Moses left, Otter stood and started dressing a rabbit. I watched and we shared a smile as he worked. It was a strange encounter but not at all unpleasant.

But I was curious to know what was happening. I knew our time together was even more limited than it was earlier and I was anxious to know why.

While Otter and I sat smiling at one another, I attempted to imagine what a life with Lone Crow would be like. Knowing I was only causing myself undue pain wasn't enough to stop me from doing it.

The daydream was beautiful. We were together. Living in a house like the ones I'd seen in the village and children were running around happily.

It was a dream that I wanted so badly. But knew it was impossible so I was glad when I saw Moses had returned. Instead of dwelling on my new sadness, I began asking him questions as he walked toward me.

When he heard my questions, he tried to hide the disappointment he was feeling. But I saw it. It was fleeting but he was not pleased. So his reaction was the reason I was glad I sounded happier than I was feeling. It didn't take long for me to understand I wanted the man to be as happy and content as possible. My feelings were not as important.

"There is a wagon not far from here. They are a day away but Pathkiller is going to check on their progress," Moses explained as he sat beside me.

The news wasn't a shock but hearing about the closeness of the wagon did cause me to sigh.

"I don't think I want to hear any more," I admitted as I picked up a stick and began moving it just above the flames. "But I do want more time with you."

Moses smiled and placed his arm around me before kissing me. "After we eat, we can go to the waterhole," he offered.

The first time he brought up the site, he did so with trepidation in his voice. The second time he offered, his tone was one of passion and need.

I swallowed hard and nodded. "I would like that," I agreed quickly as I slid as close to the man as I could. "I do not want to cry because I am happier than I have ever been. But I am so afraid I will not be strong when we leave one another," I admitted, doing my best to stop my lip from quivering.

Moses held me tightly and began rocking me in his strong arms. "It will be the hardest thing I will ever do but knowing it is the right thing for you is enough for me."

I wanted to be able to repeat the sentiment but knew if I said another word, I would be crying again. So instead of speaking, I allowed the man I loved to soothe me.

The smell of the cooking meat was enough to make me realize just how hungry I was.

Moses chuckled quietly when he heard my stomach rumble. "I do not want to leave you but I must help my father with the food," he whispered after kissing the top of my head. "As soon as we eat, we will leave."

I reluctantly moved away from him and smiled before wiping the remnants of the tears that managed to fall down my cheek.

"When will Pathkiller be back?" I asked, watching Moses stand.

We had little we could talk about that didn't make me sad and I was curious to know how long we had.

Moses turned back to me and smiled. "He will be gone for hours."

The look in Moses' eyes gave me goosebumps.

I sat still and watched as the men cooked and spoke to each other. Not many men I knew prepared meals for themselves if a woman was present so their natural actions both surprised me and gave me a new appreciation for the differences in our people. The men didn't seem to need or want my help but I found it impossible to sit and do nothing.

"What can I do?" I asked, standing up and wiping the dirt from the back of my dress.

Otter continued to smile as he worked and Moses stopped to look at me.

"You can go wake Wilma. I am sure she is hungry," he suggested.

Otter's face lit up and he chuckled when he heard Wilma's name.

His reaction confused me and from the look on Moses' face, he was just as lost as I was.

The two exchanged a quick conversation and then Moses dropped the clay pot he had been holding.

Without any explanation, he ran to the shelter and pulled the cover before looking in and turning back to his father.

Moses appeared to be upset but Otter continued to smile. The conversation was as confusing as Otter's constant grin. Moses was clearly angry and confused and Otter was speaking in calm, amused tones.

"What is going on?" I asked when I found I couldn't remain quiet or clueless any longer.

As soon as I began asking my question, I walked toward Moses.

Before Moses had a chance to answer, Pathkiller rode into the camp with an angry look on his face.

The conversation was again, strange. Otter never stopped smiling. Pathkiller was angry and concerned. And Moses was concerned at first but then seemed to be extremely pleased; excited even.

Again I was convinced if I didn't speak soon, I would burst.

"What is happening?" I asked, employing a decibel above the ongoing conversation.

I may have been meek when I lived in constant fear but was proud to learn it was a trait that I was outgrowing.

The men stopped talking and looked at me. Their expression varied as much as their tones.

Otter still looked at ease and maybe even pleased with himself. Pathkiller was angry but again concerned more than anything. And Moses looked at me with love and hope.
But none of them were speaking or answering my question.

"Wilma has left," he answered, pointing inside.

I was sure I misheard his response and looked inside to prove him wrong.

She was gone. And I did not know how to react.

"Where has she gone? Do we need to follow her? Is she going to get you killed? And what is going to happen to me?" I asked, walking from him and throwing my hands in the air in desperation.

"I know this could be terrible but I do not believe it will be. Somehow my father was able to put her on a horse and set her off in the direction of town without us knowing. The old man can be sneaky when he wants to," Moses began explaining while he reached to hold me in his arms.

"Why would he *or she* do that?" I asked, not relaxing when he touched me. "Someone go after her," I demanded as I looked from Otter to Pathkiller.

I could not understand why the only person there who was reacting appropriately was the Leader.

"Pathkiller will follow her. He returned only to tell us he saw her. And this could be the only chance we have at happiness," Moses continued to hold me and speak in soothing tones.

I stopped fighting him and unclenched my muscles before looking him in the eyes.

"We don't know what she is going to tell them," I pointed out quickly. "This could be awful and I am not there to help."

My argument started out strong enough but the more Moses soothed and rocked me, the more I was able to concentrate on the last thing he said.

"How does her escape give us a chance?" I asked as soon as my breathing returned to a normal rhythm.

Moses took a deep breath and pulled away so that he could hold me at arm's length. "We have been given permission to leave, together," he explained, stopping to gauge my reaction to the news.

I actually felt faint when the words hit my ears. And then I wondered how he could be so cruel to me.

"If we leave, your people could be attacked," I argued.

Moses looked hurt by my reaction. "Pathkiller and my father have done all they can to ensure that will not be the case," he promised before pulling my back into his chest.

I wanted to believe what Moses was saying. But something inside me would not allow the worry to fall away. I had not been given a choice in my future before and wanted to be with Moses. But still, the fear of what outcome that action would bring was enough to make me cautious.

"This is your choice," Moses said, into the top of my head.

He was trying to hide his disappointment but I heard it in his voice. And I didn't care for it one bit.

"My choice is to be with you. But I do not know if I can live with the guilt if anything bad happens because of Wilma," I admitted as I held to him.

I heard his breath catch in his throat when I answered him.

Before he could reply to my statement, I felt Otter taping both of us on the shoulder.

When we turned to him, the old man was still smiling but was holding Wilma's bible in his hands.

I wasn't sure but I thought the man was trying to calm the both of us. I knew Wilma well enough to know she would never leave her bible. So I was alarmed more than before.

Moses and Otter spoke while I remained clinging to the man I loved.

Otter was still holding the book when Moses sighed and took it from him.

I moved away slightly when he opened it and gasped before talking to his father again.

I pulled the book from his hands and saw words written on the back of the cover. It looked like she found some coal or black rock. The words caused me to drop the book and reach for Moses.

I had been so afraid to allow myself the chance of being happy that I was on the verge of telling Moses to take me to Wilma but two scrawled words changed everything.

The words were "Be Happy."

Moses kissed me passionately before reluctantly pushing me back.

"I want you more than anything, Tsisqua. You make me whole. But what we are planning on doing will not be easy. We will not ever be completely safe. But I will spend the rest of my life protecting you from all harm and loving you until my last breath."

I was crying once again. I was overwhelmed with the idea that we were going to be together. I was going to be happy.

"My life has never been easy. But you make me feel safe and loved, and isn't that what really matters?" I asked, kissing him again.

Otter smiled and hugged both of us. There was a sadness in his eyes but also happiness and hope.

"Gvgeyu'i," he said against my lips.

I was overwhelmed and happier than I ever thought I could be.

"Forever?" I asked excitedly.

"Forever," he answered.

FIN


Other books in the Native Warrior Series include:

Running Elk

Spirit Talker

Shadow Wolf

Two Feathers

Ghost Hawk

And coming soon: Three Bears

Made in the USA
Monee, IL
08 July 2020

36052867R00184